TOO FAR DOWN

Books by Mary Connealy

From Bethany House Publishers

THE KINCAID BRIDES

Out of Control

In Too Deep

Over the Edge

TROUBLE IN TEXAS

Swept Away

Fired Up

Stuck Together

WILD AT HEART

Tried and True

Now and Forever

Fire and Ice

THE CIMARRON LEGACY

No Way Up

Long Time Gone

Too Far Down

The Boden Birthright: A CIMARRON LEGACY *Novella*

Meeting Her Match: A MATCH MADE IN TEXAS *Novella* 4

Runaway Bride: A KINCAID BRIDES *and* TROUBLE IN TEXAS *Novella (*With This Ring? *Collection)*

The Tangled Ties That Bind: A KINCAID BRIDES *Novella (*Hearts Entwined *Collection)*

TOO FAR DOWN

MARY CONNEALY

a division of Baker Publishing Group
Minneapolis, Minnesota

Published by Bethany House Publishers
11400 Hampshire Avenue South
Bloomington, Minnesota 55438
www.bethanyhouse.com

Bethany House Publishers is a division of
Baker Publishing Group, Grand Rapids, Michigan

Printed in the United States of America

Library of Congress Control Number: 2017945352

ISBN 978-0-7642-1183-6 (trade paper)
ISBN 978-0-7642-3114-8 (cloth)

Scripture quotations are from the King James Version of the Bible.

Cover design by Dan Pitts

Author is represented by Natasha Kern Literary Agency.

17 18 19 20 21 22 23 7 6 5 4 3 2 1

This book is dedicated to my beautiful grandbaby, Katherine. You have been a true, precious blessing from the moment we knew you were on the way. God bless you, Katherine. Welcome to the family.

Skull Gulch, New Mexico Territory
February 1881

An explosion brought Cole Boden to his feet. His chair slammed backward into the wall. Cole ran for his office door and ripped it open.

Murray Elliot, his assistant, rounded his desk in the outer office. "What happened?"

A second explosion rocked the whole building.

Cole didn't bother responding. He charged outside into the winter chill, just in time to duck flying rocks from the mountaintop. He threw himself back inside as stones blasted right over his head with the force of cannonballs.

"Murray, get down!" Cole grabbed at the man who'd responded much more cautiously and was well behind. He tackled Murray to the floor just as another explosion went off.

The log wall of the office buckled. This building was small but solid, so the rocks were coming with terrific force. Rocks sprayed in through the open door and smashed into Murray's desk.

"What is happening?"

"I don't know." Cole glared at the man. "Something blew up. We're not blasting today, are we?"

"Nope, but we just got a supply of dynamite in."

"Where is it?" Cole imagined a wagonload of dynamite, and explosion after explosion. But no, that'd be just one big explosion.

"It's stopped." Murray lifted his head.

"Is the dynamite stored in that big cave?"

"Just like always, boss."

Cole knew explosives, and he knew they brought them in by the wagonload. And they stored them in a cold cave a good distance from where anyone worked. Even if they exploded, they shouldn't have done anything but rock that cave. At the worst it might seal the mouth of it.

Three explosions and nowhere near a wagonload had blown—which meant there was plenty more to come.

"I'm heading for the big cave. You stay in here."

"No, I'm coming with you."

"You aren't." Cole heaved himself to his feet. "It's my mine and my risk."

"I'm coming, Cole." Murray was up.

A fourth explosion sent a rock the size of Cole's head slamming through the roof.

Murray fell onto his backside, then scrambled into the kneehole of his desk. He'd been hired for his brains, not his guts.

Cole was glad he'd been delayed from running outside. But he also knew he was going now, and it was most likely a blamed fool idea.

"Stay under there until we're sure the explosions have

stopped." He hoped Murray stayed put under the solid oak desk. It should protect him even if the whole building collapsed.

Cole raced out the door to see the smoldering ruins of the newly opened mine only about a hundred yards from his office. The entrance was collapsed, and he knew men were trapped inside. Before he could deal with that, though, he had to make sure the dynamite was done blowing up.

He charged toward the cave.

He hoped and prayed his men inside the new mine were all right. If they'd been far enough in, around the corner from the blasts, out of the line of any flying debris, they should still be alive. The entrance had collapsed, but they'd shored the mines up with thick timbers. There was a good chance the inside of the mine was still intact.

Once he got near the cave, grit and dust filled the air. Choking, Cole jerked his kerchief out of his pocket and covered his mouth. His eyes burned, but he had to see. Cole raced faster, thinking of all that could have gone wrong, all the men who could be hurt.

He saw one still form on the ground, so covered with dust he couldn't identify the man. Yet Cole could see clearly enough to know the man was beyond help.

Running, stumbling over rocks, barely able to breathe, Cole finally reached the cave. Outside it was a burning fuse, heading for a wooden box, torn open, full of explosives.

He slid on his knees to beat the fuse from burning down. It ran shorter by the second. Cole fumbled for the knife he kept in his boot as he crawled the last foot through the rubble. He caught the fuse only inches from burning down. He slit the sparking fire with one slash.

He looked down the side of the mountain. The office of the CR Mining Company was near the top of Mount Kebbel, with only its snowcapped peak higher. The CR leased claims to many men, all spread over a hundred square miles. A few dozen of them were right here close to headquarters.

Cole's eyes swept down the long, steep slope dotted with mine entrances and saw boxes of dynamite burning at a bunch of them. Enough to account for nearly every box they had in storage. Cole could never reach them all in time.

Yards away, he saw the next fuse burning toward a wooden box. Thinking furiously, he saw this fuse was longer. Whoever'd done this wanted the explosives to go in separate blasts, and the boxes were far enough apart not to be set off by an earlier explosion. Men were deep in their mines, so they might hear the explosions, and they might not.

This time, with the men inside, was deliberate. Midmorning. All the miners were hard at work at this time of day and very few were outside. The explosions would bury them alive.

Fury pushed him faster. He scrambled, fell over stones, and smacked himself in the face so hard he saw stars. Then he was up again and cut the next fuse. With cold purpose he picked up a stick of dynamite, cut its fuse short, and lit it to the still-sparking fuse in his hand, then threw the stick as far as his arm could hurl it.

He watched the dynamite soar high in the air and arch down, hoping the miners farther down the slope, near the burning fuses, would hear it blow and come out to help.

His hand burned. He dropped the still-burning fuse with a desperate toss to get it away from the explosives. The stick of powder he threw detonated in midair, doing no damage but making a deafening sound.

Another fuse burned just ahead. Cole ran for it. He cut it, lit one stick, threw it, and ran on. He saw the first man poke his head out of his claim far below.

The man took in everything in a second, ran to the closest

stack of explosives, and cut the fuse before it could blow. Another man emerged. These men knew dynamite, knew what that box meant. They went to work saving themselves. Cole cut another, then another, and another. He hurled a lit stick every time, trying to alert the miners.

Then he heard another explosion. Sickened at who might've been in its path, he whirled toward the sound. The remnants of the blast colored the air below. Someone had figured out what he was doing and had thrown a single stick of dynamite to warn those farther down.

More men appeared. Fuses were cut. Sticks of dynamite were set off as a warning to all.

Finally he dropped to his knees by the last one at this higher level and cut it. His gaze swept the slope below him. He didn't see a single sparking fuse.

The men waved up at him.

"I've got a broken-down mine up here," he shouted. "Men trapped. We need help." He didn't know men were trapped for a fact, but the mine closest to headquarters was big, and a lot of men labored there. He prayed the ones inside had survived. And what other madness awaited him today? Was he asking for help that might lead others to their deaths? He leapt to his feet to go free the trapped men.

The world spun around. His vision blurred and darkened. Blood dripped from his head. By sheer grit he shook off whatever weakness wanted to knock him down.

No sparks in sight. He considered the piles of explosives and, by his own judgment, thought all the dynamite was accounted for now.

He couldn't be positive, of course, as some sticks could have been unboxed and set to blow separately. But he saw no sign of them.

He trusted his instincts about the dynamite and trusted his miners to be on the lookout. Then he sprinted back toward the collapsed new mine. Several miners that he'd just saved came up behind him, took one stricken look at him, and approached him. He knew he was bleeding but didn't have time to get a bandage.

"No, I'm fine. Come back to the new mine. It's collapsed." He left them behind to do as they wished.

Murray was doctoring a man sprawled out on the ground. Murray had been here running the mine when Cole came home from living in Boston for a few years. Cole had seen how smart the man was and had given him a raise and kept him on as an assistant. Murray had his own cabin here as part of his salary, and he even had his own claim and worked it during free hours.

Other men were working on the wounded, separating them from the dead. Yet others were digging at the blocked mine entrance. More men came every minute.

His teeth clenched, Cole rushed toward the miners who were clawing at the entrance to the mine. "Is anyone in there?"

One burly youngster with a full beard stopped digging with his hands. "There are twelve or fifteen men in there, boss. A couple of the men ran to get shovels while we start the digging."

"Twelve or fifteen?" Cole looked with dismay at the wall of rubble that filled the entrance. They had at least five feet of rock to clear if they hoped to reach his men.

"Yep, maybe more. We've lost count of who's missing. The first explosion went off right by this entrance. We saw you fighting the rest of those fuses." The youngster paused and added, "Boss, you're bleedin' pretty bad. You need to let someone wrap your . . . your whole head and face."

Cole saw the worry in the kid's eyes and wondered how bad he was hurt. Plenty bad, going by the loss of blood. "I'll be fine. You're bleeding, too." The kid's arms were bleeding from working with the stones with his bare hands. "Everyone is."

"Well, you're a little worse than most." But the kid turned back and attacked the wall of stones blocking the entrance. A man who let another man make his own choices. Cole respected that.

A clatter drew Cole's attention, and two miners, coated in dirt, came running with their arms full of shovels and pick-axes. Cole grabbed a shovel and attacked the cave entrance. He glanced over to see Murray carrying a man over his shoulder toward the company office.

He dug. And dug and dug. With so many of them working, they got in each other's way and had to dodge flying rocks. For all the danger, they still dug.

Hours passed, though Cole had no idea just how many, only that all this had started early in the day, and now the sun was past its peak.

At last one of the men shouted, "I'm through into the mine!"

They fell to working on the tiny opening with renewed strength. It soon grew, and before it was big enough to crawl through, a voice came from behind the collapsed stones. "We're here—we can see light. We're digging from this side."

A ragged cheer went up from his men. The worst hadn't happened. The cave hadn't completely collapsed and buried all the men inside.

"Keep at it, men!" Cole plunged back into widening the opening.

By the time it was just a bit larger, an arm stuck out the hole.

"Stop, everybody! Don't cut him."

"Is that you, Cole?"

"Yep, Gully."

Gully was the real boss of the mine operation. Cole was the

manager; he did paper work, along with Murray, and yes, Cole threw his back behind a pickax plenty, yet Gully had been here before Cole. The old-timer knew mining and did the lion's share of bossing on the job. Of course, Cole had been smart enough to leave him to do his job so that deserved some credit, too.

Cole hadn't even looked around. All his men out here were coated in dirt anyway, to the point of being unrecognizable. He hadn't even noticed Gully was missing.

"I think we can get a few of the scrawnier men through this opening. We've got a few hurt that'll fit through. I'll send them first."

"A few hurt bad?" Cole realized they needed more help, more *skilled* help. He'd been working in a headlong frenzy and had done little thinking.

Now it came to him. Heath Kincaid, his new brother-in-law, had healing skills. Heath had once saved the life of Cole's pa, Chance Boden, who was injured in an avalanche. Having ridden with the cavalry for a time, Heath worked alongside an army doctor and became skilled at meting out medicine.

Rosita, the Bodens' housekeeper, was good as well. His sister Sadie had tended sick people plenty of times herself. He wanted them all here and for good reason. He desperately needed help. And they could sure as certain use his little brother Justin's strong back and quick thinking.

He never let his family help with the mines . . . until now.

"You!" He jabbed a finger at one of his men. "Get on your horse and ride for the CR. Get all the help you can and have someone there send for the doctor in Skull Gulch and more help from any neighboring ranches. Send them all running for the mines. Get the sheriff out here, too."

Disgusted that he hadn't thought of it earlier, Cole turned back to the hole in the cave. "We're ready." His throat grew tight at the thought of who all might be hurt. He hadn't looked around yet except to notice Murray tending the wounded. His stomach swooped, and he leaned against the wall of the cave, letting his belly settle and his head clear while he waited for Gully to send out the first man.

A pair of filthy hands appeared, and they were slack. Cole saw someone holding the limp arms, guiding them through the opening. Cole gathered himself and blinked until his vision cleared, then grabbed one arm and someone caught the other. The man's head appeared next, supported as if someone was guiding a thread through the eye of a needle.

"Careful with him," Gully shouted from inside the cave. "I think an arm and a leg are broke. Who knows what else."

Cole quickly shifted his grip as he realized the arm he'd reached for was bent in an ugly way that could only mean a broken bone. He exchanged a look with the man helping him. He couldn't identify him. Cole probably looked just as bad. They nodded at each other and eased the man forward, others reaching up to help. All the men who'd been digging supported the man.

It was a fight to keep the nausea down just thinking how he'd gripped that arm.

Through the tight opening, Cole wondered about broken ribs, or worse, a broken back. Praying silently, Cole did his best to be gentle. As soon as they had him all the way out, Cole looked around and saw Murray flipping his jacket over the face of the man Cole had first seen when he left his office earlier in the day.

Dead.

"Murray, we need you over here."

Quieter, Cole said to the miners, "Murray's a good hand with healing. He's who we want helping with this."

He knew the men stayed back from Murray, who wrote letters and pushed numbers. True, he had his own mine, but he didn't mix with the men much. They treated Cole better because he was the boss and they probably thought they had to. But a divide existed between the men who leased their mines and those who ran them. No hostility, just no friendship.

"Bring him into the office," Murray yelled. "I'm using it as a hospital." Murray paused as he came close and looked at Cole. His eyes widened. "You may need stitches, Cole. You should come, too."

"Get back to work, Murray. No time right now for anyone to stop."

Something flashed in Murray's eyes that Cole couldn't understand. It seemed like anger or irritation of some kind. If Cole's head hadn't ached so much, he might've known what to make of it. Maybe the man was just frustrated that Cole wouldn't come along. Or maybe he'd seen too many men terribly hurt and he was just plain upset. Whatever it was, Murray would have to handle it on his own.

Four men carried the injured miner away toward the battered mine headquarters with Murray at their sides.

"Here comes the next one." Gully drew his attention back to the rescue mission.

Galloping hooves told him the man he'd sent to the ranch was on his way. Cole didn't have a man to spare right now, but someone had to go. He turned back to see another pair of limp hands emerging from the tight entrance they'd opened up.

With painstaking care they got four more unconscious men out. Cole swiped at the sweat on his brow and pulled his arm away to see a bright smear of blood. It startled him into jumping, and the move made his stomach dive and his head throb.

He steadied himself and went back to work. As the sun

dipped behind Mount Kebbel, the shadows lengthened and seemed to reach for them like shrouded hands of death.

Two more men climbed out, conscious, bleeding, and unsteady, but standing upright on their own. More of the diggers supported them on the way to the makeshift hospital.

"Let's open it up more for the rest of us," Gully ordered, sounding more cheerful. "The rest of us ain't so skinny."

Cole had lost diggers now because he'd sent them to help Murray. Those of them left tore at the opening with all their strength, though Cole had to admit his strength was waning. He was more aware with every shovelful of rocks that he had his own host of cuts and bruises. His knees ached and bled. His arms were coated with blood from falling before and cutting himself to bits digging and moving stones.

He vaguely remembered falling while he raced toward that first burning fuse and dashing his face on a rock.

Nothing that needed doctoring, though, not like these other poor souls.

He was surrounded by miners, both outside the cave and inside, so the rocks and dirt moved fast. Finally they had a gap with some height, so a larger man could crawl out.

"Enough. We're coming." Gully knew what he needed and Cole didn't, so he let the foreman give the orders. One by one, five big men emerged from the collapsed mine entrance.

Gully was the last. He was bleeding, his head and neck crimson, cutting through the thick dirt that coated him.

"Are there more, Gully?"

"Nope."

"Are you sure? I can go in and do another check."

"Every man in there is alive and accounted for." Gully caught him by the arm. "No one goes in there until I clear it. That's why I wanted all the men out who could get through that little hole. I saw some big cracks in the cave roof and it looks like the ceiling could come down at any moment."

Grimly, Cole nodded. "Get over there and let Murray take care of you."

Gully looked him in the eye, hard, studying him. "You need a doctor more than I do, boss. You look like you've got more blood on the outside than the inside." Gully took his arm in a tight grip. Almost like he thought Cole couldn't stand on his own, which was flat-out foolish because there he stood.

Cole decided he would go along if it made the man happy. He'd even lean on Gully, maybe agree to lie down a while just to put everyone's mind at ease.

Before he could move an inch, hooves pounded coming from the east, and Cole realized he'd been waiting for that sound for what seemed like an eternity, although he admitted to being mighty confused. He saw Justin in the lead.

He felt a wave of pure relief at the sight. His brother—who he never stopped fighting with—was here. Justin would take charge for a while, and maybe Cole would just sit until his head stopped throbbing.

Justin's wife, Angie, rode at his side—rode pretty well too, for a woman new to horses. Justin had been working with her.

Heath came next, riding alongside Cole's little sister Sadie. The two of them were married now. Riding even with them to make four in a row was Jack Blake and his daughter, Melanie. For some reason Cole's eyes settled on Mel—who'd kill him if he ever called her Melanie—and his vision shifted to strange and dark around the edges, as if he were looking through a tunnel. It narrowed more until she was all he could see, the only light in a black world. Her long caramel-brown braid blew back as she galloped. Her skin was tanned, even in winter. He couldn't see her eyes from here, but he knew they were light brown and that her coloring altogether was a single golden-brown glow.

She was beautiful. He'd never thought about her looks before. Well, maybe once or twice. But they'd grown up together, so you'd've thought he'd've noticed just how beautiful she really was.

Then he heard shouting, plenty of that today, but for some reason this shouting was aimed at him. Then the rocky ground punched him in the face—as if he hadn't taken enough of a beating today. And the tunnel he'd been looking through closed shut as the world went pitch-black.

Mel cried out in shock when Cole collapsed. She wasn't the only one.

But she wasn't a screamer by nature. She flung herself off her horse and rushed toward him. He'd fallen hard, and his head looked like it had bounced off a boulder. He was soaked with blood all down his shirt and arms, and covered with dirt.

Dropping to her knees, she saw Justin reaching for him on the other side.

A stout man, coated head to toe in dust, with trails of blackened blood being the only thing that kept him from being stone gray, said, "Pick him up and bring him along to the office. We're putting the wounded in there."

Justin lifted Cole in his arms. Mel knew Cole and Justin were the same size, similar in so many ways, tall with dark hair and dark blue eyes. So the feat of lifting Cole was an act of enormous strength. It was strength almost certainly fueled by fear.

Mel reached out from her side to help bear the weight, but Heath Kincaid pushed Mel gently but firmly aside and caught Cole across from Justin.

Normally, Mel didn't like backing up for a man, but in this case she admitted Heath was better able to help carry Cole.

"Let's get him inside." Justin nodded at the building with a hole in its roof.

They headed for the battered structure. Sadie rushed ahead with Angie and a few others. There was more doctoring needed than just Cole, Mel reckoned.

When they reached the building, which looked near to falling in on itself, Mel felt everything in her tamp down until she was fiercely calm. Inside, wounded men lay everywhere. Bleeding, some moaning, some stoically quiet. Some unconscious . . . at least she hoped they were unconscious and not dead.

She saw half the Boden family surrounding Cole, so Mel decided to see where else help was needed. One man was wearing a filthy suit, the only man in a suit besides Cole. The man pointed and shouted an order to someone. Mel decided he was the doctor in the crowd.

She picked her way around the wounded and went to the doctor's side. "Tell me what you need."

The man looked up at her very suddenly, his eyes wide with shock, maybe because of hearing a woman's voice, or maybe because the man looked battered himself. She wasn't sure if he was splattered with his own blood or someone else's. "Come with me," he said.

Following him, they moved to a victim lying on his back. His leg was bandaged and resting on a rolled-up blanket.

"I need you to wash the cuts on his head and neck. He'll need stitches, and the wounds need to be absolutely clean. Once you're done, call me."

"I can set stitches, Doc."

"It's Murray. I'm not a doctor."

"Today you're a doctor."

"Sew him up if you've got a notion. I've found only one needle, so we'll have to take turns."

As the doctor rushed off, Mel wondered what in the world had gotten into her that she would offer to sew. She didn't really know how to set stitches on someone, but she'd seen her ma do it a couple of times. Once on Pa's thumb, and once on a young colt that'd cut itself on a sharp splinter of wood.

Shaking her head, she figured it couldn't be that much different from sewing up a torn shirt. She knew enough, then, and help was sorely needed.

She grabbed a bucket of clean water, knelt by her patient, and went to work. She saw Pa across the room. It looked like he was getting the same instructions she had. In fact, just about every cowhand from the Bodens' Cimarron Ranch had come, and they all went to work. Pa and Mel had been visiting the CR, so they came along and sent word to the Blake Ranch for more help.

There were now too many helping hands, to the point it was hard to move. Heath took charge and ordered those who'd been here since the explosions to go to their cabins, clean up, eat, and rest for a bit.

He also said something to Justin and Sadie that Mel couldn't quite make out.

Justin abandoned Cole, as did Sadie. Only Heath hovered at Cole's side, tending him, looking so busy that Mel started working faster.

She shifted her full attention to her patient as the light faded and lanterns were turned up. Once he was sewn up, she went on to the next one. She lost track of time as she plunged into the chaos and pain.

It was long after dark when she heard someone say, "Would you like some help?"

The strong hand and familiar voice caused her to whip her head around. She leapt to her feet, and her knees buckled. She'd been kneeling by patients for hours so every joint rebelled.

Cole grabbed her and steadied her.

She realized who had her and smiled. "You're awake and moving around." They'd been friends since childhood, and she'd been horrified to see him collapse.

"I've been conscious for about two hours and helping for one. I wasn't hurt bad, just took a whack on the head, then bled too much and worked to the bone—along with everyone else—digging my men out of the cave."

"Well, good." She noticed a neat row of stitches on his forehead. He was a mess and very pale, but he looked himself again. "Who sewed you up?"

"Heath did it. Murray, the guy I've seen giving you orders all night—"

"Murray's the one in the suit? He said he wasn't a doctor, but he sure acts like a doctor."

"Murray Elliot. He's my assistant here at the mine. Someone had to take charge before help came. Heath took over and tended me, who's a better doctor than Murray. Then Doc Garner got here from Skull Gulch and he took charge. Mostly we've all been working hard enough that there wasn't a whole lot of time to judge who was the best doctor."

Mel looked around the room. Through the hole in the roof she saw the first blush of dawn. A wave of exhaustion swept over her. She took a few steps so she could lean against the oak desk. That's when she realized the room was much emptier now. There had to have been twenty men stretched out in here before. Now there were five, and they were all moved to the edges of the room. Most of the Boden cowhands were gone, too.

"D-did everyone make it?" She hated asking because she'd

worked over many of them and knew a few were in fragile condition.

Cole came to her and leaned beside her on the desk. He'd gone just as long without sleep as she had, and he'd lived through an explosion and hours of hard work digging the cave open. It made her feel like a weakling. "Every man who regained consciousness and could walk went back to their own beds in the bunkhouses. That was most of them. The ones left here either haven't woken up yet or have got a broken bone Doc hasn't set yet. Doc heard it was an explosion and feared the worst so he brought a lot of plaster with him, but still he ran out. He sent someone to Skull Gulch for more of it. He'll finish casting the breaks when they get back."

"I live out here on the mining site, Miss Blake. Got my own cabin." Gully, who'd given her the first orders, wiped his face with both hands. "I've sent the womenfolk over to my place to sleep. You'll have to set up a pallet on the floor, but there are spare blankets and you'll have some privacy."

Mel had never been to the gold mines on the CR property before. It struck her as strange that she hadn't.

"I'll try to get a couple of hours' sleep and then be back here." She headed for the door.

Cole was at her side again. "Gully's cabin is a little ways off. I'll walk you."

Mel nodded. "Is everyone else gone?"

"Justin and Heath went to sleep in the cabin I live in when I put in long days. I mean, the cabin I used to live in."

"Before your pa told you he was giving the Cimarron Ranch, including the mines, to your cousin if you didn't move back home."

"I've never slept here or at my house in Skull Gulch since."

Mel saw Cole's jaw clench. She knew he loved the old ranch

house on the CR. He loved his job and his family, but Cole made it more than clear that he didn't like his pa dictating to him. What man did?

Cole opened the door, and the two walked out of the office into the dim light of early dawn.

Mel glanced back to make sure they were alone, then asked quietly, "How many dead?"

Cole's shoulders sagged. "We found six bodies. There may be more, though. There's so much rubble, who knows if we've missed anyone? But the men have been counting, checking the mines and cabins to make certain. I hope six is the end of it."

"And you're hurt." She settled her hand on his arm. "I know you've been working, but you're barely over being shot."

Cole had been shot by a man who'd been hired to kill the Boden family. Cole was up and moving, back at work, but that was a long way from being at full strength after a near-deadly bullet wound.

"Yesterday I took a whack on the head and bled. I blacked out, which I appreciate because I wouldn't have liked being awake to watch Heath stab me in the face with a needle. When I had enough rest, I woke up. It took a while for my head to clear, but it did, and I've been working ever since."

He was too tough to admit he should have spared himself, and Mel didn't blame him for carrying on. She'd never been able to sit around with her feet up while men were hurt or dying.

Making their way across the rock-strewn ground, Cole led her a ways before she could see the cabin. There was a low light in the window. Someone had turned a kerosene lantern down but not off. Angie and Sadie helping her find her way to bed.

Before they got close enough to be overheard, Mel caught Cole's hand and drew him to a halt.

He turned, his eyes shadowed in the darkness. "What is it?"

"I just want you to know how sorry I am." She hugged him, surprising herself, and by the tension in his back, she knew she'd surprised him even more. Well, she wasn't a hugger, but if a disaster like this wasn't enough to make her one, then hugs had no place in this world.

"Six men dead. So many hurt, including you. I'm so glad you're all right. I'll be here to help for as long as you need me." She pulled back with a sheepish smile. "Sorry . . . thanks for walking me to the cabin."

Cole nodded, looking down at her. The sun was starting to rise, and she could finally see his face. Without a bit of warning, Cole dragged her back into his arms and hugged her back.

In a whisper, he said, "You know those explosions were no accident. Someone set them."

"I heard some talk about that, but I was hoping it wasn't right."

He drew back a half step. "The sheriff came out same time as the doctor from Skull Gulch. I wasn't up to walking him around, but I told him what I saw. Then Gully went out and showed him what happened. The sheriff agrees it was deliberate, yet I knew that from the first. It's mighty hard to believe this isn't connected to all the other trouble we've had."

A shiver went down her spine. "I thought you arrested the men behind the attack on your pa and the one who shot you."

Cole pushed her hair back from her face. She couldn't imagine what a mess she was after the long, wild ride and the night of helping wounded men. Even now she didn't much care, not when she thought of how close they'd come to losing Cole.

"I thought we had. But based on this madness, I'd say we must not have gotten them all." Cole looked up at the sky. Her eyes focused on his mouth. He was tall, but so was she. Because his mouth was right there, it caught her attention somehow and she wasn't sure why.

He looked down again, his dark blue eyes seeming black in the first blush of dawn. They met her eyes and held.

He stared a moment too long, and for sure she stared right back. Then he tore his eyes away by turning his head and shaking it. "Best get to bed now. We may need a lot of help, but I'm afraid it's the kind of help best done with a noose."

Mel knew what that meant. Whoever had done this terrible thing was a murderer looking at Judgment Day.

"Tell me again how those boxes of dynamite were set." Justin strode alongside Cole, heading toward the cave where the explosives were stored.

"I've told you five times." Cole was doing his best to keep up with his brother's long paces. Cole had been shot a month ago. Now he'd nearly been blown up. Normally, Justin couldn't outwork him, he sure couldn't outthink him, and he'd never been able to outwalk him.

Cole was mighty tired of getting hurt while his baby brother dodged all the bullets.

Not that he wanted Justin shot, for heaven's sake. But Cole would be obliged if trouble stopped dropping on his head.

Justin reached a stack of wooden crates full of explosives. "This is the first one I found." He knelt and picked up the stick of dynamite with the cut fuse. "You had about an inch left when you got here." Justin looked from the fuse up to Cole. "You're a reckless fool, big brother."

Luckily, Cole was too exhausted to start fighting over the

insult. "We need to get all of these covered up. The men brought them all up."

Cole took a few minutes to point out where the boxes had been set, all over the sloping face of the mountain. "They can't sit out like this, and from now on we'll have to keep them under lock and key. Thing is, I've got no way to lock them up right now, not in this cave anyway." Cole could lock them inside his cabin, but the miners needed dynamite now and again and he'd always just let them use it when asked. After what happened, though, he needed someone to oversee handing it out. Records had to be kept from now on.

"I've never worried overly about the explosives. Now I feel like a careless fool for overlooking something so obvious."

Justin stopped and turned back to Cole, and they looked straight into each other's eyes. They were a close match. They might have passed for twins, even though Cole was five years older.

They might've passed, that is, if it wasn't for everything about them except their looks. Justin wore blue denim jeans, a Stetson, a gun on his hip, with his hair overlong. He kept it tied back with a thong during the stretches between haircuts, but not today. The night had been hard on him, and the thong was missing. Justin was smart as a whip, but he'd gone to school for only eight grades—and he'd skipped every day he could. He made his living with the strength of his back and his knowledge of ranching. He was in every way a western man.

Earlier this morning, Cole had gone to the cabin he kept here and washed up thoroughly. He had a change of clothes to put on. He wore a black suit with a narrow necktie. His hair was cut neat and short. He had a gun, but it was tucked in a shoulder holster inside his suit coat. He'd graduated from Harvard and had worked in business back in Boston and helped to manage his grandparents' vast wealth. He knew stocks and investments, and he could reason things out when another man might need to throw a fist.

No one seeing them standing together would mistake one for the other.

Add to that, Cole had lived with his blue-blooded grandparents. . . . Cole and Justin had different mothers. Cole's mother, Chance Boden's first wife, had died when he was three.

Then Pa and Cole headed west, where Pa ended up married to Veronica Chastain, Justin and Sadie's ma. Veronica had been—still was—a perfect mother to Cole. She always said she'd loved him before she had loved Pa.

Cole knew western ways just fine, yet he had city manners, at least most of the time, and Justin was as rough and tough as a cocklebur.

Justin looked past Cole's shoulder, scanning the land, then came back to focus on Cole. "Is this connected to the ones who sent that avalanche down on Pa and the man who shot you?"

Cole noticed Justin didn't mention that those same men had also kidnapped Angie, Justin's wife. But it wasn't because he forgot about it. That would never happen. Justin probably just got tired of making a list of all the wrong that'd been done to them.

They'd finally come to the reason Cole had asked Justin to come check the dynamite. Cole wanted to talk to his brother alone. He didn't want to worry the women before they had some solid answers. And Heath, married to Sadie, was strong enough and a good man and plenty of help, but he told Sadie every thought in his head. The nitwit stubbornly insisted Sadie should know what was going on rather than let the men handle these things.

So Justin and Cole had come out here alone.

"We know all that trouble isn't over. They attacked us at the ranch; they even attacked Pa in Denver." Pa's leg had been badly broken in an avalanche set off by their enemies. Afterward he was sent to a special doctor in Denver, who was a good hand at breaks where the bone tore through the skin. Months later, Pa was still in Denver healing up. There'd been an attack on Ma and Pa all the way up there while others harassed the Bodens here in New Mexico Territory. It all seemed aimed at taking control of their vast land grant near the Cimarron River. But all the trouble so far had focused on hurting the Bodens, attacking them personally. And the attacks had centered around the ranch.

No one had bothered the mines.

Until now.

Justin crossed his arms in the blustery wind. It was a chilly day, though early in February like this, the worst of the bitter weather was over. So while there was a bite to the wind, it wasn't painfully cold.

"They attacked real soon after you came back to work," Justin pointed out. "Maybe you just weren't here. And if this was an attack meant to kill you, they picked a poor way. If you'd've died, it would've been a lucky hit. And that's not the way they operated before. When Pa got hurt, they'd set up that avalanche well in advance and herded those cattle through the narrow canyon, knowing Pa would ride in there to get them out."

Nodding, Cole thought back to how these varmints had acted before. "The day they shot me, they were waiting for us, not sneaking around to make it look like an accident like they did with the rockslide that hurt Pa."

Justin shook his head slowly. "Were they trying to destroy the mines? Did they hope to bury every single one of the miners working inside those caves? If they'd succeeded, you might've lost a lot of men. And that would mean you'd lose a lot of leases."

"Not a chance." Cole studied the steep slope, dotted with

mine entrances. "There's no end to the number of men willing to risk their lives hunting gold. If every miner on our property died, there'd be new ones clamoring to take their places."

"That might be true the first time there was a disaster, and maybe even the second."

"But then the rumors would start." Cole looked sharply at Justin and picked up on his idea. "The Boden mines on Mount Kebbel are cursed . . . or haunted."

"And by then you might've gone a year without anyone finding gold, which is what keeps new men coming."

"A long game." Cole murmured it. "We've been saying these men are playing a long game." They'd found out there was a connection to the death of their grandfather thirty years ago. Then they'd hurt Pa just a couple of months ago—a note left behind connected the two attacks. None of them had figured out what caused the long halt between the attacks.

"They'd be willing to spend a year crippling this mine, and in that year they could make sure one of their attacks kills you, Cole."

"Which brings us right back to what we've been fighting all along. Someone wants to kill the Bodens and take our ranch."

"And now it looks like that includes the mines," Justin added.

Cole felt exhausted. Though he wasn't about to admit it to anyone, the battering he'd taken yesterday was too much on top of his barely healed gunshot wound.

"So our troubles aren't over."

"We knew better than to hope they were," Justin cut in.

"Fact is," Cole said, "considering they showed a willingness to harm so many people, our trouble looks to be worse than ever."

"Justin and Cole are planning something," Heath called over his shoulder without looking away from the window.

Mel almost smiled at the little brother spying on his big brothers, then telling on them. Of course, the "little brother" was a full-grown man. But the rest was about right.

She rose from where she knelt by a wounded man and looked around the damaged building almost destroyed by the multiple dynamite explosions yesterday. She knew exactly what those two brothers were talking about.

"You know they're planning how to handle what happened," Sadie said, the corner of her mouth curling up in sarcastic amusement.

"I could have helped." Heath sounded a little hurt.

"They knew you'd tell me every word they said." Sadie rose, then looked down at her patient with the newly plastered leg. "The doc will fashion a pair of crutches for you and then we'll get you moved back to your cabin."

They'd all tidied up after the day of mayhem and a long night of hard work. No one had a change of clothes, but Sadie had her blond hair pulled back in a neat bun, and the few hours of rest had made her hazel eyes sparkle again. Yesterday had taken the sparkle out of everyone.

"Thanks, Miss Sadie." The man sounded as though he was glad enough to have a broken leg if it got him a minute of Sadie's attention.

Sadie seemed to calmly accept it. But Mel had been treated the same, like the men reveled in the soft touch of a woman's hand. They didn't care whose hand it was. Angie, a gentler soul than Sadie and Mel, thanks to city living, was over in the corner applying a clean bandage to a man's head. Her hair was a lighter shade of blond than Sadie's, and her eyes were blue.

There were five men left, the most seriously injured. They needed to be still until the doctor decided they could go. But whether minutes or hours, however long the doctor held them, soon enough they'd be back in their cabins.

Mel thought the men should be kept there for a few more days. She was no woman to coddle a man if he didn't need it, but resting up for a couple of days after an explosion broke your bones didn't seem too much like coddling.

Only two of the injured would be staying. Their injuries had left them dazed and seeing two of everything, besides a broken bone or two, and they just weren't up to being transferred yet. The other three were sharing their cabins with mining partners so they wouldn't be completely alone. Yet despite the tragedy of yesterday, today most of the men were back digging for gold.

Mel was glad enough to watch a while longer these few who needed the most care.

"Let's go talk to the Boden brothers." Heath headed for the door.

Angie said, "I think if Justin and Cole want to protect us, that's sweet."

"Spoken like a newlywed who's madly in love." Sadie smiled at her new sister-in-law with true affection—and maybe just a tiny bit of pity. "Not like a sister who has been handling two overbearing big brothers all her life."

Mel felt a pang of being left out. She'd known Sadie from some of her earliest memories. And because she had worked with Angie at the Safe Haven Orphanage in Skull Gulch, she knew Angie well.

Now that Angie had been married to Justin for two weeks and was living under the same roof as Sadie, the two of them were close in a way that left her out.

Then Mel remembered who she was and how tough she was

and decided she didn't care worth spit—and if she did, she wasn't going to admit it, not even to herself.

But she did agree with tormenting the Boden brothers. That was just plain fun.

"I'll watch over the patients. I'm sure Justin will tell me what I need to know later." Angie turned back to one of the wounded men.

Mel considered how she could get Angie away from Justin long enough to toughen her up. She'd shown Angie a few tricks already, and they'd helped when Angie was kidnapped. But the woman needed a lot more work. She could especially use some practice shooting.

And the woman seemed to think a gun being loud was a good enough reason to avoid them.

Mel followed Sadie and Heath outside. By the time she came out, bringing up the rear, Cole and Justin had already seen them. Both looked irritated at the sight of company. They stood side by side, turned slightly away from where they'd been talking face-to-face.

Mel was struck by the similarities. Same height, same general weight, same dark hair, same blue eyes that flashed with intelligence and strength of will.

And also the huge differences.

But right now she just saw the look in their matching eyes. It was as good as a confession.

"Don't get started nagging me. We aren't keeping secrets." Cole glared at Heath, who grinned and then glanced at Sadie, whose pretty hazel eyes shot sparks at him as she crossed her arms.

"Just planning exactly what to do." Mel jumped in.

Too bad about Mel. Sadie looked too annoyed to talk—but that probably wasn't true. Not much stopped Sadie from talking. But he'd hoped to get a chance to tell them a few things before the yelling started. And Heath seemed inclined to just laugh at them. But Mel's mouth was working just fine.

"And debating all the options." Mel plunked her fists on her hips. It was a second before Cole realized he'd let his eyes rest on her . . . fists for a bit too long.

"Comparing what you've learned and deciding how to handle it before you tell us."

Cole shrugged and managed to meet her eyes. Tarnation, what was wrong with him? He'd never given a second thought to it being hard to take his eyes off his cowboy-ish neighbor girl before. Well, maybe a couple of times. Maybe more than a couple.

"You've known Justin and me for a long time, haven't you, Mel?"

"Since birth. Not a whole lot of surprises."

He'd have smiled at her, as Mel had always been a friend and a decent match for a couple of roughhousing boys like Cole and Justin. She was Justin's age, so she hadn't spent much time with the much younger Sadie until they were closer to grown up. She could outride both of them if he cared to admit it, and he didn't.

She was lightning fast with her pistol and deadly accurate with a rifle. They'd done plenty of hunting together, so Cole knew.

He'd seen her bust and hog-tie a thousand-pound steer, handle a branding iron, stick a bucking bronco, and shoe an ornery horse. She knew cattle better than Cole and just as good as Justin. Cole decided right then he was glad he ran a mine. Maybe he could beat her at mining, so long as she didn't turn her attention to it, and why should she?

Mel was the only child of a rancher with a mighty big spread. Not as big as the Cimarron, but still a prosperous, well-run property. Her pa, Jack Blake, who'd headed back to his ranch after everyone was patched up last night, had raised her to know how to take care of what would one day be hers.

Cole had wondered many times during his growing-up years whether or not Mel and Justin would suit each other. But there'd never been the least spark between them. And for some reason—some reason to do with those sassy fists propped on her slender hips—Cole was glad his little brother was all nicely and happily married.

Then Cole tore his gaze away from Mel, and it landed on the men digging graves at the base of Mount Kebbel. Six of them. Mining was a dangerous business, and these men went into it knowing that—but this was different.

There was only the thinnest thread of relief that these men hadn't been among the handful who had families. There were cabins tucked here and there in the heavily wooded lower levels of the mountain where no gold had yet been found, though not for lack of trying. Some of the men lived there with their wives and children. Some sent money to family members back east.

But these six were bachelors, including two brothers who lived and mined together. None left wives and children behind. If they had, that would've deepened the tragedy. But Cole knew them. They were hardworking men. He didn't rent to the kind of madmen who usually followed gold strikes. This strike was old, which helped. Gold fever seemed to follow new discoveries, not modest but long-working gold fields.

His miners were good and decent men or they didn't get a claim. This land was on the Cimarron Ranch, part of the old Spanish land grant Ma's father had been given, back when this land was part of Mexico. And back then the grazing land had the value. Rugged mountains stood just west of the ranch, and while they had some pockets of grassland, they hadn't been considered valuable.

Now Cole considered the land his.

True, his pa owned it. One day it'd be an inheritance split three ways between himself, Justin, and Sadie. But his name wouldn't be on the third of the ranch under the mines, because the CR would not be divided. Instead it'd remain one piece but with three equal owners.

Still, no matter what some deed said, the Boden mine operation was his. He ran it. He set the rules. It almost filled the void left from the company he'd run back in Boston. He'd loved doing that, and it still called to him at times . . . in fact too often. And now, with a sick twist of his stomach, he was going to have to admit that gold might've been behind their troubles all along.

Forcing himself to speak, he said, "Justin and I have to assume this is connected to the attacks on us. Those were meant to kill us all and leave the CR without any heirs."

They'd found a notebook carried by the man who seemed to be the leader, now dead, which had listed each of the Bodens by name. A checklist of people he'd been hired to murder.

Heath's eyes, a wild blue color that often flashed with good humor, were somber now. "It might be about the mines, Cole. I've seen men run mad over gold, and this is madness if ever I saw it."

"We'll have to assume for now that the attacks are connected. I'd hoped the men after us would accept defeat. They've come with force five times and been driven back each time." Cole rubbed his right thumb across his bottom lip as he considered that.

They'd come once for Pa with the avalanche.

Once for all of them when Heath earned himself a bullet wound.

Once for all of them when Cole ended up shot.

Once for Justin when Miss Maria from the orphanage died.

Once for Sadie when they tried to kidnap her and got Angie instead. They'd done that to lure the rest of the Bodens into a trap.

"And those who've come after us are all in jail . . . or dead," Justin added. "At least I thought they'd need to hire more men or take time to make a new plan to reach their goal. That should've taken more time."

"That's only true if this is a new plan," Mel said. "Maybe this has been part of things from the beginning. They just started out centering the trouble nearer your ranch house. After all, none of you come out here except Cole."

Cole almost flinched. His eyes locked on hers. "You're right, Mel. They're moving this war to the far west edge of our property and focusing on the mines. And they probably always planned to."

"What are we going to do?" Heath looked at Cole as if to say, since he and Justin had been out here sneaking around and plotting, they ought to have some answers.

Justin stepped in. "First thing is, the women are going home and they're riding with you, Heath."

"You're not going to move me away from trouble," Sadie snapped, "and then face it on your own."

"Somehow, I knew you'd say that." Cole braced himself to start in hollering at Sadie, but before he said a word he saw Heath step up close enough to wrap his arm around her waist and whisper something in her ear.

A look crossed Sadie's face that Cole couldn't make any sense out of. But for all the stress and worry and danger, Sadie looked deeply happy.

She nodded. "Heath and I will go back and take Angie and Mel with us."

What had made her change her mind like that? Cole was stunned. If he ever got a chance, he was going to take Heath aside and ask how he'd managed a fractious little filly like Sadie without any screaming.

"A few of the CR ranch hands already headed back," Heath said. "But there's enough left we'll have a good solid escort for the ride home."

"We're not ready for you to head back yet." Justin clenched his jaw and fell silent for a moment, then added, "There's time. The cowhands are busy helping open up the collapsed mine, knocking down loose rocks from its roof. A couple of others from our place are helping dig graves."

Cole turned to look at their progress. "I didn't even talk to anyone yet about how those men died."

Justin patted Cole on the back. "Do you need to, Cole? I'm sure they got hit with flying rocks."

Nodding, Cole said, "Even so, I want to know who found them and where. I didn't see men outside, except for one man who was caught out close to headquarters. Of course, in the madness I probably just didn't see the others, but someone had to find the bodies. I'd like to thank whoever helped with that. I know Murray was paying more attention, so I'll ask him how they died and where. It's too easy for a man to just disappear in the West. If anyone comes looking for these men, I want to be able to tell them how they died. I owe them that much."

Cole saw the solemn agreement from everyone.

A crash of rocks spun Cole around and swept him back to the day before. He braced himself to rush toward whatever new disaster was happening. Four men came running out of the mine Cole had helped pull men from just yesterday.

Before Cole could take a step, Gully emerged. He saw Cole and waved at him. "We're all right. We're bringing down some loose rocks on the walls and ceilings, making sure it's all braced up and safe."

"Good work, Gully." Cole did his best *not* to act like a man whose heart was pounding out of his chest.

Justin took over as if he knew Cole needed a minute to calm down. "Now, we all know Pa is adamant that we live at the ranch."

Cole smirked. "Adamant . . . that's a mighty nice way of putting it. He threatened to leave the whole ranch to our worthless cousin Mike and his no-account sons if we didn't move home."

Cole had built himself a nice house in Skull Gulch, and he ran a lot of the business of the mines from there. Sadie had lived there with him because she'd worked at the orphanage in town, which was operated by Angie's aunt, Sister Margaret.

When Pa had been hurt in the avalanche and was near death, he'd warned them about the change in his will and said he was counting his orders as being in effect from that moment on. He wasn't waiting to die to enforce his wishes.

All three of his children were to live for one year on the Cimarron Ranch. He wanted them to understand and respect the legacy that had been left to them. If they refused, or if even one of them left before the year was up, that would lose the ranch for all three of them.

So they'd all moved back home—except for Justin, who already lived there.

That left the orphanage short of help, so Mel had started spending time there with the children after Sadie left. Though she'd done her best, no one pretended Mel was a natural teacher. She was more comfortable hog-tying steers than making children tend to their studies. In fact, she treated the children about the same way as she handled the cattle, though she'd never gotten her lasso out. Or, to be perfectly honest, no one had ever actually *caught* her with it out, and the children weren't talking.

Then Sister Margaret had brought Angie, a widow, here from Omaha to take Mel's place. But before she'd even been fully settled, Angie had up and married Justin.

Mel was volunteering again, though Sister Margaret was looking for permanent help. Some might say she was desperately looking.

"We talked to your pa, Mel."

"What's he got to do with it?"

"Whoever's behind this knows us. Your pa headed home already, but he swears by the loyalty of his men, especially a group of them who have been with him for years."

Mel nodded. "I know you had a couple of men who were hired by you and ended up spying and working with your enemies. And we have men come and go, too. But we've got a good band of longtime hired men, and my uncle is our foreman. Do you want to hire some of them? Bring them to the CR until the trouble's over?"

Cole tipped his head sideways. "What I want is to bring a group here to fill the cabins of the men who were killed yesterday. That would give me a tough, loyal bunch of men on the place. Your pa said he's going to ask very carefully so no one realizes what he's done. I'm hoping whoever is after us doesn't know all the hired men from the surrounding ranches. I talked about the danger with your pa, but I swore to him the dynamite would be locked up, so we hope that stops something this dangerous from happening again. Still, they needed to be warned."

"I know just who he's going to pick," Mel said. "There are three longtime cowpokes on our payroll who are former soldiers and aren't afraid of much. He'll probably include Uncle Walt, who ain't afraid of nuthin'. They'd be good men to have fighting at your side. And in the winter, we can spare them."

Cole said, "I know a lot of these miners. We've been leasing land to them for years before I came home and started working here. I trust the ones already here, and we have every claim leased right now—not including the men we lost. Now's no time to let newcomers in. I want men out here I can depend on. I'm still supposed to sleep at home every night, but there's no doubt in my mind that Pa would agree I have to stay out here. So I'm moving to the mines. We lost six men, but there are only five cabins—the sixth man shared a cabin with his brother. And the mines and the empty cabins are all together, so we can meet at night and see if we've found any evidence."

"They're all right together?" Mel asked. "What are the chances of that?"

Pretty slim now that he thought about it. "Well—"

Sadie's gasp cut him off. "I don't think you should stay here overnight, Cole."

"You don't really believe Pa's gonna make Mike his heir, do you?"

"I don't think he would now that we're living at home." Sadie hesitated too long. "But there's more to it than that."

"Why? You know he'd want me here defending our property."

"Yes, but Pa's *not* here, and that will is legal and in good order. So long as it's written up as it is, if something happens to Pa before he can change it, you're risking the ranch by staying here."

Cole froze where he stood. The weather wasn't cold. New Mexico Territory had its winter, but there were often stretches even in the middle of winter that were fine days. Cool but not cold. He was frozen because he knew Sadie was right and he hadn't thought of it himself.

He looked from Justin to Sadie and back again.

Justin shoved his hands in his back pockets. "I understand why you want to stay out here, but she's right, Cole. We can't risk it. In fact, we already stayed away one night, every one of us."

"Pa said he's being treated carefully with his broken leg. In Ma's last letter, she said he's out of the plaster, and now the doctor wants to make his leg regain its full strength. He's not going to die." But even as he protested, Cole knew the law would be on the side of that will, however good the reason was for their not sleeping at home.

"Sometimes bad things happen, Cole." Sadie came right up to him and hugged him tight. Another hug so soon after Mel's. He couldn't help but glance at Mel, and the memory of the early morning closeness was there between them.

He was stunned at how good it felt. He was glad he and

Sadie had moved back to the ranch. Justin irked him, but living with him and Sadie had reminded Cole of how much he loved them, how much he loved his parents. How much he respected the legacy that was handed down with the Cimarron Ranch.

But this was a bad situation. He needed all his cabins filled so he had a solid reason not to lease to a new miner. "So I've got five cabins, five abandoned claims, but we've got four of them covered now. If one is open and someone comes in asking—I can and do take the measure of whoever wants a lease—but now, instead of just judging if he's going to be a troublemaker, I have to figure out if he's a traitor, too. And we've just cleared the ranch of them. I don't want to let a stranger on the place." He turned to Mel. "Can you think of another man your pa trusts? Can I take another of his cowhands and not leave him too short of men?"

Mel was slow to respond, and Cole suspected it was because she didn't want to make things worse. Finally she said, "That'll really leave us short. It's not a busy time of year so we can get by, but the four who'll come are the heart of the ranch. Besides that, we always have a lot of cowpokes move on after the busy time of year, roundup and the cattle drive. You know how rootless wranglers can be. They're always wanting to see new land, so they go wandering and hire on somewhere else come spring."

"That's how it is at the CR, too. We keep a skeleton crew through the winter."

"Pa's going to be working extra hard with his cowpokes gone. He wants to help you any way he can to clear up all this trouble. But the other men he has around haven't been here as long. He's not going to vouch for them. I sure enough wouldn't."

There was another long silence. "Short of burning down a cabin, I don't know what to do."

"I do."

Everyone turned to look at Mel. Cole knew she was a tough frontierswoman, and if she had a plan, he was willing to listen. "What've you got in mind?"

"The person who moves into that empty cabin is going to be . . . me."

Mel enjoyed watching Justin's eyes spark with rage. It felt good to see Sadie staggering backward. Heath caught her before she collapsed in a heap.

And it was just plain entertaining to watch Cole nearly choke.

Mel went and started slapping him on the back. She noticed Heath didn't get all worked up. The man was too quick with a grin in Mel's opinion, and someone probably ought to slug him until he took this whole mess seriously.

Instead he made sure Sadie was steady on her feet, then said, "I'm going to do some tracking, see if I can figure out anything about the man who set those charges yesterday."

"Not man . . . *men*," Mel said. "All those explosives set so far apart. He could've done it with increasingly long fuses, but that would've taken hours and it was early in the day. If he'd done it overnight, the miners would have noticed. He started after they went to work. And they were spread all over that hillside. Some of the fuses would've had to be yards long. One man couldn't have done all that."

Cole started breathing again, and he shoved her hand aside. She'd forgotten she was still pounding on his back. He'd been through a lot lately. She didn't need to go beating on him.

"Why would you waste time saying such a harebrained thing?" Cole stepped right up to her until his nose almost touched hers.

"You mean there might be more than one outlaw involved? It's because there were so many fuses. One man alone—"

"I'm not talking about that!" Cole leaned even closer. "I mean you moving into one of my miner's cabins."

This reminded her of when she'd gone to his house after he was just barely moving while he was still healing from being shot. He'd been fractious then, too. In fact, Cole had always shown a cranky side of himself around her. Not like Justin. She'd always gotten on with Justin in such a friendly way it was almost like talking with Sadie.

Mel realized that the cool morning was starting to burrow into her skin, even wearing a buckskin coat. "You know I fork my own broncs. You know there's not a thing a man can do that I can't. You know—"

"I'll let you two fight it out." Heath glanced at his wife. "You want to come hunting tracks with me, Sadie girl?"

"I don't think Mel should—"

Heath grabbed her hand and dragged her away, whispering something in her ear.

She looked over her shoulder at Mel and grinned. Then the two left to track down a killer as if it were a romantic walk.

"What I *know* is a woman isn't going to live out here, in a cabin alone, surrounded by dozens of rough men."

"You said there were women and children down there in those cabins. You said the men were all decent."

"I'm not discussing this with you. No. You can't be one of the *men*." Cole said the word loud and strong and that made her mad. "I'm just going to have to risk staying here. Pa will be fine about it as far as the will goes."

"He will be," Justin said. "But the law's the law. Just because Pa says it's okay doesn't mean—"

"Or I can send John." Cole glared at Justin.

Mel knew John Hightree, the Bodens' foreman, would be a great one to rely on. But . . . "You're trying to pick men who aren't connected to you. Whoever's doing this has been focusing on you and your ranch and your family. If they see your foreman out here, they'll know something's going on and they'll probably fade back into the woods and wait a few months before they strike again."

"Oh, that's just perfect," Cole said through gritted teeth. "So you want to get attacked. You want to risk *your* life. Besides being here with all these men, which is as improper as anything any woman has ever done."

Mel had heard a few things in her life, and she knew there were plenty of things less proper. "I ride with these men all the time. They would protect me with their lives, just as I would protect them. And as for that fool nonsense about properness, one of them is my uncle Walt. Pa's brother. So that's a respected family member, and we'll move into the two cabins closest together. It'll be as proper as Sadie living with you in your house in Skull Gulch."

"Walt Blake? He's a mighty good man to have at your side." Justin sounded like he was on her side now that he considered Walt.

"No." Cole jabbed her in the shoulder. Then he jabbed her again for every word that followed: "It. Wouldn't. Be. Proper."

She swatted his rude finger aside.

"The men out here are a lot more dangerous than the men in town."

"You told me you make a point of hiring only decent men."

"I do my best, but I can't vouch for every single one of 'em."

"Miss Maria was killed right in town, right near the orphanage I've been working at. How is that safe?"

"Mel, it's not a good idea." Cole changed from being bossy to acting like an understanding father.

She considered swatting him again, this time in the head. She'd always enjoyed fighting with good old Cole—another thing she had in common with Justin. But this wasn't fun; it was just annoying. The stitches in his head were the only thing that saved him from getting hit.

"Listen, I'll make it known I'm working with Uncle Walt. Anyone with a lick of sense won't bother me."

"A lot of outlaws are famous for not having a lick of sense."

Mel ignored that, even though it was a mighty good point. "We'll stick together. I'm sure my pa wouldn't even consider allowing this under any other circumstances. And if there is anyone these men are apt to talk to, it'd be a woman. They might've seen something and not even realized it. Even more, maybe their wives or children saw something. And I'm good at ghosting around in the woods. You want any tracking done, or a guard posted? I can do all of that as well as any man."

Cole didn't respond. Mel knew she was right. She saw it on Cole's face that he was realizing just how right she was.

And she knew he still wanted to absolutely forbid it. Right now he was cursing himself for being so reasonable—something he was really proud of in the normal course of things.

"But will you be safe, Mel?" Justin stepped up beside Cole and rested his solid hand on her shoulder. Justin was her friend. They'd been in the same grade in school. Cole was too old, too good-looking, too perfect. He'd always bothered her in some way she couldn't define. And yes, she was good friends with Sadie, but only since they'd been grown. Sadie was years younger than Mel.

Now Justin was looking at her with real concern. She had to dig around for her stubbornness to stand up to him.

"I'll make sure to have a cabin close enough to Uncle Walt's that he can hear me call out." She turned to Cole. "Do you have cabins that close?"

He shoved his suit coat back and stuck his hands in his pants pockets, looking disgruntled. "Yes. There are two so close we could almost build a big room and connect them." That brought his head up, and his eyes flashed as if he planned to rush off and do just that.

"The extra room won't be necessary. We'll use those two cabins and say I'm here with my uncle, but we both have our own claims. If the doors don't have sturdy locks, I'll get that changed right away."

"The locks are all good." Cole sounded insulted by her question about door locks. "These are gold mines, for heaven's sake. Men with gold in their cabins want to lock their doors."

"I'll let you two argue over it, but Walt Blake is a mighty good chaperone." Justin looked back and forth between Mel and Cole in a way that seemed odd. "I'll go check the locks on your cabins right now."

She wondered what he was thinking. He asked which of the cabins he needed to check. Cole told him, and Justin headed off down the mountain.

Mel bit back a grin. Cole might not be aware of it, but letting Justin go inspect the cabin was as good as giving her permission to stay. Now if she could just convince Pa and then, just as important, convince *herself* that this wasn't an idea cooked up by a half-wit.

Cole turned back, probably to take up the fight he'd already lost when Gully, the man Mel had met yesterday who ran the mines, came up the hill, walking mighty fast for an old man.

"Cole, I need you down there." He pointed at the graves being dug. Six men wrapped in blankets lay together on the ground, waiting for a resting place.

Mel wondered what Gully needed. Maybe someone to speak a few words over the graves? Then why did Gully look as though he wanted to shoot somebody?

Cole saw murder in Gully's eyes and forgot all about Mel and her half-wit idea about moving to the mines. "What's going on?"

"Get down here." Gully jerked his head toward the gravesite, then marched right back down the mountainside.

Cole looked at Mel, who shrugged. Finally, something the woman didn't think she knew everything about.

Heading down, Mel fell into step beside him. He wanted to argue with her some more, but that was just wearing him out. He'd just bide his time and tie her to her saddle and lead her horse home, as that seemed like the most reasonable way to handle the situation.

Gully was far enough ahead, Cole couldn't hear what he said, but the graves looked finished. The men digging had set their shovels aside and left.

Crouching beside the first body, Gully looked up at Cole. His eyes then shifted to Mel. "This ain't a sight for a woman, Miss Blake."

Mel nodded. "I appreciate your warning, but I'm tougher than I look."

Cole considered nagging her about this and was sick of his own voice. "What have you found, Gully?"

As if gathering himself, he said, "My apologies, miss." He flicked the blanket aside from the first man. Cole's stomach twisted at the ugly cut on the man's head.

Gully spoke without being asked. "Just by itself this wouldn't worry me, Cole. A man hit by a flying rock has a good chance of looking like this, no doubt about it." He covered the man back up, then stood. "I'll show you four more dead men and every one of them has a wound too much like this one. A blow to the head, that same ugly cut." Gully went on to describe what Cole had just seen.

"And the chances of them all dying from such a similar wound is—"

"It's impossible, Cole."

Cole felt ice sleet through his veins, coating the anger to keep it under control. He looked from Gully to the men lying dead at his feet. "These men were murdered?"

"We know all six were murdered because whoever set off that explosion killed them. Emmett on the end died because he was in the wrong spot at the time of the explosion. But these other five . . . I'm saying these men were specifically killed by someone standing behind them, probably with a shovel." Gully paused, his voice turning cold, quiet. "Whoever set off the explosion may have done it for the express purpose of covering up murder."

But why? Cole thought it, but didn't say it aloud. They were all thinking it already.

"We need to find out if these men were connected in some way," Mel said. "They had to be. If their deaths weren't random, then they were in something together."

"They *were* connected in some ways. Their cabins are all close, their mines clustered together. I've been here a long time, Cole, a lot longer than you."

Cole thought Gully sounded resentful about that. Did he not like having a new boss?

"These men never seemed close, though. Not especially friendly to each other or anyone else."

Gully nodded, his eyes looking back into the past. "I can't say for certain, but I think they all leased their mines about the same time. I know for sure three of them did. Not together; they came in separately. I'd remember five at once, with cabins side by side." Shaking his head, he added, "Check the records in the mine office. See if they've been here about the same length of time."

"I'll have Murray get the dates," Cole said.

Gully shook his head. "You should do it yourself."

Gully was glaring at him as if angry Cole would send someone else to do work he oughta do himself. Cole knew the men didn't exactly like Murray, but he'd never given it much thought. "You don't trust Murray to handle this?"

"I didn't say that." Gully crossed his arms and stared down at the row of fallen men. All of them killed by someone. "I just think it's best to keep it quiet. Whoever did this went to a lot of trouble to cover things up. No sense making the coyote suspicious that we're on to him. Take these men's names to the sheriff, have him do some checking, and see if there's any proof they knew each other before they came here."

"Because they might've come with a plan, something to do with a gold mine."

Gully cocked his head and sighed. "No shortage of men willing to kill over gold."

Cole dragged a hand over his mouth. The words he wanted to say were best kept inside, for now anyway. Was this about these six men or was it connected to the other troubles the Bodens had . . . or could it possibly be both?

"Where were they when they died? Who found the bodies, and were they found together?"

"I can't answer any of that," Gully said. "But I will before another day passes."

Without a word, Cole went to each man, uncovered them and studied the wounds that had killed them. One could have taken a terrible blow from a flying rock, but every one of them in the same spot on the head? Finally he was convinced.

Cole looked up the hill and saw Emmett's brother coming with a group of others. "Gully," he said, "we need to pay our respects and speak a few words for Hoot's benefit. He'll miss his brother."

They took the time to do it right. Cole, Mel, and Gully shook Hoot's hand and talked quietly with him. No one came to see the other men.

"I'll bury my own brother, Gully."

"Hoot, we're not giving up until we find the ones who set off the dynamite. It's murder, plain and simple." Cole glanced at the dead. Not all that simple.

Gully nodded as he moved to the man next to Hoot's brother. "Time I got started on the burying."

"I'll check some things here and then take everything I've got to the sheriff. We need to get our questions answered. Gully, for these five, have someone clean out their cabins and store the stuff together. I'll go through everything they own to see if there's anything that should be sent to their heirs."

Or anything that could be used to track down their killers.

Cole turned to Mel, who wanted to live alone in a cabin where the last resident had been killed. He needed the help and needed that cabin leased to keep from having to answer questions about why it stood empty. But his stomach twisted at the thought of what she might face. He could lock up the dynamite, but he didn't see the sense in locking up every shovel. He couldn't believe he was in agreement that she might come and stay here. He'd have never allowed it if it were Sadie or Angie. But Mel was tough. About as tough as any man he knew.

"You need to go talk to your pa, Mel," he said, "and see if he'll agree to your wild plan."

Murder. Deliberate, cold-blooded murder.

She hadn't counted on that.

She was acting as though she was going to help them get to the bottom of whoever set off the explosions, but the truth was she had no idea how to investigate a crime, and no real interest in chopping away in a mine. She had a strong preference for cattle and fresh air.

But she did want to help. And if she wasn't any help, at least she was filling up a cabin so that Cole didn't have to worry about any new renter showing up . . . maybe even one working for their enemies.

"It sounds like it's settled then. I'll head home and be back before nightfall with the hands Pa will send." If Pa agreed to it. Oh, he'd send the hands, including Uncle Walt. But as for her coming back here to stay, she was going to have to ask him just right.

She headed to the stable for her horse, Cole striding up the trail right behind her. At the flat where the mine office stood in near ruins, she paused. There were other buildings, some in usable shape, with others needing a lot of work. Cole's broken-down new mine was about a hundred feet to the east side of his office, dug into the large wall of rock that jutted out of a long plateau. The mine looked like the last part of this area to be dug into, and she wondered why they'd left an area so close for last.

"This is a big job, Cole." It struck her just how big. The white cap of Mount Kebbel loomed over them to the west, and the Boden mines went most of the way to the top. "It's an impressive business. You've been running all this work here and I've never seen it, never even heard you talk about it much. Why is that?" She stopped scanning the area and looked back at him. "Do you want this place to be a secret for some reason? Have you had trouble with outlaws wanting to steal gold?"

Cole gave her a half smile and shook his head. "It's just my own project is all. Pa giving me charge over the ranch's mining interests was a huge show of respect. I've spent the last two years, since moving back from Boston, showing Pa I can handle it and make the business work, and that my education wasn't wasted. I wanted this to be mine—the success of it or the failure."

"How many of the men renting from you have been here more than two years?"

"A handful of the miners have been here a long time and seem to be settled, but mostly they come and go." His eyes narrowed. "Not those five who died, though . . . they'd all been here a while. I'll need to ask Murray what he thinks of them."

"Murray, the man wearing a suit yesterday who acted like a doctor?"

"Murray did act like a doctor, didn't he?" That quirked a smile out of Cole. "When I came back, he was running the place for Pa. I took over and lifted a big load off his shoulders and gave him a raise while I was at it. He's a good man, but I had a few ideas to do things different. Since I've been back, the mines have become more profitable. We've opened new mines and leased them out. We've used new mining techniques that speed up the digging. In fact, I've nearly doubled our profits since the day I started here." He clapped his mouth shut.

Mel knew why. The man was just plain bragging. He was proud of what he'd accomplished and looked fit to bust his buttons when he talked about it, yet she'd never heard him talk about it before. She'd never heard anyone talk much about the mines and that struck her as strange.

"You've been back two years now. It seemed like you were gone back east forever."

"Nearly ten years."

"Ten years and three months. You left late in the spring of 1868 and came home in September of '78." His train carrying him home had come in on a Wednesday, midmorning. The Bodens had thrown a party the next Saturday that was still legendary in the area. Talk about killing the fatted calf. She remembered the day he'd left, and she sure as certain remembered the day he'd come back. But the Blakes and Bodens were old friends, so of course they'd remember the return of the prodigal son. Though *prodigal* might not be fair. Going to college and living with your grandmother and grandfather wasn't exactly running off to find trouble.

Chance Boden thought it was, though, and made no secret of his worry that he'd never see his son again once he'd gotten used to life on the East Coast with his wealthy grandparents.

But mostly everyone in the area was proud of a local boy going off to Harvard.

Not Mel. She'd always thought it was pure nonsense. A man didn't need a college education to handle cattle. But Cole wasn't handling cattle, now, was he? She saw what Cole had created here and knew he'd used some savvy business training to manage things so well, make so much money, and find a way to do it all so that the miners who leased from him were prosperous and staunchly loyal to him.

She suspected Cole was running on anger mixed with grief

right now. But with the suspicion Gully had just raised, Cole's anger had turned to black rage.

She regretted pushing him, regretted trying to get her own way. She thought she could help, but could she really? Or was she just fascinated by this nearly secret part of Cole's life—the biggest part that kept him locked up in the office at the ranch, or here at the mines, or on the road between the two places.

And no one ever talked about the Boden mines.

So she'd noticed when Cole left and when he'd come back.

"You counted the days I was gone, huh?" Cole waited to see if Mel's eyes lit up. He always considered her light brown eyes to be unusually pretty. They reminded him of the caramel candy Ma used to make from time to time. Her hair was a match, her tanned skin as well—all golden brown.

He found himself looking more closely at his neighbor, the tough daughter of a tough rancher, and he'd been looking at her too much already.

She was just one of the neighbors, a little unusual too because she was a woman obsessed with ranching. A lot like Cole's little brother, Justin. Cole had grown up expecting she'd end up marrying Justin. They'd be a perfect match, honestly. The marriage would join the two big ranches, with their interest in ranching a strong bond between them.

To be completely honest with himself—which Cole tried to be—before leaving, he'd had a notion or two about Mel. But she'd been Justin's friend more than his, though the three of them rode around together often enough when they were youngsters. And at the time, he was already determined to go to college back east. His grandparents wrote to him often and promised a lot of things, and that had awakened a desire to see a bit more of the world and also gain an education.

His grandparents, Davidson and Priscilla Bradford, had said things, very subtle he could see now, about Pa grieving over his ma until he wasn't thinking right. And Pa running off with Cole under cover of night in some fevered notion that his grandparents wished Cole ill.

They'd laced all their worries in kindness because Cole would never have sided against Pa, and they seemed to know it. Mainly they'd told him how much they loved him and wanted to get to know him.

So he'd gone east to college, even though he knew he was breaking Pa and Ma's hearts.

Later, when he returned home, he was more than a little surprised that he'd never received a letter telling him Mel and Justin had married. Of course, that letter hadn't come because they hadn't married. And she was still as good a friend to the family as always.

And now good old Justin had married someone else. If Cole had warm thoughts about Melanie Blake, there was no little brother in his way. But there was one big barrier, and bigger with Mel than with any other woman.

Except here she was, putting herself in his clutches by moving out to the mines.

Not really in his *clutches* exactly, because if he put a foot wrong, her dangerous uncle Walt would shoot him, her only slightly less dangerous father would shoot him, his own mighty dangerous father would probably come home from Denver and shoot him, and while they were at it, Mel—who could only be described as dangerous—would shoot him herself.

And even knowing that didn't stop him from playing with the idea of her being in his clutches.

Then a solid, strong hand shoved at his chest and woke him up from whatever nonsense he was in the middle of. He realized he'd leaned toward her.

Mel stepped back, and he had to face those golden brown eyes, expecting anger, maybe a threat or two. Instead he got "I can only imagine how upsetting this has been for you, Cole."

Good grief, he got pity.

"You need someone to hold on to. I know you're grieving and ready to explode with anger. But the way you were leaning toward me, well, Cole, I can't let your upset turn into a kiss that doesn't mean anything to you. It's a hurtful thing you're thinking of doing to me."

He looked in her eyes and saw she *was* hurt. First she'd pitied him, and now he'd hurt her feelings. While he'd been braced for her to draw her gun. Maybe he should make this whole episode officially a disaster by trampling her with his horse.

Mel, a happy girl . . . no, a happy *woman*. She was twenty-five years old, for heaven's sake. She was a fully grown, tough woman who had a nice, cheerful attitude about life. He'd seen a lot of expressions on her face, but never hurt, not like this.

And maybe she was right. He was upset almost beyond sense. Had he been having improper thoughts of her because of having such a bad day?

That sure sounded insulting. His muddled brain woke up a little, and having never had a romantic notion toward Mel before today—well, not much of one—he remembered why it was impossible.

Suddenly her hurt and pity was replaced by anger as she turned on her heel and strode toward the stable where they'd put up the horses. And there he stood, left speechless because he had no idea what to say. And with his feet stuck to the ground, because the only place he could think of to go was after her, which he oughta not do unless he wanted to give her another chance to draw her Winchester on him.

He was still standing there when Mel came out with her horse saddled and the anger gone from her face, this time replaced by a blank expression that told him nothing.

She didn't ride in a big circle to avoid him. Instead she rode right up to him and said, "I'll go talk to Pa now. If he's agreeable, I'll move into the cabins with the other Blake hands before nightfall. Have them ready."

She squeezed the horse with her thighs, which Cole noticed overly, and headed down the mountain as if nothing had happened between them.

But oh yes, it had. It took a while, but Cole's mind cleared and settled on the one thing that could absolutely not be denied.

Despite his fumbling and improper behavior, he knew upsetting her and leaving her angry was the right thing to do, because despite his love for his family, his satisfaction with his job, and his father's blackmailing last will and testament, Cole knew there was a chance he might not be staying at the CR. He had loved his time back east. He'd loved the cut and thrust of business. He'd loved his finely tailored suits and the women's silk dresses and the regal houses.

But this life appealed to him, too.

His family. The mines. Home. Being here felt as natural as breathing.

Boston with its busy streets, fast-paced business deals, the pleasure he got from being respected as Davidson Bradford's grandson. He'd fit in there as well as he did here.

His parents thought that when he came home, it was all settled. But Cole had never lost the tug of the city. One of these days he was going to have to make a hard decision. And if he did head back east, Mel Blake would never come along with him.

Most any other woman from the area wouldn't, either. Even if they did, they'd find themselves in a strange life that didn't suit them. Because of that, he'd held back from involving himself with anyone, and for that same reason he'd never courted a woman back in Boston.

He thought of this dilemma far too often, yet he'd been unable to come to a decision about his future. For right this minute, though, he knew what to do. He turned his attention to where it belonged. He needed to hunt up some culprits and make them pay for killing his miners.

"You're sure that says Bradford?" Chance leaned close.

Her husband's strength, the warmth of him pressing against her, the masculine smell—it all threatened to distract Veronica from her work.

It hit her hard how blessed she was. She'd come so close to losing him. But here he was, standing sturdy, her precious husband alive and well.

God had been so good to her.

They lived such a different life here. So far from the ranch. And together mostly every minute, living quietly in a small cottage in Denver while Chance's badly broken leg healed.

There was no comparison to their lives in New Mexico, with both of them working hard all day. Chance mostly outside working cattle and running the ranch. Her inside with Rosita, keeping the home fires burning.

This would almost have been a vacation. Except that someone

had tried to kill them—and their fear he might try again—and her children being in terrible danger.

Nope, this was nothing like a vacation.

And the worst of it was their children were facing danger in New Mexico Territory while she and Chance were trapped in Denver fighting for Chance's leg. It was almost more than Veronica could bear.

King Solomon would be confounded by this mess.

Chance wanted to go home to the CR now! The doctor demanded more time so that the leg would mend completely with no lingering pain and no pronounced limp.

"I've told you and told you it says *Bradford*." Veronica looked up from the note they'd found on a man who'd tried to kill them here in Denver. They'd thought their troubles were all left behind in New Mexico, but it had followed them all the way up here. And it was written in such a terrible, cramped scrawl that it was proving to be impossible to decipher.

Her husband was a good man. And when Veronica discovered the name Bradford, Chance resisted believing the name was in this note for a very good reason—because he wanted to believe it so badly.

Cole's grandmother was an old horror. Veronica had met her twice. Such an arrogant woman, well, arrogance could be borne, but her unkindness toward Justin and Sadie while lavishing time, attention, and gifts on Cole was another matter altogether. She'd seen Justin's confusion when all the gifts came and they were all for Cole. And that was when she was sending packages. Veronica and Chance could help with the sting of that. But when Priscilla Bradford herself had arrived with piles of little-boy gifts for Cole and nothing for Justin, her second son had developed a shield around his heart and acted with gruff disgust like the toys were stupid.

Sadie just cried.

Veronica had wanted to strangle the old bat.

Chance's feelings were even more intense. He detested the Bradfords right down to the soles of his feet. They'd made him run. He'd gone into hiding to escape them. He remembered that as weakness and shame. Which had only made him loathe them all the more.

As far as the note was concerned—and the note was a long way from being untangled—Chance finally had his revenge. He was proved right after all these years that the Bradfords weren't just selfish and greedy and rude and unkind. They were evil.

Knowing that gave Chance such intense satisfaction, he was ashamed of it. It was made worse because both Davidson and Priscilla Bradford were dead now. So Chance couldn't confront them or accuse them—he could only hate.

And that was tough because Cole had loved his grandparents.

"All right then. Their name is in there, but what does it say about those low-down, snooty, child-stealing thieves?"

"You know they didn't steal him, Chance. Not exactly." But once they'd found Cole, they'd begged and bribed and promised and lured. And in the end they'd won. At least for the long time they'd had Cole in Boston. Never had Veronica hated it more than when the Bradfords had convinced Cole to come east for college. It broke her heart and scared her to the marrow of her bones that she might never see her son again.

Of course, not *her* son, not by blood. Cole was Chance's son by his first wife, the Bradfords' daughter. Veronica married Chance later when Cole was nearly five, and she'd loved the boy as truly as one born to her.

"To think those two had something to do with all this trouble," Chance said through gritted teeth, "and they're dead and beyond my grasp."

"I know you want to blame all our trouble on them so badly that you're sure your feelings are a sin."

"Oh, they are." Chance clenched his fists and his jaw with equal strength. "My anger can be nothing else."

"But you're not a sinner for being glad the Bradfords finally revealed their true colors."

"Except now we have to tell Cole, and you know how he loves them. He never saw them for the varmints they were."

"Maybe we don't have to tell him."

"I don't see how we get to the bottom of this without all the facts being made clear." Chance straightened away from her. "I've always disliked them so fiercely."

"Dislike doesn't begin to describe it. You hate their guts, admit it, Chance. Especially that old witch Priscilla."

Chance looked sideways at her and gave her a shrug. "You're right, but it's a poor Christian who feels that way. I don't like to speak of hating someone."

"Not even someone evil?"

"I grabbed Cole and snuck away rather than stand up to them. They wanted my son and I didn't think I was strong enough to stop them from taking him, not with all their money and influential friends. I thought then, and I still believe, that if I didn't slip away and lose myself so they'd never find me, they'd take my son. Which means my hate is based in knowing I'm a coward."

"You weren't a coward, you were wise." They'd had some version of this discussion a hundred times in their married life together. "You saw the lay of the land and you decided not to fight your battle where you'd lose it. By the time the Bradfords found Cole, you were settled. We were married. We had connections in New Mexico Territory, and all theirs were back in Boston. That was land a battle could be won on."

Chance nodded, but when he spoke it wasn't to say she'd

convinced him of anything. Instead he said, "We have to tell Cole we found his grandparents' names."

"And that we found the name of Don Bautista de Val and his wife, Lauressa. I remember her. If the Don was arrogant, the señora thought she was a queen." Somehow the man who'd been a partner in her father's land grant was involved in this.

"It's gonna be about the hardest letter we've ever written. I want both of us talking over every word we write. You know how Cole is about the Bradfords—he won't hear a word against them."

She knew this was something Chance always carried around, the worry about the Bradfords' hold on Cole. At least she and Chance had him all his growing-up years. Cole knew they loved him, and he'd always loved them back.

After a long time away, he returned to them. But Veronica always wondered if they really had him. He was much changed from his education and wealth. She knew too, though Cole never said so, there were things about life on the East Coast that he missed.

And now he faced a terrible danger, the kind that a man only faced in the West. Cole was as courageous as any warrior and would stand with them and fight to the end. But what about after the end, when peace was restored? Would he long for a more settled land?

She'd stirred this around in her head for years. What would make her son put down roots at the CR? They'd given him the mines and a free hand to run them. They'd kept quiet while he built his own house in town . . . until Chance had finally snapped and threatened him into moving home. Would Chance's enforced year of living at home open Cole's eyes to the legacy of the CR? Or would it drive him away once and for all?

She never stopped wondering what it would take to win him fully to the West.

Mel should have punched Cole in the face.

When he leaned into her like that, it looked for all the world as if the man was going to kiss her.

He had no business doing such a thing. She ought to refuse to help him. But for some reason she wasn't one bit interested in refusing. Which brought her back to convincing Ma and Pa. She practiced what she'd say as she galloped toward home.

Ma, I'm going to live in a miners' camp with about two dozen men. Maybe more. I didn't get an exact number. Oh, and I'll have a cabin by myself.

Mel left Cole believing it was all arranged, which made Cole as big a fool as she was. Now, as she unsaddled her buckskin, she was running out of time to think of the perfect words.

Pa, can I borrow Uncle Walt and three other men?

Pa was already planning that. But they hadn't planned on her.

Her parents had always let her go her own way. While Sadie Boden had kept mostly to the house and worn pretty dresses and learned to cook and sew and run the lovely home the Bodens had, Mel had been raised as the future owner of the JB Ranch, named for her pa, Jack Blake. Oh, they figured she'd marry, but even then they wanted her to know how to run the ranch she'd inherit.

So her folks had let her run a bit wild by proper rules of behavior, yet they were a long way out, and as the only heir, Mel had to learn. Pa wouldn't have pushed it if she'd wanted to stay inside more. Still, it suited her to work cattle and live mostly on horseback.

And now she was going to push her parents further than she ever had before. She felt a little sorry for them because she fully intended to do this.

Ma was probably in the house alone. Pa was gone working cattle most of the daylight hours. She strode toward the back door of the tidy log cabin. It was plenty big, but not a bit grand, not like the Bodens'. But that was because her pa and ma were practical people. Pa didn't want the work of building anything big—and chopping wood to keep it warm—and Ma didn't want the work of trying to keep a whole territory's worth of dust out of any more rooms than were necessary.

I'm going to be living alone, and I'm planning to mine for gold.

She stopped for a second, suddenly curious. Would Cole let her keep the gold if she found some? He'd better. If he wanted her to sign a lease, she'd do it. Any gold she personally clawed out of rock, while she was trying to help Cole, should be hers to keep. A strange flare of heat washed over her.

Ma, Pa, I think I have gold fever. I'd like to dig up enough gold to build a mansion and have a dozen servants and silk dresses.

Where had that come from? She didn't want a mansion. She had no idea what servants would do, unless the "servants" were cowpokes. If she had a mansion, most likely the servants would spend all their time dusting. Smarter to just not build the dad-blasted mansion and skip the need to dust it.

Of course, if the servants were just a fancy word for cowpokes, they could rope and ride along with her. And silk dresses? Where in the world would she ever wear one of those? A cattle drive?

Not likely.

She'd look foolish at church, too, amid the calico and gingham.

That image restored her common sense . . . but even so, the gold lured her, and if she had a touch of gold fever and was going to live at a gold mine, she was going to have to get her parents to go along with it.

She swung the door open and went to look for Ma, still with no idea what she was going to say.

Ma, do gold miners ever wear silk dresses?

She paused to whack herself in the head, then heard a pan clank into something in the kitchen. It had to be Ma. They had no servants, and no rooms for them to live in if they did get some.

She swung open the kitchen door. "Hi, Ma . . . and Pa."

At that moment she realized she'd been planning to divide and conquer. Ma was going to be hard to convince, but of the two parents, Ma was definitely easier to handle.

Pa surged to his feet, concern etched on his face. "How are things out at the mine? A few of the men came home and told us more details after I left, but we want to hear it again from you."

Mel remembered the six men who'd lost their lives and all the mental wheedling she'd been doing suddenly seemed foolish. "Cole needs my help. You said a few of our men could go out there."

"Yes, I told Cole I'd send men over."

"He's got five empty cabins, and you've got four men to send. This is no time to let strangers around the place. I told him I'm going, too."

Pa's brow wrinkled. Ma gasped quietly and narrowed her eyes, watching Mel closely.

"Uncle Walt will go along and you know we have only three other trustworthy hands."

"I trust my men." Pa sounded offended.

Nodding, Mel said, "I do too, honestly, but there were two men hired at the Boden ranch who'd come there to spy and cause trouble. Besides our older hands, we don't really know the men we've hired. So yes, I trust them. But not with Cole's life."

Pa tipped his head a bit as if to give her that point.

Mel pressed on. "I convinced Cole I'd have a good chance of helping get to the truth. He doesn't want anyone from the CR because whatever's going on, they seem to be targeting Bodens, and he can't be positive there aren't more outlaws amongst the men at his ranch. Cole thinks they've caught all the traitors, but he can't be completely sure. Besides, whoever's after them might know men who worked for the Bodens and see right away who was a danger to them."

"But they wouldn't know anyone from our ranch," Pa pointed out.

"The miners there will want to talk to a woman, and Uncle Walt, along with our other hands, will be there to protect me and keep things proper. In fact, Uncle Walt and I will be in cabins only a few paces apart. And many of the miners have wives and children there. It's not an all-male place like you might imagine, and it's not that dangerous."

Not counting dynamite. And shovels used as weapons.

Pa sank back into his chair.

Mel sat down at the table. "You've heard some of the trouble the Bodens have faced, but not all. They've been thinking all the danger was aimed at taking their land. Now, though, I'm starting to wonder if it's been about the mines all along. Focusing on the land never made sense, because if they wanted land and were willing to kill for it, why not come and pester us?"

"We're a big organization," Pa said with a slow nod.

Ma refilled Pa's coffee cup and got one for herself and Mel, then sat. The three of them had always been a good team. Right now she needed their help. She needed them to talk this through with her because they always helped her sort out her thoughts.

"Cole and Justin warned you about the possible danger around here, and yet we've never had a bit of trouble."

"Maybe they don't have enough outlaws to go after two ranches. Maybe we're next." Ma got that look in her eye that meant she was ready to grab a gun and start up a war.

It was one of the things Mel liked best about her ma. "All the more reason to help protect the Bodens, so that the varmints pestering them are in jail and can't turn on us."

Pa gave her a mighty grim look. "I want to help the Bodens, but I don't like you up there. Why isn't Cole staying there?"

Mel wasn't sure how much they knew about the strange details of Chance's will, but she quickly told them why Cole couldn't stay.

"They don't trust their own hands, and the ones they do trust, they can't spare. You have to stay here, Pa. If four men and you go to the mines, there's no possible way to get the work done. But Cole doesn't want to spread the word far and wide that there's danger at his mines."

Then she added the part she hoped would convince him. "I'm planning to stick close to Uncle Walt's side. If whoever's behind this really does want those mines, you know I'm tough. I can shoot as straight as a Comanche arrow. I don't need anyone to take care of me, but I'll have four good men doing it anyway. And Cole said the miners he has up there are decent men, many of them married with their wives living nearby. They go home every night to family and supper. It's only newcomers we have to worry about. I'll be safe, and it feels like the right thing to do to help neighbors as good as the Bodens."

Pa stared at Mel for a long moment. Then he turned to Ma. Neither of them looked a bit happy. Mel could tell they were thinking between them, connected without words. They'd always been good at that.

They each looked back at her, and she could tell they'd come to a decision.

Very reluctantly Ma nodded. "We've always given you a lot of freedom, and you've proven yourself to be wise beyond your years. So we agree, at least for now, that you can go."

Mel decided not to hang around and give her parents time to come to their senses. "Pa, come with me to talk to the men. I want to get back there and settle into our cabins before nightfall."

"I'm going to gather a few things for you," Ma said, "things you'll be needing, and send supplies for you and all four men. I'll make up bundles so you won't have to take a wagon or packhorses."

Mel hesitated for a second, then went and pulled her ma into a tight hug. "I'll be careful. You know me. I'm not a reckless woman."

Ma hugged her back and whispered in her ear, "What I know is, you're the finest part of my life, Melanie Blake. You be careful. I love you."

"You go pack some clothes, Mel, leave Ma to get the supplies together. I'll have a word with Walt."

The way Pa said it made a chill skitter down Mel's spine.

Mel loved her uncle and trusted him completely, but the truth was, Uncle Walt was known to be a hard man, a dangerous man. He only came to work for Pa about four years ago. She'd heard it whispered that it was because, after years of being a hired gun, he'd made his peace with God and wasn't willing to earn a living that way anymore. Whether it was because of the rumors or the fact Uncle Walt could freeze you to death with a glare from his cold eyes, he wasn't a man anyone pushed around.

Yet Pa was an excellent judge of character and he trusted his younger brother without hesitation. Pa loved him, and Uncle Walt loved them all right back. That was good enough for Mel. Pa agreeing to this and talking with Walt made her sure he knew everything he needed to about Walt. Even with brotherly love between them, Mel didn't think Pa would trust or respect a professional killer.

Whatever Uncle Walt's story, Mel was glad to have him at her side.

She rushed upstairs to pack. Knowing gold mining was a dirty business, she included several changes of clothes so she wouldn't have to wash too often. Without telling Ma, three of those outfits included riding skirts. Mel just wasn't going to put up with digging in the dirt while wearing a calico dress.

She hoped Uncle Walt wasn't a tattletale.

8

"There were at least three men." Heath rose from where he crouched by a clear footprint beside the spot a dynamite fuse had been lit. "I've found prints that are different on each level."

Cole nodded. "We lease for the ground beneath the mines, as far down as they want to dig. They have clear possession of the land." He looked down the slope, dotted with mine entrances. Three levels. Three bombers.

Heath had spotted a third man's footprints, and Justin had gone following them. Now he'd come back. "Heath, I might be able to pick up this varmint if I'm careful, but he steps onto a trail a lot of men walk on. Once he does, I'll only be able to figure him out if he turns off the trail alone. I could use your eyes on this."

Heath glanced at the sun, now sunk behind the snowcap of Mount Kebbel. They were working on the east side of the mountain and already in deep shadow. "I doubt I can see much from here. And we need to head home if we plan on sleeping there tonight."

Heath looked between them. "I could stay here. If the crew from the JB Ranch shows up, I'll point out their cabins for them, and I can bunk in the cabin you keep here, Cole. Your pa's will doesn't say anything about a son-in-law sleeping away from the Cimarron Ranch."

The idea bothered Cole so much, he had to face the cold fact that he didn't want to leave until Mel came back. He wanted to have a serious word with her uncle Walt.

And there was nothing he could say to Walt that Heath couldn't say and that Mel had no doubt already said. So what it came down to was, he wanted to see if he couldn't talk her out of this madness . . . madness that he had to admit was a pretty good idea. He just plain wanted to see her again, but that wasn't all. What he had tickling in the back of his mind was finding just a few moments to be alone with her, and that was a purely bad idea. Sure thing Uncle Walt wasn't going to let her out of his sight. And he wasn't going to stand quietly by while a man paid too much attention to his niece. So that left Cole telling her good night, which was no good reason to wait and ride home to the CR in the dark.

He was just getting ready to do the commonsense thing and leave Heath behind when a group of riders emerged from the woods at the base of the mountain, Mel riding in the lead along with her gunfighter uncle at her side.

Cole started down. "We'll go as soon as I show them where their cabins are."

"I can do that, Cole." Heath's voice followed him downhill, but as always there was a thread of humor in it. Cole wondered, if he looked back, if Heath wasn't laughing and maybe Justin, too. Well, Cole didn't want to know about that so he walked faster and reached the bottom about the same time Mel, Walt, and three other men pulled to a halt, all staring at him.

This was Cole's mine. He ran it. He was the one who should welcome newcomers.

Justin and Heath came right behind him.

"Howdy, Cole. Justin, Heath," Mel said. "I think we saw the cabins. We could tell which ones were empty. There are five of them with their doors open."

Five cabins all together. Five men mining side by side. All five of those men dead by the same brutal, deliberate method. Cole's mind kept circling back to these men, who knew one another for years, not showing much outward signs of a connection, yet all of them dying the same day.

He shook off his thoughts. He could do nothing about it now, and nobody from the JB needed his help.

Which didn't make Cole head for home.

And then Mel spoke again, and he kind of wished he'd headed out.

"All of us," Mel said, sweeping a pointing finger to include the men riding with her, "expect to sign leases, and we're keeping any gold we dig up."

"I hope you don't all end up being miners instead of cowpokes. Jack's gonna blame me."

The men all chuckled, and even Mel's face broke into a smile. "I might get gold fever. I might develop a taste for expensive silk dresses."

That got another low rumble of laughter, especially since she was sitting astride a gray gelding, wearing a riding skirt and a Stetson, with a Colt Peacemaker strapped on her hip. Fancy dresses and Mel Blake. For a second, Cole found himself distracted by the image of Mel in silk. He thought she'd look pretty good . . . just like now.

Cole cleared his throat. "I'll get the leases to you first thing in the morning." He lowered his voice. "Do any of you know a blamed thing about mining?"

The men looked between each other, until finally Walt Blake spoke up. "I've spent some time in a mine."

Every person there listened up when Walt spoke. It was just good sense. Walt's eyes were a light brown just like Mel's, though there was a darkness behind them. A man who'd seen too much and didn't have much to smile about. Something about him sent a shiver down Cole's spine. Not that he felt like the man was dangerous to him, for Cole had heard Walt was a decent sort of man. A gunman, yes, and tough as an old boot. But it was said he liked to defend the weak against the powerful. He was interested in justice more than money. He fought on the side of right.

And a lot of the time when Walt got into a fight, no one wanted to buy in, and the fight was over just from the mention of his name.

"Didn't care for it much," Walt said. "Never wanted to dig my way into the earth and go too far down, but I know the way of it and can give enough pointers that these men will look as good as any of your miners. I imagine some of them were new to it when they signed on, too."

"Can't deny that," Cole said, nodding. "Do you need help getting settled?"

He meant to ask Mel, but he did his best to include everyone. "Justin, Heath, and I are done for the night so we're free to lend a hand." He paused and looked from one man to the other, ending when his eyes reached Mel's. "We really appreciate that you've come. You're fine neighbors and the Bodens will do the same for you if you're ever in need. There's some danger here. If any of you want to leave at some point, I'll understand and you'll leave with my respect."

The men all nodded silently. Though Cole had spoken the promise out loud, every man there already knew it for a fact. The Blakes and the Bodens had been friends for a long time.

"We'll settle in on our own, Cole," Mel said, "but thank you for the offer of help. We'll see you in the morning."

Cole tugged on the brim of his Stetson to say goodbye, then watched them all ride away, Mel and Walt to the two closest cabins. Cole could see the cabins from where he stood.

When he reached his cabin, Walt dismounted and turned to look straight at Cole, and Cole couldn't help but wonder why. He thought he'd behaved well, but that darkness in Walt's eyes told a different story.

After they reached the top of their climb, Cole said to the others, "I should go look through my files and see just when those men who died signed their leases for the first time."

Heath nodded. "And how'd they end up side by side? What are the chances those five cabins opened up all at once?"

"If they did," Justin added, "then you'd better check just why they opened up. Were the miners who leased them before driven off? Did they leave by their own choice or were they pushed out?"

"Murray might know the answers to all that." Cole then remembered Gully's expression after hearing Murray's name, which still bothered him. He trusted both men. He was sure the distance between Murray and the miners was because Murray made himself out to be a different kind of man. For one thing, the man wore a suit. And he worked with contracts and payrolls and percentages while the miners gave the Bodens ten percent of their finds.

And yet Gully had asked Cole not to include Murray. Cole decided he'd better do what Gully wanted. Cole would handle the files himself and consult Gully only if he had any questions. Both men had been at the mine longer than Cole.

"You haven't slept all day, Cole." Justin patted him on the back in a way that was too gentle for his ham-handed brother. "You got your head sewn together, you worked all night and all day, and you've got a long day planned for tomorrow. Leave the files until tomorrow, when your head doesn't ache. Everything will make more sense in the morning."

It was the pure truth that Cole was feeling almost cross-eyed from fatigue and pain.

"You're right. Let's go home." Cole turned toward the stable to fetch his horse. Justin was on one side while Heath came up on the other. Rather than head off to bed down in the office as Cole had expected, Heath stayed with them all the way to the stable. "I thought you were staying here."

Heath flashed that reckless smile of his—honestly it didn't go with him at all. Heath was a calm, dependable, steady man, but his smile and his eyes could take on a wild look on occasion. Which they did now.

"I took one look at Walt Blake," he said, "and decided I'd be wasting my time. He looks like a man to take charge of a situation."

So they all saddled up and rode for the CR.

"Yep, a man you don't want as an enemy," Justin said as they trotted along. Another mile eastward and they would ride out from under the shadows cast by Mount Kebbel, and they'd have a bit of sunlight before the late afternoon of a New Mexico February turned to dusk. They'd be home before full dark.

"But I'm thinking he'd be about the best kind of man you could have as a friend," Heath said. "And he makes a fine chaperone, too."

Before Cole could grab him, Heath kicked his horse into a gallop. Deciding they should stay together, Cole went after him. It had nothing to do with catching his brother-in-law and shoving his teeth down his throat.

Then he heard Heath laughing ahead and, worst of all, Justin laughing behind.

Cole decided he was riding at exactly the right pace, because he didn't want to deal with either of them—not after being halfway blown up yesterday. Maybe in a few days, when the wound to his head had healed some, he'd find a way to make them stop their teasing.

In the meantime they were making tracks toward home that would soon let them put food in their bellies and let Cole sleep for the first time since he'd passed out. It'd been a long couple of days.

Cole was back at the mine before sunup.

Murray didn't start this early, so Cole had the headquarters to himself. Stepping inside, he paused to light a lantern. He walked through an open doorway, as the door had been ripped from its hinges in the explosion.

The building was empty. All the men had been carried to their cabins. Two of them were married and had wives to care for them. Two more had decided they'd be fine, or at least could survive on their own. The fifth had a friend who'd agreed to look after him until he could care for himself, only that would also keep the worker away from the mine. All five were going to be laid up for a while, as well as a bunch of other men who'd been hurt in the explosions. Cole had already seen they had supplies to keep them going until the men could return to work, including a doctor to check on them regularly. He also told them they didn't need to worry about their lease payments until they were back working.

The explosions were an attack on the Bodens, Cole had no doubt of that, even without solid evidence. Unless it was just a brutal cover-up to kill five men. Whichever it was, none of these miners was going to pay more of a price than they already had.

He studied the wreckage around him to try to imagine how to fix the place, to make the office like it once was. Tearing it down and starting again would probably be easiest.

But no. He decided it'd be faster to rebuild the roof. The corner of one wall had buckled, but it could be shored up. Cole hoped it would hold and his repairs wouldn't leave him with an office that might cave in during the first heavy snow.

Rocks that'd come in through the roof were shoved aside, lined up by the wall, under Murray's desk, and everywhere else an injured man hadn't needed to lie. But getting rid of the rocks would involve just picking them up and carrying them outside.

The furniture was in bad shape. Murray's desk had stood up to the blast, but his chair was smashed to pieces. He scanned the debris tossed into a corner, along with the two filing cabinets that always stood behind the desk. They'd fallen over and broken apart, the drawers in shambles. Cole was unconscious when they'd brought him in after they opened the mine, so he wasn't sure why both of the filing cabinets were tipped over. There was no hole in the roof right above them.

Maybe they'd been pushed aside to make room for the injured and somehow toppled. It was a mess. Stacks of files were bunched together in such disarray Cole didn't even bother to go look at them.

He headed for his own office instead. He closed himself in and let the dismay sweep over him. They'd spread the wounded out in here, too. There was blood splattered on the floor. The roof was intact, but the heavy shutters on two windows were gone. Stones looked as if they'd been scattered everywhere, then pushed aside to make room for the injured.

But compared to the front office, this room was in pristine order. His desk, chair, and files had all survived intact.

And this is where he kept all the leases, saved back from the beginning of when gold had been found in the mid-sixties and Pa had the notion to lease out claims rather than go into gold mining himself.

Cole began opening file drawers.

An hour later he had a disturbing picture of the men who'd been killed. It was curious more because of what he couldn't find than what he could.

He needed to talk to Gully.

Mel stepped out of her cabin, stretching, trying to get her muscles to stop aching. She'd just spent the night sleeping on a bed about as soft as the board-walks of Skull Gulch. She paused for a moment and thought of all the times she'd slept on the trail with a blanket her only bed and her saddle for a pillow.

Good grief, she was getting soft.

Uncle Walt was already up and out, leading both their horses, which had been staked out to graze overnight.

"I'm going to have to figure out a corral for 'em." Walt glanced up at her from where he was shoving a metal pike into the ground to hold the haltered horses. He'd picked a spot for them that had plenty of fresh grass. Her gelding had water dripping from its gray muzzle, so he'd taken them to the stream already.

Mel threw in and had her own horse staked out before Uncle Walt had to do it.

Left with nothing to do, he said, "I saw a light in Cole's office." Uncle Walt pointed up the mountain, and Mel turned, surprised that she could see the building from this distance.

"It was already lit when I got up and I've been going awhile, so he's at it early." Walt sounded as if he approved of early mornings and long hours, which any good rancher did.

"I'll get the men, and we can all go up to the office to claim our leases. Then we'll see to a little mining." Walt smiled in a way he rarely did. Mel wondered if he thought watching her dig for gold would be funny.

Mel finished with her horse and did a few morning chores. Uncle Walt appeared with the three Blake hands trailing him. Mel had known these men since she was a kid. They were the heart of the JB Ranch operation.

They all trooped up the big old mountain to get to Cole's office. It was a long hike. She should've ridden her horse.

Cole met them at the door. "Good morning. I have your leases all ready. I'd have brought them down to you in a few minutes."

"You're real banged up, Cole." Mel noticed the ugly bruise around his stitches, the scrapes all over his face. And she could tell he was favoring his belly some. He'd been shot not that long ago, which had brought on a fever that spent a week trying to kill him.

She'd've said he was all healed up from the gunshot, but it looked like he wasn't quite healthy enough for a mountain to explode around him.

"Come on back to my office." They followed him in and did the paper work in short order. Though the lease carried a charge with it, Cole said, "I'm not taking a cent from you. And whatever gold you find is yours. I know I'm causing a real short staff at the JB, and I thank you all for helping me."

There were stacks of papers on his desk, so orderly Mel was sure he'd been working on them since early morning. It was way more paper than a man needed to rent a few mines . . . which meant Cole was investigating. He was thinking about the men who'd died in the explosion or had been helped along in such a way it appeared they'd died in the explosion.

Mel itched to ask him questions and figured the JB hands oughta know what was going on so they could be on the lookout.

Walt kicked the floor of the battered office building as if he wondered if that might bring it down. It distracted Mel from her questioning.

"I've tried my hand at gold digging." Walt thrust his lease at Cole. "It pays mighty poor except for a lucky few. I can earn better money making thirty a month and found on any ranch in the West. But we're here to help you, Cole, and glad to do it."

The men with him shrugged as if they were working for Walt and not Cole, and that suited Cole just fine. These men handed their signed leases over, too.

"I'll pick up whatever part of your wages you'd earn back at the ranch." Cole wished he'd made that clear to Mel yesterday so she could tell her pa. "I'll make sure Jack knows I'll cover it. You're not doing any work for him, so it shouldn't cost him, and you shouldn't lose the money."

"Let's go back down. You can show us our claims." Mel had a lot of questions she'd like to ask Cole—and not just about the investigating he was doing. She'd also like to know how bad he felt, and had he slept well the night before, and to tell him she'd be glad to help in the office if he was feeling poorly. She'd even let him sneak off to her cabin and grab a nap if he wished. She knew he'd never admit he was all in, at least not in front of the men. But if she asked on her own, away from the others, Cole might just admit he needed an easy day.

They headed down the slope, where Cole pointed to five open holes standing side by side at the lowest level of the mountain. The two closest belonged to her and Uncle Walt.

"You men all come into my claim first and bring your

pickaxes," Walt said. "There oughta be one in your cabin. I'll show you how to mine for gold and how to recognize it if you find it, assuming there's a speck of the stuff left to find."

"And be careful." Cole glanced at Mel. "The mine entrance goes in level, but soon enough the shafts go down, a long way down. I don't want anyone hurt. Be on guard for all kinds of trouble."

Everyone split up to find their axes. Mel headed for her cabin, Cole falling into step beside her. Her breathing sped up a bit as he walked with her. All she could think about was that moment from last night when he'd leaned toward her. They were dealing with bombers and one threat after another. She oughta not waste much time thinking about anything else.

When they reached her cabin, Cole followed her right inside. She seized her chance. "How are you really feeling, Cole? You should have taken one day at least to heal up." She looked up at him and felt her brown eyes lock on his blue ones. It prompted her to smile. "You have that look."

He scowled. "What look? I don't have any look."

"That look that says me telling you to rest is the same as insulting you."

"It is insulting me."

Mel shook her head. Through her window, she saw Uncle Walt emerge from his cabin with a pickax and head the few steps toward her place. He poked his head in the doorway.

"These were left by the men who died, I reckon." Uncle Walt examined the heavy tool grimly. "It don't seem right somehow to just start right in with a dead man's tools, digging only hours after their graves have been filled in. No harm in giving a man a day or two of remembrance before the world goes on."

"You're welcome to wait if you feel better about it." Nodding, Cole said, "They were carrying their tools with them. We found them near their bodies and returned them to their cabins when we packed up their clothes." Cole's chin firmed as if steadying his emotions.

"I'd just as soon keep busy, but I don't mean it as disrespect. I want that to be clear, Cole." Uncle Walt headed out the door. "Let's go look at our gold lease. All three of the men and Mel and I are going to spend the first hour or so together learning to be miners."

Mel saw the wry smile push back Cole's guilt. "I'll come in for a few minutes and tell you what I know."

"A few minutes? All you know will fit into a few minutes?" Mel nudged him with her elbow.

"I suspect Walt will be as much help as I will, but it's best I walk you each through your mines and make sure you see where the lanterns are, and we've got lamps that'll strap on your head and light a small candle to keep your hands free. I'll show you where the pit drops down. These slopes hold some of the oldest mines and they go deep."

"Pit?" Mel didn't like the sound of that. She preferred working in the sunlight.

"Oh yes. Pit." Cole took her elbow. He led the way to the black-arched opening to the mine. It looked like a gaped mouth. A hungry mouth.

Her mine was about one hundred feet from her cabin. Before he entered, Cole looked at Mel and said, "This is the mine you've leased. Walt, yours is next to hers on the left."

The other Blake hands had joined them. Calling the men by name, Cole pointed out each of their mines. "But let's all go into Mel's mine first. Well, that is unless you're eager to get to work. You don't have to listen to me."

"You have to listen to me, though," Walt cut in. "And I mean to hear what Cole says first. And then have my own say. Lead the way, Boden."

The six of them moved inside. The entrance and the short tunnel was a passable size for one person, but with six of them, Mel almost felt the walls pressing on her. A black circle that had to be the pit wasn't far away. Mel edged toward it and looked down into pure darkness. A ladder was visible against one side, but it seemed to be swallowed up after just a few feet. She couldn't see anything down there, and a wave of dizziness swept over her. She straightened away from the hole. She'd climb down it eventually, but she decided then and there she'd refuse to look down while she did so.

Cole mainly talked about safety, pointed out the lanterns they could fasten on their heads, the lanterns they could carry, and the matches to keep them both lit.

Mel swallowed hard and acted as if a mountain looming over her head didn't bother her. And a thousand . . . no, probably a hundred thousand pounds of rock over her head was fine. Oh for heaven's sake, it had to be hundreds of thousands of tons! She wondered if landing a pickax in the exact right spot would bring the whole thing crashing down.

Cole pulled something out of his pocket and held it close to a lantern. "This is what you're looking for."

Every one of them leaned close except Walt. A small black stone, about the size of Cole's palm and flat like a skipping stone, lay in his hand. A bright line cut through the center of it. A bright gold line.

"This is it. Gold. You find veins of it as thin as a hair, and I've seen them as thick as a man's arm. These mines aren't played out, not exactly, but the big excitement of a gold strike is long over. There is a modest amount of gold in this mountain, and a hardworking man can chisel out a living. You're none of you going to strike it rich."

"How can you be sure, Cole?" Mel asked, her eyes studying the glittering metal.

"As to that, I reckon I can't be sure. All I know is that no one's done it for about ten years. The first four years they were taking a lot of ore out of here, but unless someone hits a new lode, I'm expecting each of you to earn about what you'd earn busting broncs and running a branding iron. And the work is dark and hard." Cole looked up and smiled. "Not saying a cowpoke doesn't work hard, mind you. I know ranching. But at least you get to do it above ground."

The men nodded, and not a one of them looked to be all that excited about the work that lay ahead.

Forcing herself to sound calm in the black cave, Mel said, "Okay, now that we're where no one can hear us, how exactly are we going to manage pretending to dig for gold and at the same time poke around to find out more about the explosions and who set them off?"

Cole looked at her with horror. "You're never going to do that. You are all here to fill up those cabins. I don't want any of you to do a thing to put yourselves in danger. If the men talk, you can listen for anything that sounds like a clue, or like they saw something they should've told me, but it's my job to get to the bottom of whoever set off the dynamite. You just dig in these mines and fill those cabins so I don't have to take on any new leases from men I don't know and can't trust."

Mel mentally skidded to a stop. "That's not what we agreed to. I came over here to ask questions, pry a few secrets out of your men, in case any of your current lease holders are in on this."

"No, absolutely not."

"I thought we agreed these men might be more apt to talk to a woman."

Cole looked desperate as he sought out Uncle Walt. "You know we can't let her do anything to endanger herself, don't you?"

Uncle Walt's eyes narrowed just a little, but it was enough to cause complete silence and rivet everyone's attention on him. "She's not going to be in danger. And she's not going to take orders from you." Then he looked at Mel. "But you are going to take orders from me, little girl. That don't mean you can't ask a few questions, but you're not to wander from my side. Is that clear? One word from me and your pa and ma will yank you right back to the JB."

Since Mel figured it was going to be impossible to slip away from Uncle Walt, she accepted the inevitable. "It's clear as glass. I am not going to make it hard for you to protect me. I know my only hope of appearing respectable is to clearly be here with my uncle. So you don't have to worry about me doing anything reckless or stupid."

Uncle Walt looked at her a little too long with those same narrow eyes. She got the distinct impression that he wasn't going to take anything on trust.

Which was exactly what she expected him to do, so she didn't let it hurt her feelings. Uncle Walt was a straight-talking man, and if he trod on someone's delicate feelings, he figured it was worth it to make sure he was understood. Mel was a little like that herself.

"Now, I'm going to get to work," Cole said. "Walt, take over with your mining lessons. If you have more questions, send someone for me. I'll be glad to help in any way I can, and I've got a foreman here at the mine, name of Gully, who knows a whole lot more than I do, and he's aware of everything that happens, so you can talk to him, too. Thank you all for coming over here."

Cole started to turn and then, as if he couldn't move, he took a long look at Mel. Even in the shadows of the dark cave, she read too much in his blue eyes.

Then he was gone.

"All right, you bunch of greenhorns."

"Greenhorns?" Mel said with a snort. "I've been roping and riding longer than you have."

Uncle Walt quirked a smile at her on his weathered face. "I reckon I got you beat by twenty years or so, girl, or thirty, but you've been at it long enough. Just not when it comes to digging for gold. Now grab your axes."

She hefted the pickax. The thing weighed a ton . . . and confound it, she was going to have to pretend to enjoy chopping up a mountain.

She'd sure as certain better find some gold in here.

10

"Heath, you're here." His sister's husband was picking up the door to his office building. It'd been tossed aside in the hurry to get the wounded inside.

"I'm here, too." Justin came out of the stable. "Got the horses put up. You should have waited for us instead of riding over here alone."

"Hmmm." Cole grabbed one side of the door Heath was hoisting around just fine by himself. He wasn't about to admit he'd come wide awake long before sunrise thinking he'd fulfilled his pa's wishes for sleeping at home.

Justin had tools handy, and they made short work of getting the door rehung.

Pounding overhead drew Cole's attention. He looked up and saw nothing. The sound was coming from the far side of the roof.

"We helped Murray get a ladder up to the roof on the other side of the building. There are three good-sized holes up there. He said he could handle all the repairs himself, but we told him we'd do a few things."

Justin jerked his head toward the open space between the office, the stable, and the mine entrance.

"What is it?" But Cole followed and spoke low. He was getting suspicious of everyone now. Murray had been with the mine long before all the strange goings-on had started.

"We got a letter from Ma. She's worked out some of that cramped handwriting."

The same handwriting had been found in a notebook they'd taken off the man who'd shot Cole.

"What did she find?"

"It don't make a lot of sense, but she figured out a lot of it was in Spanish, sort of mixed up like it was written by someone who spoke both languages and was just making little notes over time, which is part of why the languages jumped back and forth maybe."

"Okay, makes some sense I reckon. But that doesn't matter." Cole got the feeling Justin didn't want to get to the point. And that was strange because Justin was a straight talker even when a person wished he'd find a little tact. "What's in the note?"

Justin crossed his arms and looked Cole in the eyes. He'd had some trouble getting used to his little brother being all grown-up. Cole left for college at age eighteen and Justin was thirteen, not close to full grown yet. While Cole had gone to college, Justin quit going to school and started working full-time at Pa's side. Cole had left a little brother behind and come home to find a man. Justin wasn't educated in books, but he was mighty educated in cattle. He was smart enough that he could have done college work as well as Cole. Instead he was a tough, skilled, coolly intelligent rancher.

They'd been trying to figure out how to get along ever since Cole's return.

More honestly, they'd been trying to figure out how to get

along their whole lives. They'd spent most of their growing-up years tussling—with Cole usually pulling his punches and tormenting his little brother in a way that got Justin in trouble with Ma.

Now it was almost instinct to settle disagreements with their fists. But they were a match now, and Cole didn't dare pull any punches because Justin sure didn't.

So mostly they didn't throw any.

Anyhow, Cole knew neither one of them was out for blood; in fact, they both enjoyed fighting.

"You're not going to like it, I didn't like it, and Ma said in her letter that she didn't like it."

"What?" Cole ached in every joint and muscle. His head still throbbed, and if he didn't have so many chores ahead and so much danger to face, he'd've slept till noon today. That left him mighty short on patience.

"She's sure she read the name . . ." Justin hesitated and swallowed, not like he was scared exactly by what he had to say next, but more like he dreaded it and honestly felt bad about it.

"Just tell me, Justin." Cole's stomach twisted a little because he didn't think he'd ever seen that exact look on his brother's face before.

Justin watched Cole closely. "She read the names . . . Davidson and Priscilla Bradford."

"What?" Cole felt like his eyes almost bugged out of his head. "What do my mother's parents have to do with this?"

He fought down suspicion. No one in this family had ever liked his wealthy Boston grandparents. Pa had even said that he'd come west to save Cole from them—not to save his life but to save him from being under their influence. Pa had never suggested Cole was in any actual physical danger. In fact, Grandmother and Grandfather Bradford had doted on him.

Even from halfway across a mighty big country. Grandmother had visited him twice, once when he was about twelve, and again when he'd been seventeen. And getting here was no small journey, as the train didn't come until much later. Besides the visits, the Bradfords sent letters and generous gifts—to Cole and no one else.

They never acknowledged Justin or Sadie. Although it bothered Cole and he shared whatever he could, he'd liked getting things all his own. After all, his little brother and sister had no Bradford blood in their veins.

"Ma read that?" He kept his voice flat. Waiting to see if Justin was casting his grandparents in the worst light. Those old folks had been good to him while he lived in Boston, and they'd left him a fortune, and yes, he'd stayed until his grandmother died. But he hadn't been under her thumb. He'd known she wanted him to stay in a civilized land and take over all the Bradford holdings. But he'd always planned to return to the West and to his family he'd missed so fiercely.

That didn't mean he'd put up with this family he loved tearing up about the Bradfords. He realized his fists were clenched and forced himself to relax.

Heath interrupted, "I'm going to go follow some tracks. I could be at it for hours because I'm going to have to watch for where our bomber left the trail. When you two quit bickering like a pair of little girls, some help would be welcome."

Cole broke off the glare he just now realized he was burning into Justin. He took a long, deep breath to calm down and, leaving the repairs to Murray, said, "I'll come."

"Me too." Justin fell in beside Cole and trailed after Heath. He sounded way too kind when he said, "I won't tell you more if you don't want to hear it, Cole. I'm not sure what's going on. Your grandfather has been dead eight years, your grandmother two. There's no way I can see they could be involved with this. But Ma is sure she read your grandparents' names. You know she wouldn't lie about that."

Cole breathed in and out steadily. "What else was in the note?"

"Your grandparents being in there is strange and what else she found is even stranger. There was a mention of the old Don."

"Don de Val?" Cole stopped, as surprised by that as by his grandparents' involvement. "What possible connection was there between de Val and the Bradfords? Don de Val owned half the land grant before he went back to Mexico. He left before any of us were born—that's counting me up in Boston. What's he got to do with anything?"

"I've no notion. But he's in there, and Ma read his wife's name, too. Lauressa de Val. The names are distinctive, de Val and Bradford, and repeated a few times. I guess that's how she made them out. But the rest of the writing isn't giving up its secrets without a fight."

Justin snorted. "Ma mailed us a magnifying glass along with what she'd translated. What I can't figure out is who wrote those notes? No one is going to send a letter no one can read expecting action. It don't stand to reason. So Ma said she wondered if these writings were personal reminders for someone that got sent on somehow. Do you know your grandma's handwriting?"

"I do." Cole felt his spirits lift. "It was so pretty it was ridiculous. Not like that cramped handwriting at all. Grandfather's was like it came out of a Spenserian copybook. It was cleanly written and easy to read. They both had the handwriting of people who had been trained to write in the finest schools and who took pride in precision, though Grandmother liked to add a few flourishes."

He couldn't help but smile as he thought of the graceful artwork of his grandmother's hand. Then he had another thought. "That cramped handwriting really is strange. If we ever saw anyone with that handwriting, there's a good chance we'd recognize it. And didn't you say it was a combination of English and Spanish? I'd say it's a mighty good guess that my grandparents didn't speak a word of Spanish. Though both could speak French, and Grandpa read books in Latin quite often."

Cole had studied Latin in college and spoke French decently, yet he could read and write very little of it. He didn't tell Justin that.

"Good. Maybe mention of the Bradfords is just someone talking about all the possible factors in their plan. If your grandfather didn't write it himself, then someone making notes to themselves might've thought your grandfather would make a dangerous enemy or a powerful ally. That doesn't mean he was involved."

Cole was almost addled. Justin was being mighty nice. Not taking an easy chance to speak ill of the Bradfords, but doing his best to absolve them of guilt. In fact, Justin was being so nice, Cole had to ask, "Is there more? Did Ma come up with anything else?"

"She said it was starting to make some sense once she figured out it was Mexican and English mixed and she was recognizing more letters. She wants Pa to stay and spend a little more time healing his leg. There are exercises the doc has him doing."

"He could do that at home." Truth was Cole would like having Ma and Pa back.

"But the doc somehow measures any improvement, then changes a few things. Ma said she's never seen anything like it, and she can tell it's working. She's fretting that they won't do as well on their own."

"Then I hope they take the time they need." Or at least Cole knew he oughta hope that. He'd like them back here. Pa was the smartest man Cole knew, and that included his wealthy grandfather and all the professors at Harvard.

"Pa's pushing at the doc and Ma mighty hard." Justin strode alongside Cole down the steep slope dotted with leased-out Boden mines. "He's slap out of patience with Denver and wants to be back in New Mexico Territory on his own ranch. Ma said his leg won't be injured by the train ride, but he's got a pretty bad limp and a lot of pain yet. She's hoping more of that will be fixed by the treatment he's getting. Pa just figures he can ride and shoot as well with a bum leg as a good one. And aches and pains don't stop a man from much."

"My Bradford grandparents and the old Don and Señora de Val." Cole shook his head. "Two couples who don't know each other and are long dead. What in the world is going on?"

"Señora de Val isn't dead," Justin said.

Both of them nearly stumbled to a halt. They exchanged a long look.

"She isn't dead, is she?" Justin repeated. "Ramone spoke of her."

"Spoke ill of her, in fact. Made her seem like a mighty cranky woman." They were silent a few moments longer before walking on until they reached the mountain's base. They passed the cabin where Mel was staying. Heath was visible down a heavily traveled path.

Then Cole remembered the search through his files this morning. "I've got more I want to ask you before we join Heath."

"What's that?"

"I went through my filing cabinet to find out when these men, the ones who died, signed their first lease. I was hoping they all came in on the same day, but it's not that clean cut."

"Nothing about this is clean." Justin sounded weary from all that'd gone on. Cole knew just how he felt.

"They came in within about a year and a half of each other. The men who dropped their mines had moved on, a couple of them just up and left. Men who'd been here a long time. Two headed out together, and from notes I found, there doesn't seem to be anything to question in that. A third died from a fall off his horse."

That made them both fall silent for a while.

"There'd've been no trouble with five men in eighteen months coming and going."

"Nope. The mines turn over, it happens a lot, but to have their mines and cabins all next to each other—that's not gonna happen."

"So they opened up the leases slowly, and five men drifted in to fill the openings. Do we assume they banded together to run the men off?"

"Or killed them." Cole shook his head. "We have common sense to tell us something was going on, even all the way back then. But I want to know more, and Gully is the man who'd have answers. He was here."

"Murray too." Justin glanced up at the headquarters. They could hear the sound of a hammer from here. Murray hard at work rebuilding the office.

Cole felt like a traitor not to include him in their investigation. "There's a divide between the miners and Murray. They just see him as soft, a city slicker. They treated me that way when I first got here, but I rolled up my sleeves and dug alongside them enough they decided I could be trusted. It's not Murray's fault he prefers a pen and paper to a pickax."

"I saw Gully riding north when I came in. The Boden mines stretch a long way over this mountain. I reckon he'll be a while."

Justin clapped Cole on the shoulder. "We'll get to the truth, big brother. For all the scheming that's been going on, they haven't won the fight yet."

"That's the absolute truth. They've done plenty of damage, but we've whipped them every time. I'll talk to Gully later." Cole pointed ahead at Heath. "Let's catch up with him and show him what reading signs looks like."

He grinned at Justin, who smiled back. It had been about the friendliest talk the two of them had ever had. They both knew Heath could out-track them anytime he wanted to, but they weren't too bad at it. No sense in letting their little sister's husband think he was in charge.

11

Mel tossed the pickax down in disgust and flipped her long braid over her shoulder. It kept dangling in front of her while she chiseled. "Uncle Walt, do you really want any gold?"

They were in his mine. They each had their own but had agreed to stay together, for Mel's safety and of course the ever-annoying concern of behaving properly.

Mel had never been fond of the word *proper*, and now she was getting downright sick of it.

"Don't you want to find enough gold to buy your own ranch?" Uncle Walt held up what looked to Mel like a piece of gravel. Shiny gravel.

"Is that gold?"

"Yep."

"How long are we going to have to dig to get enough to even bother to count?"

Walt laughed. He pointed at the wall. "This here is a seam of gold."

Mel picked up the lantern and moved close to the wall. "It's about as wide as a hair."

"I'd say maybe three hairs, but yep, it's thin. Chances are it's about as deep, too."

"So how much is that worth?"

Uncle Walt shrugged. "Your pa's been known to pay his men with twenty-dollar gold pieces. You've seen them." He held up the gravel-sized piece again.

Mel nodded. "So if we dig out enough gold here to equal one of those coins, we'll have twenty dollars?"

"Yep, and depending on how deep the seam is, I doubt we'll get a coin's worth out of it."

"But maybe half a coin, ten dollars' worth, and you'll earn that with one day's work."

"I can see you figuring it out, Mel. Your pa pays thirty a month and found." Mel knew *found* meant food, and Pa also provided a bunkhouse for the men. So Pa paid with money, food, and a home.

"And you can make ten dollars here today." Mel did some figuring. "If we had this luck every day, we'd make ten dollars for thirty days in a row. That's three hundred dollars a month—ten times what Pa pays a cowpoke. If a body was careful he could live a few years on three hundred dollars."

"And if his luck held for a year, he could make over three thousand."

Mel nodded. "He could make it if the gold held out."

Walt turned back to his modest gold strike. "If I find a seam like this every day . . . and if I don't go mad from working underground like a mole all my life. But if the gold holds out, then yes, I can make enough in one month to live all year long. If I keep working a whole year, I might have enough to live for ten years. If I find a big fat seam, I could be a rich man who never has to work again. You can see the lure of it, can't you? The chance to get real rich, real quick."

"So then why do folks come and stay for years? Why don't they all get rich and leave?" Mel smiled even as she asked it. She went on, "It's because they don't all find even this tiny thread. They chisel until they get tired of working like a mole and go find a job that pays slow but steady."

"Yep. They usually start ambitious and a little gold crazy, but then they come to their senses after working their tails off and living mighty poor. For some it takes longer than others. For some they find just enough to live, maybe even get ahead slowly. For some they hear of a new gold strike and run off to find it, try their luck there. They can't shake off their love of wandering and their lust to get rich quick. Not a lick of common sense figures into it."

Mel went back to the first thing Walt had said. "No, I don't want to buy a ranch of my own. 'Course, I'm expecting to inherit one, so why would I need two? But how about you, Uncle Walt? Do you want one?" She shuddered to think of how long they'd have to dig to carve the cost of a ranch out of stone.

"Nope, I'm mighty happy with your pa. Finding my brother and being allowed to be part of your family is the finest life I've ever had. I wouldn't change a thing, no matter how much gold I found. I reckon, though, if I found enough it might be hard not to change. That's why I'm hoping we don't do well down here."

Mel looked around from the thin seam of gold to the arched cave with no sign of any more seams. "I think you're going to get your wish. In fact, if you want to finish chiseling out that gold, I'll go get a noon meal started. We can take a break to eat." She looked again at the tiny seam and rolled her eyes. "A long break."

"Wait, I'll come with you. I can dig out ten dollars later." Uncle Walt chuckled. "I'll have more fun talking to you while you cook."

"While I cook?" Mel glared at him as they climbed the ladder and stepped out into the warm sunlight. She sighed with relief. "Blue sky. It's never looked prettier to me."

He caught up to her, and she smiled at him. "If you're not mining, then you're going to have to help me cook."

Uncle Walt laughed out loud. "Yes, Miss Melanie."

"Don't call me—" She saw a strange bit of color lying in a mesquite scrub. "What is that?" She rushed over to the tree to look down at what was lying there. It was a kerchief, or some scrap, but of a strange red-and-yellow color. An unusual thing to find.

Uncle Walt was beside her a second later, and he bent down and plucked the scrap of cloth out of the scrub. "Was this here earlier?"

Mel's eyes met his. "I don't know. You think someone was hanging around out here? Maybe planning to set more dynamite?"

"Or someone lost a kerchief the other day when they were up to mischief in front of this mine."

Six men brutally murdered was a lot nastier than mischief.

"It's an odd enough color," Mel said, "that someone might recognize who it belongs to."

Uncle Walt held it out to her. "Whoever it belongs to, I'd like to ask a question about what he was doing out here. Let's go see if we can find the Bodens."

"Take this coin and this note to Dr. Radcliffe."

The little waif reached for the coin eagerly, but Veronica pulled the money back. While it felt mean-hearted, she'd learned quickly that to get Finn's attention, holding a coin in front of him was the best method. "Finn, there's more. I'll pay you extra if you will very carefully mind me."

The boy's eyes lit up. Veronica's soft mother's heart wondered if Finn had a home or lived on the streets. She'd seen him loitering around in an alley when she stepped out to go to the general store and replenish their food cupboard. She'd offered to pay him to carry her parcels, even though she didn't really need help.

It was all she could do not to feed the little boy every meal. Overly thin, dressed in rags not warm enough for the season, Finn worried her. He had plenty of spirit and seemed like a decent boy who ran errands for her nearly every day, even when she had to make errands up. She always saw to it he had a slice of bread and a glass of milk every time she could offer him one, with an apple and a few cookies to take home.

No doubt he had nice parents nearby who appreciated the bit of money he earned. But he should be in school, and his coat wasn't thick enough in the cold Denver February.

Veronica intended to find out if he needed help. And if he didn't have a home or family, she planned to take him in.

"I'll listen close as can be, ma'am. Sure, and it's glad I'd be to work more for you. I'll follow your instructions real careful." He had an Irish lilt to his voice that Veronica never tired of listening to. It was a match for his red curls and freckled face. He was a polite little guy, and as much as she wanted to help him, she had to be careful not to draw him into their mess.

They'd had no trouble since moving here, but they'd been vigilant about secrecy. Even Dr. Radcliffe didn't know where they lived for fear someone might follow him here on a visit.

"Do you know the small diner about three blocks from the doctor's office? It's called Dewey's Diner."

"Sure, I know it." Finn sounded excited, or maybe hungry.

"I want you to get my note delivered to the doctor and wait for him to write one back."

The man now under arrest for trying to kill Chance had found them before, even though Veronica and Chance had been in hiding. Veronica suspected they'd followed the doctor then, even though they'd gone to great lengths to keep their location a secret. If the attacker had cronies working with him, they might try that again. Because of that, Doc Radcliffe hadn't come to their house and they hadn't gone to his office.

"Instead of running back here fast, I want you to go into the diner and get a meal. Eat it slowly. I am afraid someone might notice you at the doctor's office and follow you. But if they see you go in to eat, they'll decide you aren't headed anywhere special, least of all to us. There might be men looking for my husband and me. I don't want you to lead them to us, for your safety as well as ours." She handed over two bits, besides what she'd already given him.

"Are you sure it's okay to stop and eat, ma'am? It'll be a fine day when anyone can sneak up on Finn." He pointed to his own puffed-out chest with his thumb. "I'm mighty careful at watchin' behind me. If someone is following, I'd spot him and make sure he's good and lost before I head over here."

"You watch carefully besides stopping to eat. Watch that you're not followed. But taking time to stop and eat will seem less suspicious to anyone who might follow. If you make some obvious attempt to slip away from someone tailing you, it might attract their attention and they'll start to wonder about you."

"I'll eat, ma'am. I've never been to a diner before."

"Well, take plenty of time and enjoy your meal. Uh, Finn, I have another job for an adult." Veronica was no hand at lying, but held the truth in highest regard. And right now, making up a job was a plain lie. "I'd like to hire your ma to do it, if she's willing." Veronica had asked this question in a different form a few times now, trying to get Finn to admit if he had a ma or not.

"Sure, and me ma's busy at home, ma'am. I take care of the both of us." The little urchin's eyes shifted down and he talked to his feet. "She don't want no job."

"Well, can you ask her? She might surprise you."

Finn shrugged one shoulder, turned, and dashed away.

Scowling, Veronica watched him go. Then an affectionate smile replaced her scowl. Finn was tough, and he didn't want to talk about his mother. Maybe if she kept letting him do little jobs for her, the day would come when he'd trust her. That was her hope and prayer.

"So you wrote to the doctor, Ronnie?"

She turned to smile at her husband. "Yes, just like we discussed. I told him in detail how you were progressing and asked for the next exercises he wants you to do. We have to be nearly done."

"That man is going to keep me here, doing strange stretches and motions with my leg, until I die of old age." Chance walked with a limp and only rarely did he slip and let her see his pain. She wanted him to have every chance to completely heal.

With a frown, he said, "I'm just about done putting up with it. My leg hurts less every day and what's left of the pain I can live with. And I don't limp anymore."

"Not much anyway," Veronica said.

He narrowed his eyes at her. "And I can do the last of his exercises on my own. For heaven's sake, I'm doing them on my own already. Dr. Radcliffe only knows what we tell him in the notes. And Doc Garner in Skull Gulch can help with anything more I need. They can write to each other. The mail travels fast these days."

Veronica approached her fussy husband. "Being patient and

doing as you're told has turned you into an old grizzly bear." She pinched him gently on the chin.

It coaxed a smile out of him. "You don't seem all that upset with me, wife. I think I've been growling around for so long that you don't even pay attention anymore."

"Oh, I pay attention, husband. I just don't let it upset me overly." Her smile faded. "Did you see Finn when I asked about his ma?"

Finn was a little shy around Chance. But Chance lurked. He was always worried. Someone had attacked them before and it could happen again. "Yep. What do you think? Is he living on the streets? I've heard of such things."

"Sit down and get off that leg." Veronica guided him. He rolled his eyes but let her prop up his healing leg on a footstool. "I can't find out if he's got a ma or not." She looked up at her husband. "You know I want to take him home, don't you?"

He smiled and nodded, and Veronica knew she'd get no trouble from him.

"We'll take him if he wants to come. I'd be glad to do it. But Ronnie," he added, his shoulders sagging, "I know I'm better than nothing, but I've made a fair mess out of being a father."

Veronica gasped and tugged a chair around to face him. "What in the world do you mean by that? Your love for our children is as fine as any father on earth."

Chance waved his hand. "I love them. I've loved those children with everything I've got. But I've gone wrong. I shouldn't have changed my will. Yet all I could see was that I'd failed. Somehow I raised them not to love their home, not to understand the roots we've put down."

"I was in agreement when you made those changes." Veronica considered it. "I wanted them home just like you did, especially Sadie."

"Especially Cole." Chance spoke right on top of Veronica. They smiled at each other.

Veronica leaned forward and took Chance's callused hands in hers. "Maybe it was wrong to trap them at home. But, well, if you did a poor job as a father, then I'm just as bad of a mother."

He scowled. "I'll not let you say such a thing."

"I have prayed for our children with all my strength. I started praying for Cole from the day you walked through the door with him."

With a faint smile, Chance asked, "Did you pray for me, too, Ronnie? Just a little?"

She had to laugh at that. "I did, though I admit at first I mainly prayed you'd let Cole stay in the house with me while you went to work. I fell so in love with that little boy." Reaching up, she rested her palm against his cheek. "You were just that single step behind. I fell in love with you soon enough."

Nodding, Chance said, "I know the kind of father God is. I can't be that perfect, but I wanted that as my goal, that example to try and reach. I've fallen far short. If I hadn't, our children would want to be home with us. I wouldn't need threats."

"Then I think as soon as we get home, we need to rewrite the will."

"Just like God lets us choose whether to believe or not, we have to let our children choose whether to embrace the CR or not. With Sadie married, I'm hoping she'll settle down at home. John's last letter said she and Heath are living in the ramrod's cabin. But Cole . . . we're going to lose him."

"Or if we keep him with our threats to give the ranch away, we'll lose him anyway, because he'll resent us." Veronica vowed to pray harder, more faithfully. She wanted first and foremost for her children to be believers in God. She knew that was most important. But after that, she wanted them near her. She wanted them to love being at her side.

"It has to be his choice, I reckon." Chance looked down and closed his eyes.

"We should rewrite the will now and send it home. Not keep them dangling like they are," Ronnie said, the defeat nearly bringing her to tears, because they were going to lose Cole. He didn't want to be in New Mexico Territory.

With a resigned shrug, Chance said, "We'll be home soon enough. I say we wait and fix things when we get there. Keep them together a few days or weeks more and hope our three stubborn children learn to be a family."

Chance sighed. She knew how he longed for home.

She did too, but she wanted him well and that meant following doctor's orders. Two of her children had gotten married, and she'd missed the weddings. That left an ache in her heart, especially since she'd known Heath, but not well, and she'd never even met Angie.

"You know, Chance, my pa as good as blackmailed us into marrying, and that's worked out fine."

Chance lifted his head and gave her a fond smile. "So you're saying a little bit of parental meddling can work out all right?"

"It did once. For now, let's leave things as they are until we get home."

"You know what would settle that boy down?" Chance said.

Cole, that stubborn boy—yes, he was thirty, but he'd always been her boy. "What?"

"Well, two of our children are properly wedded. Maybe we need to make it a project to go home and take over Cole's life and see him properly married like his brother and sister."

"But to who?"

12

Cole watched Mel stride down the trail right for him—with her gunslinging uncle beside her. She'd tossed her Stetson aside and had coal smudged on the golden tan of her face. He stood side by side with Justin and wondered if the Blakes had had enough of digging for gold already and were heading home.

Mel drew close and lifted something in her right hand. He couldn't tell exactly what, but she was waving it around. She nodded and said, "Howdy." Her eyes went to him and stayed a bit too long. "We found this almost hidden in some scrub by our mine entrance." She handed the scrap of cloth to Cole.

"A kerchief?"

"If that's what it is. It was in a strange place—I doubt the wind blew it there—and there was no good reason a man would be standing behind the tree line right outside my mine. We wondered if someone was watching the place, or if someone, maybe the man who set the explosives, might have dropped it."

"It's a mighty distinctive color and pattern," Walt added. "Any of you seen it before?"

Before anyone could answer, Heath came back down the trail;

he'd gotten a bit ahead. "I reckon if I'd ever seen it before, I'd remember. Not a normal mix of colors for a kerchief." Before Cole could study it closer, Heath said, "Walt, you strike me as a knowing man. Have you done any tracking?"

Cole's head whipped around to face Heath. Cole suspected Walt could do most anything.

"Have I done any tracking?" Walt's eyes narrowed as if Heath had called him a city slicker. "I can track a rattlesnake across solid rock. I can track a duck across water an hour after the duck flew away. I can track—"

Heath laughed, and Walt fell silent but with a twinkle in his eye.

"I see you can track. Good to know. There are plenty better than me, but the Bodens ain't among 'em."

Justin snorted.

Cole rolled his eyes. "You've gotten mighty cocky, Kincaid."

"Not so cocky I can't step aside for a better man. Walt, whoever set those explosions stepped on this trail. I made out three sets of tracks I could follow for a while, but it's a well-worn path in places. Near as I can tell, no tracks have left the path—not up to where I've been studying. They have to get off it sometime, and when they do, that's my chance to pick up the trail again. You have time to take a look?"

"I got time to do anything that keeps me above ground. Let's go back to where we found that kerchief and see if there are prints. Then show me what you found and why you think it's the varmints with the dynamite. We'll find boot prints and get to it." Walt turned to Mel. "You stay close to one of these Boden boys until I'm back."

Cole's trust in Walt's judgment sank as the man walked away. Walt oughta be able to figure out that leaving Mel alone with two men was as improper as all get-out. Especially when one of them was Cole. Of course, Justin was an old married man now. Maybe that made him a proper chaperone. Cole had been forced to sit still for Grandmother's lectures about all these rules back east, but he hadn't always paid attention.

He realized he was staring right into those eyes with no idea how long he'd been doing it. "Ahem . . . can . . . can I see that kerchief?"

Mel jumped a bit, like he'd startled her. She had definitely been staring back.

"I'm going to look at the cabin Mel moved into." Old married Justin slapped Cole on the back hard enough to make him stumble forward. Cole had forgotten his little brother was even here.

"I'll make sure you've got everything you need, Mel." Justin walked off before Cole could tell him to stay. Not that he had any interest in telling him to stay.

"I don't need a thing," Mel muttered, not loud enough for Justin to hear—almost as if she had no interest in telling him to stay. She held out the kerchief, and Cole got a close look at it for the first time.

He forgot about everything else. "I've seen this before."

"Where?"

"Shh." Cole was thinking. "I don't think it was a kerchief. Was it one of my men's shirts?" He shook his head slowly, digging for the memory. "It's such a bright red plaid, I can't believe I'd forget any of the miners wearing it, so I don't think that's it." He examined it more closely. "This might have been cut out of something bigger."

"Can I—?"

"Shh!"

A strange sound came from Mel. Not unlike the low-throated sound a wolf makes right before it pounces on a fleeing jackrabbit and bites its head off.

Cole looked up. It was coming from Mel. "What's the matter?"

Something was definitely the matter. He could tell by the cold glare and the bared teeth.

"Stop shushing me like I'm a noisy child."

"Uh, I-I'm sorry?" He shouldn't have made that a question.

Cole thought back to how many years it'd been since he'd given a woman much thought. He'd always known he was coming home to New Mexico Territory, and the women he met in Boston were citified to the bone. He didn't involve himself with any of them. Although if he'd found a woman with an adventurous spirit, he might've given her a chance.

Adventurous women weren't the type his grandparents had paraded in front of him. He knew they were trying to bind him to their world on the East Coast. So his skill with women might be more than a little rusty. In fact, if he was a hinge, somebody would be running for the oilcan right now.

So he wasn't quite sure what he'd done wrong, but it didn't take a genius to look at her face and know he'd sure as certain done *something*.

"You're sorry?"

Cole liked to speak straight, and he'd've thought Mel did, too. So he quit worrying about the rust on him. "When I have a puzzle like this cloth, it helps me to find a quiet place and let my mind drift. I dig out memories when I do that. I wasn't thinking of your feelings when I said 'shh.'" He saw her open her mouth, most likely with an observation about his manners, or the lack thereof, so he rushed to add, "As you've no doubt noticed." Thinking about his no-account skills with women had led to thoughts of his grandparents, which made him ask, "You met my grandmother the two times she came out here, didn't you?"

Mel's head jerked back a little. "What makes you ask about your grandmother? You think she had a dress like this?"

That near to made him laugh. His grandmother in plaid cotton? That'd sure never happen. "No. I-I just remembered you met her, and I wondered if she struck you as the kind of woman who would . . ." He didn't know if he could ask. It was unthinkable.

"Who would what, Cole?"

He cleared his throat. "No one's going to deny Priscilla was an arrogant woman who got her way. She had her whole life set up to make sure things always went exactly as she wished, and as soon as she wished it."

"I don't know what you're asking, but I remember her well. I met her when she first came to visit. I was probably seven at the time, and Ma brought me over to play once when you were kept in from work to spend time with your grandmother. My ma would stay for coffee and cake with your ma. But your grandmother was so intent on you that you didn't get to play with us and she never had coffee. I remember my ma whispering to me that we needed to come over mighty often while your grandmother was visiting because your ma was having trouble being sociable with her."

Cole smiled. "My ma, the friendliest woman who ever lived. The most welcoming, generous woman I can imagine, couldn't ever make Grandmother happy. I remember the constant barbs about the house and the food, about where we lived and how there was no decent clothing or conveyance."

"Conveyance?"

"It's a fancy word for something to ride. In this case she meant she was disappointed in the train. She and Grandfather owned their own train car."

With a tiny gasp, Mel said, "They owned it? A person can own one of those cars?"

"Yep, and make it mighty comfortable and not share it with anyone. The Bradfords, my grandparents, had one with two bedrooms, and I often traveled with them down to New York City and other places. But tracks hadn't been laid anywhere near Skull Gulch back then. She'd had to leave the train car behind back in St. Louis and come on the last stretch in a stagecoach. Then she'd expected to be met by a comfortable, enclosed carriage for her ride to the CR. Well, Ma and Pa didn't have one of those. Grandmother had to ride in a buckboard. From the fuss she made, you'd think Pa had plunked her backside down on a bed of nails."

"I remember she brought you presents. You were twelve, but she brought toys that seemed like they were for a much younger child. And clothes. Crates of clothes in all sizes. She wanted them to grow along with you, as if she was worried you'd run out and be reduced back to western duds. There was a velvet suit . . ."

Cole blushed. "I tried to burn that, but Ma took it and used it to make doll clothes for Sadie."

"And then your grandmother Bradford came back one more time when you were seventeen." Mel looked grim. Not a good memory for her.

"After the war, and she talked me into going back east to live with her and go to college."

"We didn't see you for ten years. You couldn't even make it home for a visit." Mel paused, let out a sigh. "But what made you think of her?"

"I know you didn't like her."

"She was horrified by me because I wore pants."

"Well, knowing her just that little bit, do you think she's the kind of woman who could hire a gunman? Pay someone to kill a man? Her or my grandfather? He never came out here, so you never met him, but they were alike in many ways. Could they . . . ?" Cole's voice trailed off.

Mel inhaled sharply. "What in heaven's name made you think of that?"

Suddenly Cole liked the idea of having someone outside the family to talk with about this. His family had always been on the opposite side of his when the Bradfords came up.

"We have two notes, one we found on Dantalion—the man who shot me." She flinched, then reached out a hand to rest on his arm. "Heath searched him before he died trying to escape. And we have another note in the same cramped handwriting, found on a man who tried to kill Ma and Pa in Denver."

"Someone attacked them up there? And it's related to the trouble you've had here?"

"We think so, and a big reason why is the handwriting that we're finding almost impossible to read. From letters and wires back and forth with my folks, we've decided just because of the oddness of the handwriting, it was written by the same person. That means there's a connection."

"Is your grandmother's or grandfather's handwriting like that?"

"No, I've already considered that. It's nothing like their hand. But Ma found the names Davidson and Priscilla Bradford in her note. They found the name Don Bautista de Val too, and his wife's. We've known all along that there was money behind the attempts to kill the Bodens, and both the Bradfords and the de Vals had plenty of money."

Cole shook his head then, his mind made up just from speaking out loud. "No, I won't believe it. I won't ever believe the Bradfords would hire someone to harm my family. Steal me away from them maybe. In fact, the year Sadie was born, Grandmother sent me a letter for the first time. She'd been searching for me for years, she said. Pa had already told me I was born to his first wife and she'd died. But to me, Ma, I mean Veronica, was the only mother I knew. I loved her as much as if she were my mother by blood. I had vague memories of my life back east, but I didn't really know if the memories were true or if they came from things Pa told me. But I realized later that from the first letter I received from my grandmother Pa kept a guard near me if he couldn't be with me himself. I never was allowed out alone. At the time, Pa said it was just good sense not to ride alone or take walks by myself in a country with outlaws and varmints big enough to carry off a man. Later I realized Pa was worried about me being kidnapped by my grandparents."

Cole crushed the scrap of cloth and stared right through it. "But could they have done just such a thing only with more deadly results? Hired someone to try and . . . and cost Pa the land grant?"

"You think they were powerful enough to steal land from your pa from half a country away?"

"The land grant wasn't always solidly in our hands. A few things have to work together to endanger the grant. Usually a weak governor who lets others do things in his name will open us to a threat to the CR. Justin knows the governor and says he's a decent man, but maybe not watchful enough of the men who advise him. Maybe when I was back east my grandparents could have hatched a plan to run Pa and Ma off the CR so I wouldn't have a ranch to go home to."

Nodding, he knew some of it didn't fit and he had no proof of any of it. Even so . . . "It makes a certain amount of sense. Grandfather Bradford used his money to get what he wanted. He knew the governor of Massachusetts well and was a personal friend to the Boston mayor. Both were at our home for dinner many times. Grandfather could have found the right man to back as the governor of New Mexico Territory. He could have thought to strip the CR from my family. Maybe they were working quietly, but when Grandfather died, his plan turned to something ugly, something deadly, funded with my grandparents' money and maybe the money of the de Val family, too." Cole's eyes came up and locked on Mel's. "I need to talk to Justin and Heath about this. See if they think it's nonsense."

Her eyes glowed with compassion. As if she knew what it cost him to think ill of his grandparents. He had no illusions about their arrogance, their influence, and their wealth and how they had manipulated him to stay in Boston. But he'd made his decisions with full awareness of what they were doing, because he'd seen the kind side of them as well, and also the lonely side. They really had loved him, and he'd loved them back. And he'd loved the opportunity to see the city and get himself an education.

By the kindness in her gaze he thought Mel realized all of that.

He took a step in the direction his brothers had gone, and because she didn't move, that meant he took a step closer to Mel.

He held up the kerchief. "Talking about my grandparents distracted me from thinking about this kerchief, which in turn distracted me from my first thought when we got left alone together. I will admit that when we're alone, I have a few notions that'd cause your uncle Walt to shoot me dead."

"I don't think Uncle Walt would shoot you dead. He'd probably just wing you."

Which made Cole take another step forward.

A gentle smile broke out on her face. A smile Cole had never seen before. Mel had a great smile, big and bright and wide.

He'd also seen her give a fine smile while she bottle-fed an orphan calf. And she had a special one for her ma and pa. But this one was something different. Something just for him.

He liked it real fine.

"Go ahead and think about that kerchief for as long as you want," she said. "I'll hush up. I'll let my mind wander about this or that while you do your thinkin'."

"This or that?" Cole got just a bit closer, and the next time he did that he was going to be in big trouble. He really had no business being alone with her like this. Uncle Walt should be horsewhipped. "You want to tell me exactly where your mind is going to wander?"

"Nope. I'm not interested in doing that at all."

He forced himself to do the right thing. "I'll leave off my thinking for now. I want to find Justin and Heath and talk with them about how my grandparents could fit into this mess."

"And then later you can study that clue *I found.*" She seemed to enjoy that smug little reminder. "And then we'll know who attacked you and we can round 'em up."

Nodding, Cole said, "I sure wish it was that easy."

Her smile faded. "So do I."

13

Mel turned to find her uncle coming straight for them. "You've looked at the tracks around where we found this cloth already?"

"Yep." Uncle Walt was moving slow, studying the ground alongside the trail. He raised his eyes. "You two get off the trail. There are already plenty of footprints muddling things up, I don't need more."

"Sorry, I figured it was trampled beyond what we could harm." She stepped off the trail, Cole right behind her. Justin came toward them from the direction of Mel's cabin.

"Justin, Heath, I want you to break off tracking for a minute. I want to ask you a question."

"I'll keep on," Uncle Walt said. "It's slowgoing so you can catch up, Kincaid." He went on, eyes locked on the ground, while Mel stayed.

"I have a suspicion," Cole said, "about why my grandparents' names were in the note Ma has. I want to talk it over with you and see if you think it's possible."

Justin crossed his arms and watched Cole close. Heath found a tree and leaned against it.

"My grandparents always tried to get me to stay in Boston. You know that, Justin."

"I mostly remember what an old bat your grandmother was when she showed up here with nothing good to say about our house, our parents, our clothes, or our speech, but with a wagonload of gifts for you and nothing for me and Sadie. Well, I was a kid back then and it stung. When I got older, I calmed down about it and knew she was your kin and none of mine, so it made some sense. But then I got older yet and decided I was right to begin with. She knew you had a little brother and sister. I can remember how she showed you those gifts, right in front of us. She wanted to hurt us. She wanted to aggravate Ma and Pa, who were nothing but nice to her. She—"

"Okay, stop. I know you don't like them and I know why. I've heard it plenty of times and, what's more, I agree with you. Let me finish what I want to say."

Justin clamped his mouth shut as if forcibly holding back the words.

"I don't believe my grandparents would hire a killer. I just don't. They were a lot of things, but not that."

Justin remained silent, but Mel had a good idea what he was thinking.

"But what if they were trying to get the land grant overturned? What if they were buying influence, getting the right people elected and appointed, with the idea that if I didn't have a home to go to, I might settle down in Boston for good. Or even if they just hated Pa, they might want to do him harm by taking his ranch away. That I can believe about them, but not that they hired killing. And after they died, what if money they'd sent for that nasty but not murderous plan got turned aside by others with uglier goals?"

Heath tilted his head. "I don't know your grandparents at all, though they don't seem like kind people, neither are they wise."

"Grandfather Bradford was a college graduate," Cole snapped. "My grandmother spoke several languages and was an avid reader of the classics."

"Whoa there, Cole." Heath held up his hands, his eyes not as fun-loving as usual. "I didn't say they weren't smart, I said they weren't wise. If your grandmother wanted to buy influence with *you*, being generous and kind to your family would have gone way further than treating the people you love poorly. It wasn't wise of her. Neither was it wise to think she could drive your family off this land and that would change your decision to return to them. Family isn't a place, it's people—if you're lucky, it's people you love and who love you. If your folks lost their ranch, a wise woman would know you'd run for home to help."

"I would have." Cole looked at Justin. "If you'd lost the CR or even if it was threatened, I'd have come and fought beside you."

"I reckon you know them better than anyone else, Cole," Justin said through gritted teeth. "So if you're sure they wouldn't hire a killer, then let's say they didn't. Instead, they ordered your home destroyed, Pa and Ma's lives ripped up. Your little brother and sister thrown off the only land they'd ever known. That may not be killing, but it's a hateful thing to do. Cruel and cold as the grave to my way of thinking."

Justin might've been madder than Cole. Mel didn't blame him. If someone had tried to steal the ranch from her family, they'd have been mad enough to start a war.

Cole's jaw tightened until Mel worried his teeth might crack.

"I'd say," Heath said, breaking the ice-cold silence, "you're the one who knows what your grandmother is like. You wouldn't have come to us with this story if you didn't think it was possible that however twisted the plot became, your grandparents at one time at least were behind it."

Cole nodded so tightly that it was almost impossible to see the motion.

Mel wished she'd gone with Uncle Walt. She wasn't a bad tracker and this was family business. But her uncle was out of sight, and she doubted anyone would let her wander off, what with a man planting dynamite in the area.

"So what does the old Don's wife have to do with this?" Cole finally managed to say.

"If your grandmother was, as you said, buying influence, maybe Don de Val was, too." Justin finally got his jaw unclenched. "His wife was an old terror, I remember hearing that. They were gone back to Mexico before I was born. Before you were born, come to that. Ma knew them. When the Don looked to be losing his ranch, he and his wife were both angry about it. I heard Ma say they went off in a fury to Mexico, their pride all tangled and twisted up. Maybe Don de Val wanted to see our grandfather lose his land and that was what drove the first killing . . . when they killed Grandpa Chastain thirty years ago."

Cole had his eyes focused somewhere in the past. "Maybe the Don started this, and since his death, the folks behind all our trouble have been using his money and the Bradfords'. Now that they're all dead, these outlaws have the money and are using it for far worse things than it was intended."

"You said that wrong," Justin interrupted. "All four of 'em aren't dead. The Don's wife isn't."

"She's still living?" Mel asked. She knew neither of them, as they'd been gone before she could remember. But her folks had spoken of them a few times, though not like they were friends.

"Yes, she is. Ramone talked of them," Justin's eyes were suddenly alert. "He said the Don was decent to him. Treated him like a servant, but at least he was fed and clothed. But Señora de Val was a different story. She always hated him and cast him out of her house within hours of her husband's death. Considering he was a child born on the wrong side of the blankets, Ramone didn't blame her much, but to me it wasn't Ramone's fault how he was born, and a father has a responsibility to care for the children he sires."

Mel remembered that Ramone had been innocent of the attacks on the Bodens. Ramone was a hired hand on the CR back when Cole was just a young boy. He'd kept quiet about being the old Don's son.

"We need to talk to Ramone." Cole tugged off his white Stetson and slapped it against his leg.

"Let's go to town," Justin said, then started climbing up the mountain toward his horse.

"Hold up there! We found something." Walt moved fast, next thing to running. "All the tracks have faded but one. We need horses and men. I found where he left the trail, and it climbs a ways into a canyon. There are good sentry spots on the way in and I'm not going in blind. We need to scout it out and make sure we aren't walking into a shooting range. And that'll take all of us."

Cole and Justin exchanged a glance. "Ramone will keep." Justin said it, but he didn't seem to like it. Then he headed uphill to the stable.

Cole was on his heels. "Heath, we'll bring your horse. No sense all of us walking all the way up there."

"Mine too," Mel yelled after him.

Cole stopped and turned to her, frowning.

Mel arched her brows. "Or are you going to leave me here all by my helpless little self?"

His eyes narrowed. Which meant he'd gotten that she was

using his own words against him. "We'll bring your horse, and you can ride with us right into an ambush. I sure hope your pa is agreeable to this."

Walt said, "She rides with me and that makes her safer than she'd be in the cellar at my brother's ranch."

Mel heard what he didn't say. Yes, he'd take care of her, but Walt didn't think she should be here at all. Cole clearly agreed. She decided to enjoy herself before she got sent packing for home.

"Mel," said Walt, "you're not armed. Go back to your cabin and fetch your gun."

She noticed she was the only one who wasn't armed. The Boden brothers each had a gun on their hip. She couldn't remember ever seeing Heath unarmed. And Walt, well, there was a mighty good chance Uncle Walt slept with his gun in hand.

Mel decided from now on she was going to do the same. As much as she wanted to help Cole and wanted to spend time with him, this was a serious business and she'd better be ready for a fight.

Cole never had a job he didn't want to boss.

He knew that about himself and he kept it under control around Pa, mostly. It was more of a battle with Justin.

Now he found himself taking orders from Walt. And not regretting it one bit. The man knew how to scout a trail. They'd gone a long distance away from the mines. Now Cole looked at the tight entrance to a canyon that might lead to a hideout. "I've never seen this trail before."

"Well, as I understand your property, this is off Boden land. It's a long ride away from the mines, too. Easy to see why you never rode out this way."

"And the three men you're trailing rode in there?"

"At least one came through here. And it makes sense they're keeping watch of this passage. So we're not riding that way. There are some likely lookout spots that cover this trail. If we stay back from it, we can maybe get the drop on them or at least slip past them. But be careful, and count on them being watchful. Cole, you and Mel go up that way." Walt kept his voice down, which really got Cole's attention. Sound didn't carry far in the mountains, not as a rule. Walt must think the trouble was close by.

"The rocks give good cover, and the mountain isn't so steep you can't climb up there from the main trail." Walt flicked his eyes between all of them. "Justin, go to the south of the trail with Heath."

"I'll come with you, Uncle Walt."

"Nope, I'm going to swing wide and beat you all to the top of the mountain. I want to go in alone. We know there could be three men, if not more. Maybe I can thin the herd some."

"No, you should scout things out but stay back, Walt." Justin scowled at him. "You're a tough man, but we're tough too, and this is Boden trouble."

"Trust me, I'm careful. And I work better alone. Let's head out." Walt turned and rode his horse toward the south, then veered uphill.

They wouldn't be able to get their mounts all the way over the top, but they could go a ways.

Cole nodded at Justin, and the foursome split up. Cole and Mel managed about a third of the trip before a stretch was too steep for the horses. They tied them near a stretch of grass that'd keep them occupied, then headed up on foot.

"There." Mel grabbed him by the front of his shirt and dragged him to the ground. Her whisper had a streak of urgency to it. He saw where she was pointing and looked about fifty feet up. He spotted footprints on a rocky track that led behind a man-sized boulder.

A lookout must be posted behind the rock . . . just as Walt had warned.

They went on, keeping rocks between themselves and the sentry. Cole got high enough he could look for a likely spot for a second guard on another peak. He couldn't see anyone, but he had to be sure. How could they sneak up on this varmint without alerting another guard?

Cole inched toward where their man must be, pausing to study the terrain before moving on, keeping well down and out of sight of any possible lookouts. Anger stirred within him. He might be within moments of catching the men responsible for the death of six miners.

Crouching lower with each passing minute, Cole finally dropped to his knees. He looked at Mel, who knelt beside him, pointed to her and then up the hill. A boulder loomed ahead, the footprints obvious now. The sentry was right on the other side of it.

Taking a deep breath, then hesitating because he knew Mel would be exposed, Cole kept his mouth locked shut. It'd be a waste of time to try to get her to stay hidden. He needed to trust her. She was a savvy woman and could hold her own.

He nodded, pointed to himself and then the downhill side of the boulder. He wanted to remind her about other guards, but he'd be insulting her, and the whispering might give them away.

They separated. Cole started crawling, letting more and more of the front side of the boulder show, until he could see . . . nothing. There was nobody there.

Boot heels were clear enough, though. Someone had been up here and not long ago. But they were gone now.

She stood from behind the big rock. "No one on the far side either."

Justin poked his head out from behind a boulder, grimaced and nodded, then vanished.

Mel turned, and Cole followed her gaze to a mountain valley thick with lush grass. Cole blew out a quiet whistle at the beautiful pasture. "A herd of cows could thrive in here."

Mel gave the view the quiet moment it deserved, then said, "Let's see if Walt left anyone down there who needs catching."

Justin and Heath stepped out in an opening down the mountain a ways, ahead of them.

"Let's go." They both headed down in a hurry to catch up, still careful in case there were other sentries.

They met at the bottom. Cole saw a sturdy cabin so new that the fresh-sawn logs weren't weathered yet. The high walls of the canyon blocked the worst of the wind.

All four of them ducked behind the nearest boulder. Mel just happened to choose the same one Cole did.

A bit of snow was blown up against the north side of the biggest rocks, and a thick stand of aspens had knee-deep snow surrounding them. The trees stood on the far side of what Cole guessed was a twenty-acre stretch of land.

"We haven't seen hide nor hair of Walt yet," Justin said. "If he got ahead of us, I'd guess he might be in that cabin."

No smoke came out of the cabin's chimney. And it was cold enough a fire should've been going day and night.

"We use all the boulders possible for cover." Cole crouched low and headed for the next closest one just as Walt poked his head out from behind the south side of the cabin.

He gestured with his gun in silence. All four of them moved faster but still tried to keep a barrier between them and the cabin.

Heath got there first and went north. Cole darted behind the cabin on the south. Mel followed him as Justin went after Heath.

Walt spoke quietly when Cole and Mel reached him. "The cabin's empty, but someone just hightailed it out of here. His tracks are fresh, and it looks like two more horses rode out a bit earlier. I climbed to high ground and watched a man ride through a gap in the canyon wall. Justin, you come with me. There are two horses in the barn. I've got 'em saddled and ready. Maybe we can catch the varmint. The rest of you ride for Skull

Gulch and tell them what you've found. Tell Sheriff Joe I'll be in and will vouch for these men, whoever they are, setting off that dynamite. The signs all read that way. Heath, you can tell him what you saw too with the tracks. Two of us with the same story will carry more weight."

"If we catch up to the man who just ran off, I'll bring him right along," Justin added. "If we don't, we'll study his trail enough to tell you something."

Cole nodded. "The sheriff knows all about the explosion and the men out here who died. He'll be glad to have someone to arrest. Wait . . . we're forgetting about Pa's will. It's late in the day. Justin, you'll be heading in exactly the wrong direction."

"What's your pa's will got to do with this? Your pa's alive and well."

"Heath, you'll have to go with Walt. Explain what's going on while you ride."

"No, Heath goes with you. I need someone who read that sign to talk to the sheriff."

"I saw the tracks," Justin said. "I can tell the tale as well as Heath."

Walt knew that wasn't true. They all did. With a snort of disgust, Walt headed for the barn and a few minutes later emerged with two horses.

"Cabin's empty. You three have a good look around before you go. I didn't take time to be thorough when I was still thinking a lone gunman might be around. These are the only horses left and they're crowbait." Walt handed a pair of reins to Heath, then swung up onto the skinny horse. It wasn't prime horseflesh and didn't make the gunmen hiding here look prosperous. Heath's was a heavier animal, its hooves thick and its back wide like a plow horse.

"Mel, I'd take you along, but I don't want you riding after

a man who might be holed up and aiming at his back trail. I doubt I'll get back to the cabin tonight. I don't want you riding alone, and Justin and Cole need to stay together all the way to town to talk to the sheriff. They'll have to go a long ways out of their way to take you to the JB. Best stay at the Bodens'."

Mel nodded. "Be careful, both of you. We'll pick up your horses."

Cole watched them ride away. "I don't like the idea of them riding after a man who might be holed up, aiming at his back trail."

Mel heard Uncle Walt's words repeated exactly, and her stomach gave a sickening twist of fear.

"I feel like I'm sending others to fight my fight," he added.

Justin slapped Cole on the shoulder. "You can't send men like Heath and Walt anywhere and you know it. Stopping them would've been the trick."

"That's especially true for Uncle Walt." Mel's fear eased a bit. Walt was a hard trail-savvy man. He'd be fine and he'd protect Heath—and Heath probably didn't need any protecting. "C'mon, let's go look around the cabin, then get to town. It's gonna be a long day, but at least it's better than mining for gold."

Just as Walt said, the cabin had nothing in it. No mysterious notes written with scrawled, cramped handwriting. No packs of gold nuggets. No evidence that there was any connection between these men and the explosions, except for incriminating tracks that not many men could read.

They had to walk until they reached their horses. Then they rode for town, knowing the day was wearing down around them.

The sun was dropping behind Mount Kebbel by the time they reached the sheriff's office in Skull Gulch.

Mel swung down, saddlesore from the grueling day. And it wasn't over yet.

They hitched their horses, and then the three of them headed to the jail. The sheriff must've seen them coming, because he swung the door open before they reached it.

"What happened?"

Justin and Cole took turns telling their story. Mel threw in a few words, too. The sheriff knew about the explosions already, and knew enough about Walt Blake that he believed every word the Bodens said about where the trail led.

"I expect Walt to be in at some point. Whether later tonight or tomorrow sometime, I can't say. He was chasing a man living in the cabin with two others, and we know it was three men's tracks we followed, so we want that man."

"If anyone can bring him in, it's Walt."

"Let's head for home." Justin tugged his hat low on his head.

Mel felt funny riding to the Bodens' and calling it "home."

She rode along anyway. “Rosita won’t be planning on me for supper.” And she was so hungry her belly button was rubbing against her backbone.

“She’s expecting Justin and me,” Cole said. “Justin, you can skip your third helping for once so that Mel has something to eat.”

“She’s also expecting Heath, and Rosita always makes plenty. There’ll be enough food for everyone.”

Mel wasn’t really worried about the food. But she was a boiling caldron of worry, and Cole Boden riding along beside her was the source of most of it.

Since their horses had rested while they talked with the sheriff, they were able to set a faster pace. Even so, it was full dark by the time they reached the Cimarron Ranch. Mel was glad to see lanterns glowing in the windows of the main house and also the bunkhouse.

John Hightree, the Bodens’ foreman, came outside to greet them. “Howdy, Mel. Cole, Justin, you’re late. I had a notion to send out a search party.”

“You’d’ve been looking in the wrong place.” Cole gave him a quick rundown on the day.

“Heath just got here. He told me most of it. Go on in and eat. I’ll see to the horses.”

“Thanks, John.” While Mel liked to see to her own horse, she badly wanted to follow the glow of that warm light.

They headed inside together. Mel was surprised to see the family just sitting down to dinner.

Rosita smiled as she carried a large bowl of beef stew to the table. “It’s good you’ve come, Mel.”

Sadie gave Mel a big hug, then grabbed a platter of biscuits stacked high. She set them on the table and went to a seat snugged tight against Heath’s.

"Yes, it's nice you're staying," Angie said. She smiled as she placed plates on the table.

Justin came in, washed his hands in a basin of water, then hugged Angie and gave her a modest kiss that didn't match the heat in his eyes.

Cole threw out Justin's water and refilled the basin. "You're next, Mel."

Soon they were all seated at the table, Cole at the head, Justin at the foot, with Mel finding herself on Cole's right next to Heath and Sadie. She looked across the table at Rosita, Angie, and Justin.

Cole led them in a heartfelt prayer for their pa's healing and safe return, the well-being of the whole family and all those around them, for the men who'd died and those who grieved, and finally for strength sufficient for the task ahead.

"Now," Cole said before he put so much as a bite of stew on his plate, "let's talk about what my grandparents might have to do with all this."

"Cole's grandfather's name shows up again." Veronica straightened from the writing and set her magnifying glass down with a sharp click. "Right along with Señora Lauressa de Val, the old Don's wife."

And if she was reading it right, they needed to see the rest of these notes—which her children had in New Mexico. The urgency of it was almost a lightning bolt. She felt the very hand of God sending chills up her spine and ordering her home.

She lurched to her feet. A groan escaped as her spine straightened and cracked in about five places. The pain brought her hands to the small of her back. She'd been bending over this writing for hours.

Chance came up behind her and rubbed her back. "It's time for a break. Let's at least walk around inside the house. We can't go outside, but we can still move around a little."

"No, there's no time for a walk." She was too anxious to think about her aches and pains. "We've got to go home."

With a twist of his big hands, he turned her to face him. "You're the one who's been fussing about the doctoring I need. I've been ready for weeks."

His leg was healed, Ronnie knew that, but it hurt and had limited movement. He wasn't well.

"I've changed my mind. And now that I have, I want to be there. You pack everything you can." Ronnie pointed at Chance, as ready to go as if someone had stuck a spur in her flank.

"Finn is usually around this time of day. I'll have him hire us a carriage to take us to the train station. I've checked the schedule, and a train leaves at two in the afternoon that's going south through Skull Gulch. It's nearly noon now. We have time to make it if we don't lollygag."

Chance gave her one long look, and whatever he saw convinced him to get moving. "I'll gather everything two people can carry."

He headed for the bedroom. They'd brought little more with them than a change of clothes. But they'd made purchases since arriving here. "We've paid rent until the end of February. We can leave anything we can't haul along and have it shipped to us later."

"I'll be back to help as soon as I find Finn." Ronnie caught Chance's arm before he could leave. "You know I want to invite him to come along with us, don't you?"

"Yep." Chance gave her a warm smile. "Another young'un around the place would be good, Ronnie. Ask him."

"I'm just worried he's alone, living on the street. I can't just take him. He speaks of his mother, and I can tell he's lying, but I'm not sure what he's lying about." She shook her head. "I am getting a straight answer out of him today."

She ran out of the room, straight for the front door. Neither she nor Chance wandered around outside. They'd caught the first man who'd attacked them, then slipped away to live in a place no one knew about, not even the doctor. All Chance's treatments had been arranged by sending notes through Finn and answering the doctor's pointed questions about Chance's leg, then getting more notes with details for new exercises.

At first, Veronica had gone out to buy necessities, but since they'd met Finn, he'd done most of their running for them. Their first trip of any distance would be when they headed for the train.

She swung open the front door and nearly knocked Finn off the porch. He jumped, his eyes wide with fear. Ronnie had to wonder what crazed expression she had on her face. She'd wonder later—right now she needed his help.

"Finn . . ." She gave him rapid-fire directions and pressed a five-dollar gold piece in his hand. Then before he ran off to earn his money, she dropped to her knees in front of him.

Yes, she was in a tearing hurry, but she had time for this one thing. She caught him by the shoulders. "Time is up for us to get to know each other better. Now, I've got a direct question for you. I'll have no choice but to accept whatever you say as the truth."

She ran a hand through his wild red curls. "Mr. Boden and I have a nice big house in New Mexico Territory. There is plenty of space for one fine young man. You. You've spoken of your ma, but I've yet to meet her and I can see you're living a rugged life."

She looked deep into his eyes. "Are you alone in the world,

Finn? Do you really have a ma and a home? Or are you living on the street like so many unfortunate children? Because if you need a home, I'm offering you one."

"Missus, I'm fine." His eyes shifted, and she just didn't know . . . was he too proud to let a family take him in, or did he really have a mother somewhere who wanted him?

Ronnie held up her hand to stop him from talking further. "You've got from now until you get back with that carriage to give me an answer. Think about it. I've got two grown sons and a grown daughter. I miss having a youngster in the house. Now go and get back fast. There's more money for you if we make that train on time."

With a single jerk of his chin in agreement, he turned and dashed away.

Ronnie took a few seconds to worry about the young'un. He needed help whether he had a ma or not. She'd give him money, but would he know what to do with it? Would it make him the target of thieves? She just didn't know how to handle the situation.

Whirling away from one problem, she charged toward another. Chance had a trunk fully packed and was working on the two satchels they'd brought from the CR.

There was little left to pack. She quickly wrote the doctor a note, explaining what had happened, and folded it. If Finn came with them to New Mexico, she'd mail it from the train station. If he didn't, the boy could do one last job for her and maybe earn himself a generous amount.

Chance dragged the trunk to the front porch, Ronnie following with the satchels, her reticule, and with a quick stop in the kitchen she added bread, apples, and cheese, enough to feed them all the way to Skull Gulch.

Finn came running up moments later. Behind him was a

shoddy cart, drawn by a single pony and driven by a man who looked like he sold vegetables at the local shops.

Ronnie gave it two seconds' consideration and decided this would do fine.

They stepped outside where Ronnie was struck by the cold. She'd been nearly housebound for most of her time in Denver, and the weather made her miss New Mexico Territory even more.

She'd told Chance all about Finn, and now when the boy approached, she asked, "Have you made your decision, Finn?"

He gave her such a scared look that she was prepared to grab him and drag him with her if he said no.

"Missus, I really do have a ma, but she's ailing something fierce. There's just the two of us and we live a few blocks from here in a bad way. I can't leave her, so my answer is no, unless . . . c-can we t-take my ma, too?"

Ronnie gave Chance a wild look.

He said, "Will she come? She's got no time to think about it—she'll just have to climb in the cart and go."

The cart that was already nearly full with their trunk and satchels.

In a halting voice, Finn replied, "She's mostly not awake these days, and we'll have to carry her. I doubt she'll even know we're moving her."

The boy's words about broke Ronnie's heart.

"Hop in, Finn." Chance caught Ronnie by the waist and hoisted her into the bed of the cart. "Give the driver directions."

16

Mel checked the load in her pistol and then snapped it shut.

"I'm gonna teach her how to shoot." Mel stepped up beside the sweet city girl who'd married into the Boden clan. They definitely needed to toughen her up.

Angie said, "I really don't—"

"I'm a crack shot," Sadie said. "I can teach her just as well as you."

"Justin has spent—"

"I can shoot the head off a rattlesnake at a hundred yards." Mel wasn't even bragging, and her old friend Sadie knew it.

"If you'll just listen," Angie began, louder this time, but Sadie ignored her.

Sadie grinned. "We can both advise her."

"Well, as to that, a few times—"

"Yep, and the two of us don't need to waste lead practicing." Mel handed Angie her pistol.

Angie rolled her eyes.

Which struck Mel as rude.

Then the little, genteel city woman raised the gun and blasted away at an aspen scrub growing out of the base of Skull Mesa. She fired three shots so fast they sounded almost like one and tore the aspen clean off at its trunk, then turned to arch a brow at her friends.

"Nice shootin'." Mel smiled. *City Girl might be tough enough already.*

"It looks like Justin got here before us." Sadie slapped Angie on the shoulder.

"Are we going to take time to climb Skull Mesa tonight?" Angie did love the top of that mesa.

Mel slung an arm around Angie's other shoulder. "It's a little late. Not much to see from the top in the dark."

"Justin and I have gone up a couple of times."

"I didn't know that." Mel looked at the mesa rising up beside them. "I've only gone up once."

"When did you two climb it?" Sadie asked. "You never told me or I'd have gone along."

"We . . . uh . . . well, we decided just the two of us might go." Angie's cheeks turned a surprising shade of bright pink.

Mel wondered why.

Sadie grinned, punched Angie lightly on the shoulder, and gave her a look that reminded Mel they were both married women.

She'd always been able to outrope, outride, and honestly outthink most any woman she met—and most men, too—but right now there was plenty these two knew that she didn't.

"The wind's picking up." The weather was a good change of subject, and she grabbed for it. "Let's head in."

Angie handed her gun back to Mel, who holstered it. She hadn't brought her Winchester from home, but she oughta see how Angie handled that.

"You need more shooting practice, Angie?" Justin led the way out to the mesa, with Heath beside him and Cole bringing up the rear.

Justin and Heath were the ones going out to see their wives, after all. Cole was just along for the walk. He looked past his brothers—he counted Heath as a brother now just to keep things simple—and saw Mel, grinning and holstering her gun. Tougher and better at the frontier life than either of the other women. And if Cole was being honest, probably tougher than any of the men, too.

Not stronger, though. He could still beat her in a wrestling match.

And then the thought of wrestling with Mel distracted him so much he only stopped walking toward her when he ran into Justin. His little brother glanced back, irritated.

Cole moved to Justin's side, doing his best to act like nothing had happened.

"I'm doing fine. You've helped me so much, these two are impressed." Angie's blue eyes flashed with good humor as she jerked her head toward Mel and Sadie with a wide smile. Her blond hair had come loose from its braid a bit from standing out in the wind. The fine ends fluttered around her face.

The women lined up and they were a picture. Mel in her dusty trousers, who never wore a skirt except to church. Cole could look at her and not see why any man would look twice at a stone made of gold when he could have a woman golden on the outside, with a heart of gold within.

Angie was in the middle, a beautiful woman, but so thin she looked fragile. She'd had to teach them all she wasn't, which she'd done when she escaped from three men who'd kidnapped her, getting to the Bodens' in time to warn them that her kidnappers were lying in wait to dry-gulch them.

His little sister, Sadie. Sassy, pretty, and as tough as a girl could be who'd had two bossy big brothers ordering her around all her life. She was the image of ma with her yellow hair and brown eyes shot through with flecks of green.

Looking at them in a row like this was a fine sight. And not one part of that sight was as fine as Mel Blake.

"Do you think, Heath," Sadie said, giving her husband an overly friendly smile, "we could take a picnic to the top of Skull Mesa sometime? Just sit up there and spend some time together?"

Heath nodded. "I'd like that. But we need to pick a time we're sure no one would be shooting at us."

"Or bringing an avalanche down on our heads," Justin added. He shoved his hands in his back pockets in a way that made it seem as though he wanted to reach for his wife.

Cole looked up at the mesa. "Or blowing us up."

"Let's head back." Heath reached for Sadie's hand and pulled her along. She said something to him Cole couldn't hear that made him glance back at the mesa.

"Really?" He spoke too loud, then went back to talking quietly.

It had turned to dusk with a few stars shining overhead.

Justin pulled Angie's arm through his elbow and followed after Heath, whispering something that made Angie giggle and lean against him.

Watching them go gave Cole's heart a pang. He glanced at Mel. They could pair off just as easy. There was an awkward moment, and it would've been the most natural thing in the world for him to reach for her so they could walk arm in arm.

But he didn't.

Mel set off, and Cole fell in beside her. They spent the whole walk back to the house talking about the weather.

❧

The boy was right about not living far away. They pulled up in front of a crumbling wreck of a building, half gone from a fire. Chance knew with one look that no one rented rooms in the building. They lived here without permission.

"Stay with the cart, Ronnie." He leaned close so that Finn couldn't hear. "You've got your gun loaded and at hand, right?"

He didn't want to give her his gun, as he might need it in this seedy place. He had no idea that he and Ronnie had rented a house so close to a derelict neighborhood.

"Go." She nodded and pulled back the corner of her coat to show a gun holstered around her waist. "And hurry. Our driver looks like he's tempted to make a run for it."

As he followed Finn up a rickety flight of stairs, Chance grew increasingly worried about the building collapsing on their heads. Several rooms were without doors, and Chance saw a few men sleeping on the floor.

One man, leaning dejectedly against a wall, lifted his head and narrowed his eyes until he reminded Chance of a wolf.

Chance ignored the ache in his leg and moved faster. They climbed to the third floor. Finn led him to a room with a door, the first closed door he saw in the place. Finn produced a key. The locked door made this the fanciest apartment so far.

A creaking floorboard from below made Chance glance behind him. "Hurry, Finn. I think there might be trouble brewing."

Finn turned the key fast and rushed into a room as bare as the others Chance had seen. Finn rushed to his ma, rolled up in a blanket on the floor. Chance didn't spend time assessing her condition. He was no doctor, and his skill ran to the injuries a man got from being bucked off a horse or kicked by a cow. Any help he gave her might make things worse. He picked her up, shocked at how light she was. A soft moan escaped her lips, but that was the only sign of life.

"Ma's name is Bridget Finn. I'm Sean, by the way, but I like going by my last name." Finn looked at his ma with eyes full of love and fear.

"Let's go, son." Chance turned to leave, determined to get all of them out of there just as soon as he could. He headed down three flights as fast as he could go, considering the stairs were in such terrible shape and it was putting pressure on his leg he hadn't felt since the cast came off. They'd made it down only one flight when a man holding a knife stepped right into their path.

Chance's first inclination was to knock the varmint's teeth out. He couldn't imagine anything lower than pulling a knife on a man carrying an unconscious woman with a child at his side. Lucky for this polecat, Chance didn't have time to beat some manners into him. Instead he shifted Bridget so he could draw his gun. The arm that was hooked under her knees now brandished a pistol.

"Drop the knife or I'll shoot. I'm not going to give you even one second to think about it. Chance cocked the gun with a sharp click.

The man tossed the knife off to the side.

"Now clear a path. Right now!"

The man spun around and ran off into one of the doorless rooms.

Suppressing a sigh of relief, because Chance sure as certain didn't want to shoot anyone, they hurried on downstairs. When they got outside, Chance saw Ronnie standing up in the cart, facing the alley on the other side of the street, her gun drawn and aimed at a pair of men who'd emerged from the alley.

He rushed forward, his own gun still drawn, and roared, "Now there are two guns on you! Do you want a fight?"

The men vanished into the alley like rats.

Ronnie saw Chance and smiled. He felt as if the sun had just come out and the day warmed to summer temperatures. With a smirk, she sat down, brushed off her skirts as if there'd never been any trouble. Chance was as relieved as a man could be—while holding such an ailing woman.

A furrow appeared on Ronnie's smooth forehead when she saw the unconscious woman in Chance's arms.

He said, "Meet Bridget Finn and her son Sean."

Ronnie gave Finn a quick glance.

"Can you take her? She weighs next to nothing. Hold her in your lap so I can keep my gun drawn and an eye out until we're well away from here."

Ronnie sat on a small box seat right behind the driver. Chance handed Finn's mother to her, and Ronnie studied the woman, pushing back the blanket she was wrapped in to see her face. She was frighteningly thin, her eyes closed even with all the commotion. No fever. No sign at all of what exactly she was sick from. Ronnie gave a frown at the hectic red curls to match Finn's.

Finn jumped into the cart and squeezed in beside Ronnie on a seat barely big enough for one. Chance took up what little was left of the cart's bed, sharing the space with their trunk and satchels.

He stayed on his knees so he could look in all directions. The cart, drawn by the now-overworked pony, was set into motion. No one pestered them as they drove through the run-down neighborhood, maybe because Chance was so alert.

Chance spoke quietly to the driver without consulting Ronnie. "Take us back to where you picked us up."

The driver didn't hesitate for a second.

They quickly returned to the rented house. Chance holstered his gun.

"We can't take her on the train, can we?" Ronnie met his eyes. She wasn't really asking. She knew as well as he that the fragile woman wouldn't survive without a doctor's care, and soon.

He jumped down from the cart, striking the ground hard enough to wrench his newly healed leg. "We'll miss the train today, but we can take another train and go back home as soon as we're sure she's properly cared for." He reached up for poor, ailing Bridget Finn.

With a nod, Ronnie went to help Finn down, but he'd already scrambled over the edge of the cart bed.

"Go for the doctor, Finn. Go straight for him this time. Don't worry about meeting him somewhere or taking notes back and forth. Just bring him here fast for your ma. Don't worry about paying him, either. The doctor will come regardless."

"Thanks, Mr. Boden." Finn nodded so hard his hat flew off his head. He grabbed it and ran.

Chance had little doubt the boy had been wanting the doctor to see to his ma for days, maybe weeks, but money had stopped him. Pride would have stopped him now, as the little redheaded urchin had more than his share of it. But that was for himself. For his mother, he'd let them help.

Once Finn was gone, Chance, holding Bridget, asked the driver to help with the trunk. Ronnie rushed ahead and held the door open for him.

As he passed her, he said, "What you just did . . . I agree with it, but if someone's watching that doctor trying to find us, this'll do it. We have to get home."

Ronnie looked down at the sick woman and back up at Chance, the desperation clear in her expression. She wanted to be back at the CR. Her children had been at risk from the first, but she'd pushed Chance to stay in Denver and completely heal. Now her control had snapped. She needed to get her hands on that other note they had. That could be her excuse. In truth, she was just plumb out of patience and wanted desperately to be home, where she could fight at her children's side.

But she had Finn's ma, who was gravely ill and couldn't be left on her own, not right now.

She followed Chance to the bedroom. "We can't just abandon her and Finn."

And that was the plain truth of it.

Chance could almost hear Ronnie's heart pounding with urgency to go. "We'll arrange for someone else to care for her as quickly as possible, maybe hire a nurse. The doctor will have some ideas, too. For now, do your best to explain in a letter what's going on so the children have some warning. We'll get home as soon as we can."

17

Sadie spoke first. "Cole, we know you loved your grandparents."

Cole was glad she was doing the talking. Justin didn't know how to say a single word that didn't make things worse. For the most part, Cole appreciated Justin's straight talk, but his grandparents were always a sore subject.

"We wouldn't make something up. You believe that, right?"

"I know there's something going on here that involves them, yet I can't be sure you won't put the worst possible face on anything you learn. I know you didn't like them and I understand why. They were never nice to any of you, and they were overly nice to me. But although I understand, I also knew them better than you. I knew the best of them."

Justin gave a nod and said, "And what you said about your grandparents maybe having bad intentions but not this bad—I think you're on to something there."

"What are you talking about?" Sadie had never liked being left out.

Now there was no point excluding her even if it did keep her safer. Since Heath had fallen for her, he told her every word they spoke. The varmint probably tossed in a few things he'd made up on his own.

So Sadie got to hear everything now.

Cole told her their theory about the Bradfords trying to force Ma and Pa off the ranch while Cole was gone.

Sadie kept her voice calm but her eyes flashed with temper. "So you can see them using their money to influence people to drive us off our land? Pa and Ma consider this land a family legacy to be cherished, fought for, even to die for, so that's no small bit of treachery."

"I can." Cole was determined to be honest and not jump into defending his grandparents. He'd done it so often it was a habit hard to break. "And it makes me furious. But I really did know the Bradfords. I understand how they liked to wield power. They had a ruthless side. They'd be up to supporting a governor's campaign and finding ways for money to be shifted to him, ways that'd make him their pawn once he said yes to the first small bribe. There was a lot of that kind of buying influence in Boston, and it's all perfectly legal. I can imagine them doing it here."

He paused and looked each of them in the eye. "But trying to overturn a land grant is a long way from hiring a killer. Besides, even if they did do such a horrible thing, it would have been to get their hands on me. All they ever wanted was to bind their only grandchild to them. They wanted to cut me off from my family. But I got shot, remember? My name is in that book right along with all of you. My grandparents never gave anyone money with instructions to do such a thing. So I'm saying whoever's doing this might have started off with my grandparents' money aimed at influencing some politician, but since their deaths it's gotten out of control."

Mel asked quietly, "What about your grandpa Chastain? Was their money involved in his killing?"

A deep silence fell over the room.

Justin broke it. "I don't see how. I got a real strong feeling that it took them years to find Cole. Remember when the first letters started coming? It was around the time Sadie was born. I wasn't that old, but I remember how upset Ma and Pa were."

"I remember it. I could read, and Pa let me read it myself." Cole still had the letters, though they were at his house in town. He thought of his grandmother's flowing, beautiful handwriting and took comfort in that tiny proof she hadn't mailed out instructions on how to wipe out the Boden family.

"You know what I'm wondering?" Heath asked.

"What?" Sadie always paid a lot of attention to her husband. Cole was almost used to the idea of Sadie being married. He liked and respected Heath well enough. Even so, she was too young, and Heath wasn't good enough for her. Cole had the feeling he'd've thought the same about any man she married.

"I'm wondering what Don de Val's wife's handwriting looks like." Heath arched a brow at Cole. "Her name is in those notes too, right along with your grandparents."

At that, Cole looked around the table, his eyes pausing now and then.

It was Rosita who asked, "How would we get a sample of her handwriting?"

They all sat thinking on that when Angie said, "Maybe Ramone has seen it."

Justin smiled with pride at his bride's quick thinking.

"Maybe," Sadie added, "Ramone has even seen Señora de Val's handwriting enough that he could read it."

Cole felt his spirits lifting.

Justin smiled. "And Ramone said she was terrible to him. So he'd have no loyalty toward his father's wife."

"By all accounts," Cole said, his eyes meeting Justin's where he saw the same excitement shining there that he knew was coursing through him, "he thought she was a nasty old bat."

Ramone lived in Skull Gulch now. He was the son born on the wrong side of the blankets to his mother and Don de Val while the old Don was married to Señora Lauressa. Ramone had a sister too, Maria, who'd died at the orphanage when someone involved in the treachery had tried to kill Justin.

Years ago, back in Grandfather Chastain's day, Ramone had been a cowpoke on the Cimarron Ranch. Ramone had run off the day old Frank Chastain was murdered, and those looking for someone to blame settled on Ramone because he'd run.

Now, all these years later, Ramone had returned, and the truth about Grandfather's murderer had come out. All those years ago, Ramone had witnessed the murder and nearly been killed himself. Ramone was brutally injured with a slashed-open face that left him scarred and blind in one eye by the killer, a man by the name of Dantalion.

Dantalion promised to blame the murder on Ramone. Rather than fight, or get word to the Bodens about who'd done the killing, Ramone disappeared and spent most of his life in Mexico City.

For years, Ramone had lived and worked for his father. And he'd been coldly tolerated by Señora Lauressa, the Don's wife, only because her husband had insisted. She cast him out as soon as her cheating husband died.

"All this most recent trouble," Cole said, "started mighty soon after Don de Val died, didn't it? Maybe the one who changed the plans was Señora de Val. Once her husband was gone, maybe she could do things he wouldn't allow."

"The timing is almost perfect." Justin's eyes narrowed as he rubbed his chin.

"I feel maybe for the first time," Cole said, his sharp-thinking businessman's brain adding things up, "we're headed in the right direction. Maybe this is the clue we need to finally get to the bottom of this mess."

"It is too late tonight to ride to Skull Gulch and question Ramone," Rosita proclaimed as if she were the head of the household. And since Cole's folks had been gone, she mostly was. "Save it for tomorrow morning. I will go with Justin to talk with Ramone."

"I don't think I'd better do that, Rosita. I think I've pushed Ramone about as far as I dare." Justin turned to Cole. "You go with Rosita instead and see if you can get any information out of him."

"I don't want to take a day away from the mines. That's more important right now."

Mel thought of the attacks on the Bodens. The avalanche that injured Chance. The gunshot that nearly killed Cole. Heath shot. Angie kidnapped. A mine explosion . . .

The secret to all of it seemed to be hidden in some notes Heath had taken from Dantalion before he died. They'd never shown the note to Ramone. Now it was possible he might help in ways none of them had considered yet.

"No, Cole," Mel said into the tense silence. "I don't think there is anything more important to do than this."

A hush fell over the room. All of them remembering.

Cole set his napkin on the table and stood. "Rosita, be ready to leave at first light."

"It feels odd sleeping at your house." Mel came into Chance Boden's office to continue discussing their suspicions with the family.

She stopped so fast she might've left skid marks on the oak floor.

"Where's everybody else?" Only Cole was there, settled in behind his pa's desk, working over a ledger of some kind.

She'd cleaned up the kitchen with Rosita, Sadie, and Angie. The men had offered to lend a hand but the kitchen was already too full, so the women shooed them away and made short work of the dishes.

Mel had helped stow away the last dishes, and as she thanked Rosita again for the delicious meal and gave her a warm hug good-night, she straightened to realize Sadie and Angie had left ahead of her.

There had been talk of a meeting in the library, but now she stood there with no one but Cole. "Where is everyone?" she asked again.

"Newlyweds." Cole smirked a little. "They all turn in mighty early. Sadie and Heath have taken over the house Alonzo used to live in."

"He was a ramrod, wasn't he?" Mel said.

"Yep, and he betrayed us. We aren't hiring anyone new until we find out who we can trust. So the house isn't in use, and I leave the upstairs to Justin and Angie and sleep down here in Ma and Pa's room. You're gonna end up in a bedroom in the back of the house near Rosita."

"I know the rooms. We played all over this house when I was a kid. Rosita's making up the bed right now."

"Can't say as I blame my brother and sister for wanting some private time. They haven't been married long and probably haven't had a word just between them since this morning. We used to gather in here at night, but lately it's only me."

"Well," Mel said, clearing her throat, "I reckon I'll go. It's been a powerful long couple of days, and I've got gold to dig tomorrow."

Cole said, "I heard Walt wants to head down into the pit in your mine tomorrow."

"Walt talked about it. We found a vein of gold in his today, thin as a hair."

Cole gave Mel a slight smile. "You're lucky. Most everything on the same level as the mine entrance is played out, which is why they're digging down."

"Good night, then."

"Wait, before you leave, you need to stay with Justin or whoever rides out to the mines tomorrow until you find your uncle Walt."

Mel shrugged. "I reckon I can stick to Justin."

"I won't be going because of questioning Ramone. Not sure about Heath. He seems to like to stand guard out there, so he might be going along."

Since he seemed to want to talk, she let the blaze burning in the huge stone hearth draw her. She did need sleep, but she wasn't quite ready to go to a strange room. That pried a smile out of her, because last night she'd done exactly the same thing at her little cabin.

After holding her hands out to warm for a minute, she admitted to herself that she didn't want to go because she wanted to stay here with Cole. And that was foolish, so she gave herself a mental shake and turned to leave. She walked straight into him. She'd been so focused on not looking at him, she hadn't noticed him come to the fire.

He caught her upper arms as if to steady her, even though she was steady as a rock. He didn't let go but instead looked down at her for a long, silent moment broken only by the crackle of the fire at her back.

Finally, without saying a word, he lowered his head toward her mouth.

"Cole," she said against his lips, "we can't do this."

She turned her head aside and rested her cheek on Cole's broad shoulder. Her hands stayed on his chest, as she wasn't quite ready to step back but knew she should.

"It's all wrong." Cole's words so exactly echoing her thoughts brought her head up. She looked into his eyes and saw regret.

It was as if he'd slapped her. It certainly cleared her mixed-up longing. She stepped around him and forced herself to walk.

"Mel, wait. I didn't mean . . ."

"Let's don't talk about it, Cole." She didn't look back but moved faster toward the door just ahead. She needed to escape badly.

She quickly reached the door and stepped into the hall. Only then did she glance sideways at him. There he stood, right where she'd left him. He'd made no move to come after her, and she knew why. He was drawn to her just as she was drawn to him, and it was exactly as he'd said—all wrong.

"Hola, Señor Cole, Señora Rosita." Ramone swung the door open, his one working eye, nervous, looking away from Cole to Rosita.

When Ramone was in profile, looking at Rosita, Cole was struck by what a handsome man he'd been. Then he looked straight at Cole and the devastation of his wound was a horror.

What would it do to a handsome man to suddenly be so disfigured? Yes, it would be an awful thing, but Ramone had once enjoyed a decent life. He'd married and had children—one of them the betraying vermin, Alonzo, who'd kidnapped Angie and used her to lure out the Bodens, hoping to kill them. Alonzo was now in prison, and Justin ended up marrying Angie. His anger at Alonzo lingered and might've overflowed onto Ramone. It was just as well Cole's little brother hadn't come.

But Ramone had daughters, too. By the few accounts Cole had heard, they were happily married back in Mexico City. Ramone had a job that kept him supported most his life. And many men came out of the war and out of the tough life on the frontier with scars or missing fingers, arms, legs. Still, they stood strong and kept going. But Ramone seemed to fold up every time he was faced with adversity.

"Welcome." Ramone stepped back, his expression etched with fear at the sight of Cole.

Cole let Rosita go in first. Ramone hadn't taken part in any of the wrong that'd been done to the Bodens, and he was innocent of Frank Chastain's death. And yet he'd known things he should have told the sheriff, which would have helped put right a wrong that allowed a murderer to roam free for decades.

Ramone was no villain, but he was a coward, and there was no reason to believe that would ever change.

Cole said, "Sit, Ramone."

There were two extra chairs in the small cabin. Rosita sat at the foot of the table, Ramone at the head.

Cole sat between them and started talking. "We've found some strange notes among the possessions of the men who attacked us. We've got a few questions for you."

"Sí, Señor Cole. Ask me. I will help if I can."

"How well did you know Señora de Val?"

Ramone jerked his head back so hard he might have fallen off his chair if it hadn't been close to the wall behind him.

"Señora Lauressa?" Ramone swallowed hard but forced the words from his throat. "She is *el diablo*. She did everything to drive me away from my work. I only stayed because *mi padre* scorned her orders and demanded she keep away from me. I feared her and she wanted it that way. But it was all behind the old Don's back. She never defied him openly. I would have gone, but I did not know if anyone else would ever give me a job. *Mi padre* said no one would because I was so ugly."

"Your pa sounds like he's as much of a devil as his wife," Cole said grimly. "Tell me about her, Ramone. Not just how she treated you, but how she treated others who angered her. How did she act about Don de Val's unfaithfulness? Was she vengeful? Did she hold a grudge?"

"Señora tolerated Papa's unfaithfulness because he gave her no choice."

"Did she accept it easily or did she make people suffer through misplaced anger?"

Ramone had nodded through Cole's questions. "She was not just angry, but dangerous. Her punishments came suddenly and ruthlessly. I believe she would have ordered executions if she'd had the power."

Rosita gasped and whispered what Cole thought was a prayer.

"My wife and I had Alonzo and also three daughters. They all married but they live quietly. They never came back to our house, though we went to see them. None of them wanted to draw attention to their families for fear of Señora de Val."

"She'd have turned her anger on women grown and gone from you?"

"Yes, she wanted them as servants, did her best to ruin their chances of marriage. Don de Val had other children with other women, and she drove them all away when the Don wanted to give them jobs. Only I stayed because of my scar. I had little choice."

"Did you ever see a sample of her handwriting?" Cole's question brought Ramone's head up as if startled.

"Her handwriting? Why?"

"A simple question, Ramone."

"I did see her writing. *Horrible.* Did she write so to make people fail her? Some, yes, but also she . . . I think she was *estupido*, her handwriting *no es bueno*. She can read and write just a little only. She had a perfect accent when the Don was nearby, but when alone with servants she spoke *Inglés*, then mixed in *Español*. And write the same. The Don had many servants, so she gave orders, no need to write."

"But you had to read it?"

"She takes pleasure in writing me notes, and then act angry when I fail her. So I learned but it was not easy."

Cole looked at Rosita with barely contained excitement. "I have a note I want you to see." He pulled it out of his pocket and handed it to Ramone.

Nodding, Ramone stared for only seconds before he said, "Sí, this is Señora de Val. I have never seen its like."

"Can you make out what it says?" Rosita asked.

His one eye widened as he looked at the note. "I had forgotten just how bad it is. I have done my best to avoid Señora de Val in recent years. It will take time, but yes, I believe I can figure out what it says."

Sick at what Ramone might find out about his grandparents, Cole tamped down the urge to grab the note and run. Instead he produced a pencil and paper from the same pocket where he'd kept the note and passed them to Ramone. "We'll be back. I have business in town."

As he rose to leave, Cole saw something that almost knocked him back in the chair. He reached for a piece of fabric lying on a small table. A lantern sat on top of it and next to a book so that only a few inches of the cloth showed. Lifting the lantern, he picked up the cloth. "Where did you get this?"

Ramone stood, looking confused. "That bit of cloth?"

"It's a pattern I've seen before."

"It's a Mexican fabric that was used much in *mi padre's hacienda*. Don de Val used it, thought of it as his colors. I owned many things with that color at one time. This is something I sent to Maria years ago." He referred to his sister, another illegitimate child of Don de Val. "It was among her things when she died, and they came to me later."

"That's where I saw it. Maria had this at the orphanage."

With cold anger Cole clenched the cloth in his fist. Another connection between their trouble and the house of de Val. "Can I keep it, Ramone? I'll bring it back soon."

Ramone waved his hand at the cloth. "I do not want it. A reminder of unhappiness, both my sister's death and the cruel household of my father."

Cole and Rosita left. As they walked away from the house, Cole looked back uncertainly. "Maybe I shouldn't have just left Ramone that note. What if he destroys it?"

Rosita kept moving. "We are in his hands anyway, Cole. If we get his translation of it, we only have his word for what it says."

"What if . . . ?" His voice faded.

Rosita stopped and rested a strong, brown hand on his arm. "What if there is something in there about your grandfather and grandmother? Are you worried you will learn something about them you do not want to know?"

Cole didn't answer.

"Or," Rosita went on, "are you afraid you will learn something about them you have always known but ignored?"

He didn't want to believe they'd hire killers, but the more he admitted they'd be party to destroying the CR, the more he was seeing the ugliest side of them. A side he'd deliberately looked away from all his life.

Cole looked down at her for a long moment. "They wouldn't hire murder, Rosita. I don't believe it."

"And if the note says different?"

Cole closed his eyes. He tried to be honest with himself. He knew the way his grandparents had wielded power. "I'll worry about that when we have our answers."

18

Cole went out to the mines alone and felt as if he had a target on his back as he rode.

He reached the office, fought down the urge to go see Mel. What for? To tell her they were all wrong for each other again? A better idea was to just stay away from her. And he had plenty to do in the office.

Murray was at his desk when Cole walked in. "Things are almost back to normal." Cole looked around, impressed.

"Yep, patched the roof and that hole in the wall."

"Looks like it'll hold."

"A heavy snow might bother us, but the worst of the winter is over. I've got the filing cabinets repaired, too."

Cole hadn't even noticed. The cabinets were standing up, the drawers all closed. "Some of them were smashed . . ."

"I found enough scrap wood to build new drawers. It's not fancy work, but they open and close well enough and I got all my paper work put back in order."

Cole thought of the questions he'd had about his own files yesterday and again made a hard decision about telling Murray too much. He probably wouldn't have trusted Gully either if Gully hadn't been the one to talk about the men and how they'd died.

"I appreciate all the hard work, Murray. It's good having a man around who knows how the place runs."

"I oughta know. I used to run it." Murray smiled and said that without any rancor. Cole hoped the man's tone was honest. He'd taken over from Murray, no doubt about it, and that might've stepped on his toes. But Cole had given Murray a raise and less work, which should have been a good trade-off.

Nodding, Cole said, "I'm going to see how things are going outside before I settle in to work."

"Need me to come along?"

"Not this time. Right now I'm going to talk to Gully. I'll talk with you later about what still needs fixing."

Cole wanted to kick himself for the suspicion. Gully and the other men were influencing him and that wasn't fair. He stepped outside to the ringing of an ax and saw a stack of logs piled near the collapsed mine. All close in length, all about six inches in diameter. He found Gully working with a crew putting support beams in place. Looking around at the work being done, he asked, "Can you take a break, Gully? I hate to disrupt your work. You are all making good progress here. Thank you."

He made sure to look the two men he could see in the eye. The main room was all finished, and a tunnel that wasn't more than twenty feet deep had log support beams as far as Cole could see. Hammers rang out from farther in.

"Finish shoring up the tunnel just to where we've gone over the roof for cracks," Gully said in the voice of a Civil War general. "If I'm not back, don't do it alone. Take a break and wait for me." Gully gave Cole a nod. "Let's go."

They emerged from the mine, and Cole had to force himself

to walk away from the office in a direction that did not lead down the mountainside to Mel's claim.

"Those five men killed together were all here before I started." Cole pulled a slip of paper from the inside breast pocket of his black suit coat. "I've got the dates they signed their leases. Two of them came together, the others one at a time over about a year and a half." Handing the paper to Gully, with names and dates printed, he went on. "Who did they take over for? And are all of them dead? What can you tell me about them?"

Gully studied the dates. "I remember when the third man arrived. We'd had a man die." Gully's light blue eyes rose to meet Cole's. Gully had a white head of hair and gray bushy eyebrows. He wore an overgrown mustache but was clean-shaven otherwise. A miner's lamp was strapped to his head, ready to light.

"A death led to an opening in that mine, right next to the first two men?"

"Yep. And he was a well-liked man and an experienced miner. He fell off his ladder climbing down into the pit. It hit us all hard."

"They killed him so they could get his lease." Cole's heart started beating faster. "What about the other two?"

Tapping the fourth name on the paper, Gully replied, "This one I recall coming. The claim he took over, I knew the man who had it and he moved on after the death of the other man. He never wanted to go into the mine after that. Said he was sick of living underground and wasn't making money enough to risk his life anymore. I understood how he felt and didn't think too much about it when he headed out. The new man who came in I barely met. He was a quiet one, kept to himself. Like I said, none of these five seemed overly friendly. In fact, considering they lived and worked so close and had little connection to the area, it was almost strange that they weren't friendlier with each other."

"That leaves one more."

Gully shook his head, thinking. "I don't remember why that miner left. I don't think I ever knew. He was just gone one day. I remember Murray introducing the new man to me, and I asked about . . . Louis, I think was his name. Murray just shrugged, said he hadn't paid his lease. Murray went to check and, sure enough, the cabin was empty. He waited a month before renting it out."

"That story wouldn't get my attention much." Cole took the note back and pocketed it. "Miners tend to move on suddenly, except—"

"Except," Gully interrupted, "when you look at it with the other five claims." Gully's eyes turned an icy shade of blue. "I wonder where they buried his body. . . ."

Cole avoided Mel all day, not counting when Walt told her to stay overnight at the Bodens and so he rode home with her along with Justin and Heath.

There was no repeat of the meeting in front of the fireplace.

The next morning was different. He found Mel ready to ride well before sunrise, and not a soul was stirring in the house.

"I should be out there," Mel said as if he was invited, only so long as he could keep up. He couldn't let her ride alone, and she was grabbing Rosita's biscuits and stuffing them in her pockets. So he did the same. They headed out together before dawn, eating their breakfast on the trail.

Justin and Heath were purely poky about getting going in the morning these days. Cole liked to be riding in time to watch the sun come up.

He should have tried to think of a way to leave her behind,

but what was the point? Mel was coming and there was no escaping it. What's more, he just couldn't let her ride alone.

And he remembered that itch between his shoulder blades from yesterday when he rode out alone. He didn't like that either. Two alert riders were a lot safer than one.

He knew he was the worst kind of rat to pay his attentions to her that night when he couldn't make any promises. Not yet. Not until he'd decided whether to make his life here.

God, help me to know your will.

How many times had he prayed that? But this was the first time it'd been about Mel.

He looked at her.

Mel noticed and smiled a bit too sweetly. As a rule, she wasn't all that sweet. She rode quietly, and Cole thought he'd do his best to ignore her the whole way. Nevertheless, he was finding her harder to ignore with every minute that went by.

"Cole, will you tell me about your grandparents?"

Even harder to ignore that. "I talked about 'em enough. What can I tell you that you don't already know?"

"I've heard bad things and seen some of it myself, but you loved them, didn't you?"

"I did." He thought of the cruel plans he now suspected his grandparents had for his family and the CR, and his love was tarnished now.

"Well, whether or not they were using their power and influence to throw your family off their land, you can still love them. But there must be more to them than that or you wouldn't care so much, so tell me about their good side."

Cole turned silent for a moment, hating what he was about to say. "I've never admitted such a thing before about my grandparents' ruthless side as I did yesterday. It only came when there was no possible way to deny their involvement. I had to ask myself just how far would they go to separate me from this ranch? My grandfather was a very rich man, and he used that wealth to make connections with politicians and anybody else who would help him make more money. He didn't even need the money. It was . . . it was like a game that he played, and money was how he kept score."

Mel moaned so quietly, Cole wasn't sure he heard it. He turned to look and saw her frowning. "What is it?"

She gave a tiny shrug. "It's just such a sad way to live. Was he a man of faith?"

"They went to church every Sunday, but"—Cole didn't like to admit this—"I never heard either of them speak of God in their day-to-day life. Not even to pray before a meal. Their faith, whatever it was, they kept to themselves."

"Hopefully they kept it to themselves *and* God."

Nodding, Cole said, "I always knew their values were wrong, but even so, they were kind to me. Yes, they doted on me and tried to spoil me, but they were always kind. Grandmother spent time with me when I was between classes. She wanted to know everything about college. Grandfather took me in with him to work. He owned banks and railroads and steel mills. He owned immense stretches of land, tall buildings, and ships. His holdings were so vast it was hard to grasp, but he was determined I would grasp it all. More than just grasp it, he wanted me to understand his company completely and learn how to manage it all. He spent time teaching me with patience all he knew. And he talked about my ma and how much he loved her and how much he wanted to shower all that on me."

"Then they both died?"

"Grandfather died just weeks after I finished my studies at Harvard, and his dying wish was that I take care of Grandmother and look after his company. After he died, I found out he'd left everything to me. Grandmother inherited the right to live on in their Boston mansion, and she was granted a generous income, but I owned it all. By that time, Grandmother was in her eighties and in poor health. Although I planned to go home after college, I'd promised Grandfather, and she had no one else, so I stayed. She lived nearly six more years. During that time, she was very dependent on me, and running the company was, I'll admit, exciting."

"Are you saying," Mel asked quietly, "when your grandmother died, you didn't want to come home?"

Cole had to admit the woman was a good listener. She'd heard things he hadn't even said. But he'd been thinking them. He gripped his saddle horn and looked at the ground. "I left things behind that I enjoyed."

"But you did come."

"I missed everyone out here the whole time I was away. I figured on spending summers at home, and I can see now that my grandparents went out of their way to make my going home difficult. They took me on trips, and Grandfather gave me jobs and paid me well for them. Also, the trip home was a mighty long journey. So I never made it. I never hesitated to come, though, once it was possible. I made preparations for it while Grandmother was still living. The holdings were all mine, and I'd been arranging my affairs, selling off parts of the company for a couple of years. Finding managers I could trust to take control until they were sold. Grandmother wouldn't have liked it, but she was failing, stone deaf, and had taken to her bed. She wasn't aware of what I was doing. When she died, all I could think was that finally I could come home."

"But you're thinking about going back, right? I mean, you like the business world. You miss it."

Cole didn't want to say how much he missed the businesses.

They were all sold now. Anyway, he couldn't very well run them from here. Everything was gone . . . everything except the money. Besides the pile of cash sitting in a bank under his name, he had investments spread out here and there. And yet here he was in New Mexico Territory. Beyond using some of his money to build himself a house in Skull Gulch, he needed none of that wealth.

He let out a deep sigh. "I did like it, and I was good at it. But there's plenty of business involved in running the mine. Pa saw I was interested and gave me full control of it. I expect once we get to the bottom of these attacks on our family, we . . . uh, I mean *I* can settle down here for a lifetime. I love my family, and I missed New Mexico."

"You sound like you're trying to convince yourself, Cole."

He didn't know what to say to that.

"And not being sure that this is the life you want is why you said it was wrong to kiss me, is that right?"

Hoofbeats pounding from behind drew his attention to Heath, who was catching up. While Cole had forgotten all about him, he was real glad to see him now.

"Thought we were riding together," Heath said, his eyes flicking between Cole and Mel.

Without comment, Cole said, "Let's pick up the pace. I want to get to the mine and then go straight to work."

He kicked his horse into a ground-eating gallop. He couldn't keep this pace up for the whole trip, but it felt like he was running away from all Mel's questions, which struck him as a mighty fine idea.

Mel found Uncle Walt sitting in the sun outside her mine.She wasn't at all sorry to leave Cole behind, the idiot. "You don't look like a man itching to find gold."

He sat on the ground, his back against the mountain, his legs extended. He'd been watching her approach.

"I am a man who rises early and works until I can't see. So I've been at it a while, digging around like a mole. I wanted some sunlight before this dad-blasted mountain starts casting us in shadows—which starts before the noonday meal. You got here early."

"Yep, I was mighty anxious this morning. I just couldn't wait to come back and find all this gold I left behind."

Uncle Walt cracked a smile—and he was a serious man. "Today, Mel, we're going down into the pit."

Mel flinched. "Can't we just hide in the caves for a few hours and *say* we went down in the pit?"

Another smile. "I approve of your lack of interest in gold mining, girl. But what do you figure this fuss is really about?

The gold boom was over ten years ago and it was a rush if there ever was one."

"I remember it. I was used to riding the range with some freedom, but during those years Pa watched over me mighty careful."

"But that eased off and those with gold fever moved on to the next strike. Yes, there are veins of gold. I showed you one. Most of the men here make a small, steady income, yet I haven't heard of a real strike for years."

"So men may find gold, though they'll work long, hard hours for it and never strike it rich."

"Sounds like punching cattle or farming. For that matter, it sounds like most all jobs," Walt said.

"Except with gold there's that dream you'll hit the mother lode."

"It happens, just not real often. No one's ever sure when it comes to gold. But that's not why I'm going down. The attacks you've told me about were always aimed at the ranch. This explosion here at the mines don't make no sense. They didn't even directly attack Cole, and earlier attacks tried to harm family members."

Mel nodded. "Maybe they'd've been happy if Cole had gotten himself blown up, but their methods made that a long shot. Of course, they've arrested the men they knew were involved in their earlier troubles, so maybe this is the same trouble except a different group is running things now, one with different methods."

Walt seemed to mull that over a bit. "I've already been down into the pit at my cave. Hate it down there. I looked all around and didn't find a thing that interested me. I don't have access to all the mines—they're spread all over the mountain for miles and miles—but this is the area that had the dynamite set. I just want to look around enough to make sure there isn't something here worth driving the Bodens off for."

"All I see is a comfortably earning mine—if you're willing to work long, grueling hours. Not a big strike. Let's . . ." Mel fell silent and turned to stare at all the cave entrances. She crossed her arms and lifted her chin. "Let's go down into the pit. Maybe someone found something and talked about it to the wrong people."

"Bring all the light you can. We can each carry a lantern hooked over our arms. I'll light mine for the climb, and we'll handle yours and these contraptions for our heads once we're down there. I've never seen this head lamp before but let's give it a try. I think I've figured out how they work. We'll need every bit of the fire we can get. It's too far down into the belly of the earth for even the faintest ray of sunlight."

With no enthusiasm whatsoever, Mel nodded and did as she was told.

"I'll go first with the lit lantern. Don't wait for me to get to the bottom. Come along quick so my light works for you, too."

Mel watched Uncle Walt descend in a narrow circle. Her throat went dry as he got smaller and smaller and the light dropped farther away. Before she could do much more thinking—for fear she'd come to her senses—she cautiously stepped out onto the ladder and, clinging ridiculously hard, went after him. Might as well get this over with and fast.

There turned out to be two lanterns already down there. By the time she reached the bottom, Walt had them both going, and the candle was burning on his head lamp. He left his own lantern sitting on the floor, so they didn't bother lighting Mel's.

She saw two pickaxes, too. She'd forgotten all about bringing that, which made her a failure as a miner.

The pit was bigger than she'd expected. "I thought this would only be . . . maybe the size of the tunnel down. Honestly, it's bigger than my cabin."

Her uncle nodded slowly. "The man who dug it was a fierce worker for a fact. It's way bigger than the mine I found at the bottom of my cave. I asked around about the men who died and was told this particular mine made a steady income. Enough to pay the lease and keep the miner fed plus a little extra."

"But no more than that?" Mel felt her brow furrow.

"There was no big pile of gold in his cabin, so unless he rode off to a town big enough to have a bank, or buried it somewhere, I reckon not." Walt helped her light her own head lamp, then turned to the wall, the beam from his forehead glowing in a circle on the wall, brighter than the already well-lit space.

"I'm going to spend a few hours going over this place, do a bit of chiseling. I'd appreciate your help."

The tone of Walt's voice almost gave her permission not to help. Even to climb back up to the surface and sit in the sunlight for as long as it lasted. Instead, she got to work.

An hour passed in silence, broken only by the clinking of their axes, though Mel had to admit that time was hard to judge in a place with no sun and sky in sight.

She had to force herself to pay attention to the wall. More than once she caught herself daydreaming, her eyes unfocused, her ax idle as she wondered if the pastureland was greening up and the north spring running, or if the spring calves would start dropping soon.

Then she pulled herself back to the job at hand and again started looking for a gold vein in the wall. Minutes later, a swing of her ax knocked a chunk of granite away, and a glint caught her attention.

"Uncle Walt, come look. Is this gold?" If so, it was a nice wide vein.

He came to her side and studied where her light was focused. "Yep, gold for sure. Let's get to digging."

Hacking away at the wall, they finally broke loose a solid little nugget.

"This is more than a twenty-dollar gold piece, Uncle Walt. I think it might make five of them."

"I reckon you've earned yourself a hundred dollars in an hour's time."

Mel grinned at her uncle, then turned back to study the gold nugget in her hand.

Walt moved a few paces over to chisel some more, and with a swing of his ax suddenly a huge slab of the wall fell away, a rock as big as a man.

Walt jumped back as the boulder tumbled toward him. He was quick for an older man and dodged the rock with no trouble. It rolled a bit, then stopped.

Mel's head lamp, along with Walt's, focused on the boulder. That was when she realized the rock glittered.

Staring at it, Walt whistled quietly.

"Is that what I think it is?" she asked.

"Yep, I believe so." He turned and aimed his head lamp at the wall where the boulder broke free. A portion of the wall shone a bright gold. "Look—that seam's as thick as my finger. And who knows how deep it goes. There's gold in this mine, girl. A lot of it. What's more, we found it mighty easy."

Walt turned to her, and she met his gaze. "Hard to believe the man in here before us did all that digging but didn't find this thick seam for himself."

"Real hard to believe, Uncle Walt. A man who just died in a very strange way."

The silence was as absolute as the darkness beyond their lantern light.

At last, Walt broke it. "My understanding of these leases is that the men pay a monthly rate and give the Bodens a share of any gold they find. A common way of leasing claims. And Cole is known all around as the man who takes the smallest percent of any discoveries."

"So if this man had been finding a sizable amount of gold, Cole would surely know that, wouldn't he?" Mel said. "Yet he didn't seem to know a thing about it when he let us sign our leases."

Walt leaned his ax against the wall. "I think we oughta go have a talk with Cole."

❧

"She's awake." Finn ran out of his ma's bedroom so fast he bounced off one wall and nearly slammed into another. He skidded to a stop, smiled at Ronnie, turned and ran back. She was right on his heels.

Chance was only a step behind her.

"Mrs. Finn," Ronnie said, moving to the thin woman's bedside, "we've been so worried. Can you take a swallow of water?"

Dr. Radcliffe straightened from listening to her heart and rested a hand on Bridget Finn's skinny shoulders. He'd been to their house three days in a row while they doctored Bridget and waited for some improvement. "You saved her, son."

He practically glowed under the doctor's fine praise. "I did?"

"She had a fever. Isn't that right, Mrs. Finn?"

"Yes . . ." Her voice was little more than a croak, but it was as Irish as her unruly red curls. "All I'm rememberin' is feeling hot and miserable, so I went to bed."

"I brought you water, Ma. I tried to get you to eat." Finn pressed close to the bed, until his next step forward would near to tuck him in with his ma.

"The fever broke," Dr. Radcliffe said. "You survived that, Mrs. Finn, but you were too weak and exhausted to wake up. You wouldn't have lasted much longer if not for your boy here. He brought you help."

Bridget reached a trembling hand to her son, and he caught hold. "Thank you. A ma never had such a blessing as you, my fine laddie."

She spoke in such a weak voice and with the brogue it was hard to understand, but the love came through clearly.

Bridget's eyes went to the doctor, Chance, then Ronnie. "May God rain down blessings on you and all your kin. I'm forever in your debt, but I've no means to pay." Worry creased her brow.

The doctor got busy packing away supplies in his black bag. "Repay us by getting well, ma'am. It's good to see you on the mend now." Closing his bag, he turned to Chance. With a slight jerking of his head, the doctor left the room. Chance followed.

Ronnie could see they had something to discuss. "I'll be back with some warm broth, Bridget. We'll build your strength up in no time." She hurried out, not wanting to miss what the doctor obviously wanted to say to Chance.

"So that will be at least a week." The doctor saw Ronnie and smiled.

"What will be a week?" she asked.

"A week before a nurse can come. Mrs. Finn had influenza—there's a lot of it going around—and I just told your husband I've had many requests for private nursing and we fill them as quickly as we can. I'm afraid it'll be at least a week before someone's free to help her. And I understand it's not just nursing; you want someone to live here so you can leave? That may take even longer."

The pressure Ronnie had felt to get home was starting to rattle her all the way to her sturdy backbone.

Dr. Radcliffe turned to his other patient. "You know that once you leave here, Chance, your leg is unlikely to show continued improvement. I think you can get much better than your current level of pain, and we can make your limp less pronounced."

"A lot of old ranchers limp, Doc. I've got kids at home who need my help."

The doctor's mouth thinned with annoyance. "Well, unless you think of something, you're stuck here for the week it'll take me to find nursing care for Mrs. Finn." He dropped his voice and looked past Ronnie toward the room Bridget was in with her son. "She's in far more fragile shape than I let on. She's going to need care for a long while yet in order to regain full health."

"She doesn't need to regain full health, Doc," Chance said. "And we wouldn't have to wait a week if she's up to traveling. I hope she'll agree to come along with us. We'd like to take her and Finn home with us. If we left now, would she survive the trip?"

"Not in the shape she's in now, no. You just can't put her through it."

"I rode up here on a train with my leg broken. I survived it."

"And it's a wonder you did. You were badly injured, yes, but you were a strong man in otherwise good health. She's just stepped back from the brink of death, and she might still teeter over the edge if we're not careful."

Chance looked at Ronnie. She almost shouted at both of them because the delay was maddening. Instead she clamped her mouth shut and nodded.

"Good then. Now, Chance, let me examine your leg and see what changes I can make in your exercises to strengthen it."

"Before we do that, are you sure no one followed you here?" Chance asked. They'd gone to great lengths to keep their distance from the doctor.

"You've warned me, and Finn *especially* has warned me and given me advice about watching for someone. I've been careful not to invite any undue danger." The doctor smiled.

A chill ran up Ronnie's spine. From his tone, she could tell he wasn't taking their warnings seriously. They knew for a fact that the people after the Bodens had come this far north before. There was every reason to fear a second attack.

Ronnie watched them go to the chairs that sat facing the kitchen fireplace. Chance had had his cast off now for a while, with most of the stiffness worked out of his leg. But even though her husband wasn't one to make a fuss, she could see he was in pain. He tired easily and struggled when he had to stand for long stretches of time.

Ronnie went to the stove and skimmed some broth off the pot of vegetable beef soup she had prepared for supper. If there was a way he could be better, she wanted that for him. She'd held out and nagged him into staying so the doctor could treat him. If Chance had his way they'd have gone home before the cast came off.

But reading that garbled note had brought back some bad memories. Though she still didn't understand all of it, she remembered Don de Val and his wife. Ma and Pa had kept her away from them all her life. She'd met them only a handful of times and always with Ma or Pa close at hand.

The old Don was a cad with women. Ronnie's ma was dead and gone before Ronnie was grown, yet her pa had made it clear he didn't want the Don to see her, let alone be near her or, God forbid, ever for a second be alone with her.

The Don's leering eyes had landed on her once when she was sixteen. She hadn't been in his presence for years when they'd met on the trail, his gaze traveling up and down her body. The look had chilled her to the marrow of her bones.

If anything, Pa loathed Señora de Val even more. He'd sounded as if he was joking when he spoke of her, but under the humor, Ronnie could see it would be best never to have dealings with Lauressa. In fact, if she ever saw her coming, Ronnie oughta hunt a hole and wait for the woman to pass by.

Lauressa de Val.

Ronnie hadn't thought of her in years until she'd seen her name on the note.

A stunningly beautiful woman, Ronnie remembered that much. Black hair and dark eyes that flashed with a strange, hard light. She was much younger than her awful husband and spent her life primping and dressing herself in fine gowns. Her daughter had also been lavished with expensive finery.

When Ronnie saw the name Lauressa, the gnawing need to get home and protect her children, just as her father once protected her, had grown into a battle. Until then, she'd been the only one stopping Chance from ignoring the doctor's orders and returning home. Now that was in the past. Her wish for her husband's healing was overridden by her fear for her children. She needed to get home, only now she couldn't. A woman's life was at stake.

She didn't say anything. She was too busy biting her tongue.

Like a spider spinning its web, Hattie lifted her hand from the paper, admiring the spider's scrawl of her coded handwriting. It delighted her to torment those who must obey her.

Their fear delighted her.

She folded and sealed the letter, then laid it on a silver salver. Tohu picked it up, careful not to touch it while her hand was near.

"Send it to Santa Fe as always, Tohu."

The man nodded. Her personal guard, her sole trusted servant.

Hattie eased back in her chair and took a moment to think through all her plans. Some that had been thwarted, others that succeeded well. It was with relish that she enjoyed the freedom, finally, to do all she'd wanted. Finally she could avenge herself.

"The carriage is ready," Tohu said, holding open the door.

At last she could go back home. No one had questioned her heritage after all these years. She'd made the perfect exiled Spanish Countess Lauressa. But she knew it for the lie it was. She'd acted her part well and outlived the foul man she'd married, eager to have his wealth for herself. Then she'd found he'd betrayed her one final time.

A prickle of fear quickened her regal step. No one need know she wouldn't return, most especially her creditors. Oh, there would be money enough once she got away from here. But she had no intention of giving any of it to her creditors. She had need of it.

She paused at a mirror before leaving this office for the last time. It had been simplicity itself to fool everyone. Her coloring was perfect, and no one who knew what she'd done ever denied her talent. She ran a hand under her chin, still quite firm, touched lightly at the fine lines at the corners of her eyes and noted the gray streaks in her hair. She'd aged but had many years left. Of course, she'd been a near child bride to a rich old man.

She'd spent a lifetime pampering herself, preserving her looks so well there were those who whispered she'd made a deal with the devil for eternal youth and beauty.

Her age was a mystery, along with everything else about her. While she had fooled people all her life, she'd grown tired of it. She'd rather wield power boldly than use her sly talent. She had far less help than she'd hoped. Word had reached her about Dantalion's death. Her old friend, gone. Then came the news of Watts, who'd been captured.

Without Dantalion, well, she would have sent Tohu to take charge, but her need to leave was great. Yes, there was money here, and every time she thought about it, fury nearly overwhelmed her.

The anger washed through her now. She fought for control, sorry for still looking in the mirror. It made every year show on her face. Her hands fisted until her nails cut into her palms. Her jaw clenched to stop her from screaming. She stood alone in the majestic entryway. She'd called this despicable place home for almost thirty years. Oh yes, there was money, but she couldn't touch it—her old fool of a husband had been very careful with his legal wrangling. It made her want to tear someone's heart out.

Finally the rage eased, leaving her head and heart pounding. But she could move now without reaching for someone's throat. She could speak without screaming.

What she had done at least kept anyone else from getting the money, and that gave her satisfaction.

Time would pass. She'd find a way to get around the secretly written will that was a sop to a horrid man's legacy of unfaithfulness. Maybe he thought his generosity after death would protect him from everlasting punishment.

Ha!

For now, she had to leave the money. She had to finish what she'd started.

That was fine because she was beyond trusting others with her mission. Leaving suited her, even if it was a step ahead of her creditors. She would now handle this herself. Once done, she'd be home where there was vast wealth waiting for her, beyond what she'd cheated out of the Bradfords over the years.

Then she'd settle into a comfortable home—also something she planned to take for her own. A home she'd always despised for the arrogance and the way the Bodens had flaunted their oh-so-perfect family while Hattie had to endure the unwelcome touch of her betrayer husband.

20

“I think the gold is played out.” Mel dropped her pickax in disgust.

“You’re just spoiled because you found the first batch so quick. Now you think it all oughta be that easy.”

Mel shrugged. “I wonder what Pa’s doing right now. It’s time to get the cattle to a fresh pasture. I hope he wasn’t too shorthanded to get the herd moved.”

“No, you can’t go home and spend a day working with your pa.”

“I didn’t say I was going to do that.”

Uncle Walt snorted. “You’re the one who wanted to be a miner.” He barely missed a swing with his ax as he goaded her. “Well, you’re here now, so get to mining.”

Mel tried to think of some other excuse to get them out of here. They’d been chiseling for days, and she was more than bored, fed up with spending hours in this dark hole.

She leaned her shoulder against the wall of the stupid pit. The rock shifted beneath her weight. She quickly jerked away, staring at the wall. “What . . . ?”

"What happened?" Walt asked.

Mel aimed her head lamp at the rock. She was a long time studying it. Was it another boulder all ready to come down? At least finding gold was more fun than chiseling and hacking with the ax for nothing.

She stepped right up to the rock wall. "See that?" She pointed to a crack, then let her finger slide down all the way to the floor of the pit, then back up to about the level of her neck and across. "Looks like a . . . a door of some kind."

Walt walked around Mel, and she saw his eyes follow the crack all the way to the floor in a rough but straight line.

"What could it be?" she asked while using her ax to pry at the jagged crack in the rock.

Walt pressed on the slab in a different place from where Mel had leaned but with no result. "It's not moving. The slab or door, or whatever it is, is too heavy." He turned to her. "I've never been much interested in gold, but I love a mystery. And this here is a good one. Climb up and fetch Cole, Heath, or Justin, but no one else. We're gonna need their help with this."

"That means the man who owned the lease on this mine needed help too, doesn't it?"

After a moment of silence, Walt said, "I wonder who all was involved . . . because those men who died, someone's behind the killin' of 'em. And I really wonder what's behind this door?"

"Maybe it's a tunnel we can follow that'll help us figure out who the killer is." Mel rushed over to the ladder and started climbing.

Cole looked up, startled, when Mel burst into his office building. He and Murray had settled back in to regular work, most of the time. Cole still kept a few things from his assistant, and he still had some questions that'd never been answered.

"What is it?" He rose from his desk. He'd been working in his shirtsleeves. Tugging on his suit coat and straightening his tie, he came around the desk toward her. "Something scared you?"

She shook her head. "No, I just found something and want to show you."

Cole glanced at Murray, who was watching them through the door of Cole's office that Mel had left wide open. He didn't hesitate in getting away from the man before Mel told him any more. He moved to follow her outside. "Keep at it until you're beat, Murray. Whatever's left we can finish later." Cole went without giving his assistant a backward glance.

"Is Heath here? Or Justin?" Mel was striding toward the slope that led to the mines.

Cole picked up his pace to catch up with her. Looking around to make sure no one could hear them, he caught her by the arm. "Heath is. He's helping clear out the collapsed mine. Do we need him?"

"Maybe you'd better just come for now. We might need more help, but we can decide that later."

"What's going on? Did you strike it rich again?"

Mel finally looked at him but without slowing her walking. She smiled. "Nope. I doubt it's that easy or more folks would do it. We found . . ." She glanced behind them, to her left and right, and dropped her voice to just above a whisper. "We found a door, I reckon. That's my best guess. A hidden door at the bottom of the mine I leased."

"A door?"

"Yep, or some such thing, down in the pit. Uncle Walt and I couldn't open it or even budge it. The wall's all chiseled up, but still I noticed a crack that follows the outline of a door. I found it by chance mostly. So my uncle and I need your help to see if we can maybe open it. We think what's behind there could lead us to a few answers."

Cole nodded, and soon he and Mel were climbing down the ladder into an unusually bright light below.

It turned out that Walt had found some extra lanterns and was working on a section of the wall. After filling in Cole on the progress he'd made, Walt said, "I got the door to move a little." He stopped and pointed. "You see this fine crack right here?"

Cole stepped over to get a better look. Mel came up close behind him . . . too close. Suddenly he was having trouble paying attention to Walt. Giving his head a mental shake, he focused once more on the tiny crack. "That might not mean a thing. If the rock got loosened, it'll give a bit. Maybe it's just another slab like what broke off last time."

"Watch this." Walt pressed on a spot at about shoulder level and the crack widened. It narrowed again when he pulled back.

Cole took a half step back. "The crack goes all the way up?"

"Yep, about neck-high; then it crosses over and back down. I don't know how we open it up, but I got a strong feeling we need to. Someone went to a lot of trouble to conceal something, and I have to ask: what did they need to hide so badly?"

Cole looked at Walt Blake, who had fire in his eyes. Which made Cole mighty curious, too. "And you hoped I could help you open this wall?"

"I'll bet my best pair of boots it's a real door and it opens somehow. There's probably a trick to it, might even swing on a hinge based on how the crack got wider when I leaned against it. If we can't find an easy way to open it, then we'll just have to do it the hard way—swinging a pickax."

"Considering the gold I found," Mel said, "I wonder if there'd been a bigger strike down here, and the man you had leasing it went to great lengths to keep it a secret. We talked about him slipping out with a saddlebag of gold from time to time, which maybe he took to Denver to stow in a bank. Or he could've buried it in the mountains somewhere. But what if he found a way to hide it right down here?"

Cole turned back to the door, or whatever it was. "I have a hard time believing someone built a hiding place with a stone door, with a secret hidden lever or something."

"That certainly would take time and a fair amount of skill." Walt crouched and studied the crack near the bottom, focusing his head lamp on it and holding his lantern close at the same time. "But that rock came off clean in a slab the other day. Some rock cracks all the way through, and this reminds me of that slab."

Mel ran her fingers down the seam. She stood on Cole's right, with Walt hunkered down on his left. They were packed together, examining the door inch by inch.

Mel was pressing with her fingertips when suddenly she flattened her hand and held it just off the stone's surface. "I think there's a tiny stream of air coming through here."

Cole extended his hand next to hers. "I feel it, too."

Walt stood and leaned his back against the secret door. "What would be behind this wall, Cole?"

He shook his head slowly. "All I can think of is more rock. This pit wasn't even here when we started mining here. No one struck an old burial or ancient cavern or secret tunnel because there was no one around—no holes, no digging, nothing before the gold strike began. Pa and Justin and I used to ride over here. This place marks the far reaches of Pa's land grant, and he knew every bit of it like he knew his own face. I'm telling you, there was nothing."

Walt was silent for a while, not paying much attention to their door. Finally he said, "I'll bet you'd've sworn there was nothing on top of Skull Mesa neither, and yet there was an ancient village up there. I've heard of native folks who lived on cliff sides as well, who built their homes into caves that they could get to only by climbing ladders. Who knows what's hidden in these mountains."

"What do you suspect, then?" Cole asked.

"I'm wondering if your miner didn't break through into a whole other cave down here, a chamber of some kind."

Cole scanned the mine's walls. "Well, it's been chiseled plenty, that's for sure." He ran his hand over the numerous gouge marks, the exact kind of marks that covered all the walls in these caves, marks left by the pickax. They helped to conceal the seam in the wall with the so-called secret door.

"So far we can't find any kind of lever," Walt said, "so instead let's turn this wall into a pile of rubble until we can see what's behind it."

With arched brows and a smile, Cole said, "Sounds like the most commonsense idea any of us have had yet. And if it's really just a slab of rock, we won't have to chisel long to break through it." He grabbed an ax and approached the wall. "Now stay back. I'm not going easy here to tease out a fine vein of gold."

Mel and Walt both stepped back. Cole noticed Mel went to a wall a few yards away, well out of distance, and picked up her own ax. She began chipping away at a different section. Maybe that was where she'd found her gold, or maybe she was just a hardworking woman who couldn't stand being idle for too long.

It took thirty minutes of concentrated hacking before a big chunk of rock busted loose and fell inward, away from Cole. He peered straight into pitch-darkness.

Cole spun around. "Walt, get over here with your head lamp."

Walt rushed to Cole's side and aimed his head lamp into the

space. The light revealed another wall several feet back. Moving his head, he lit up the corners. "There's a room here all right, but I can't see anything in it."

"Move back." Cole went back to swinging his ax. The stone was battered enough it crumbled away fast, until soon Cole had created an opening about three feet high and a third as wide, nearly big enough to climb through.

Excitement made him swing even harder. A few minutes later, the whole slab cracked and collapsed into rubble at his feet. Again he was staring into blackness. He glanced at Mel, then Walt. They both looked as eager as he felt.

"Nothing quite like finding a secret passage," Walt said. He thrust his lantern at Cole and stepped to the side to aim his head lamp into the space.

Mel took up a lantern for herself.

Careful of the rubble, Cole led the way into the heart of the mountain.

21

"What's going on in here?" Cole ventured deeper and deeper into the black cave.

At first his lantern showed nothing but chiseled-up black walls, clearly a man-made tunnel. He followed it carefully, aware of pits that might drop off suddenly under his feet. But so far the floor of the tunnel felt solid as they headed straight into the mountain.

"It's wider here." Cole stepped forward far enough to let Walt and Mel join him.

Standing on his right, Mel said, "Another tunnel goes off this way."

"One forward, too," Cole added.

"And to our left . . . except what's this?" Walt went to the entrance to the tunnel on his side where he crouched down. He pulled away a black cloth. They all gasped.

"That's gold." Cole dropped to his knees beside a heap of gold that looked to fill a bushel basket. "That's a fortune in gold."

Mel came up beside him. "And a fortune in gold is a big old motive for murder."

Cole sat back on his haunches, looking at something plenty of men would kill for. "It'd be mighty interesting to find out if those five men have tunnels that all intersect to this area."

Mel nodded. "Maybe those piles of dynamite weren't set in random cave entrances. Maybe they were carefully chosen, hoping to block off the entrances."

Jerking his head up, Cole said, "Yes, carefully chosen by a man who's in it with them but doesn't want to share the treasure they built up. Except the loads weren't all set in front of these five mines."

"He might've thought that would be too obvious."

"Whoever set the explosives might have a tunnel connected to here and might be watching what goes on in these tunnels mighty carefully."

Walt rose to his feet with surprising speed for an older man. "I'm going right now to get the rest of the Blake cowpokes who're here and find Heath. We have to explore these tunnels and post a heavy guard until we get this gold out of here and find out if there's more, and also find out who has access to the tunnels."

Walt was gone the moment he stopped talking.

"Six of us aren't enough." Cole, still crouched by the gold, turned to Mel. "We'll need men posted here and at the cave entrance in case someone saved back some dynamite. We need men exploring the tunnels and we need it all done right now."

"But who among your miners can be trusted with so much gold?" Mel knelt down and picked up one of the gold nuggets and turned it over in her hands.

Cole thought of a few reliable miners, trustworthy men, especially if he agreed to divide it evenly. And he thought of

Justin and Heath. Heath at least was here. John Hightree would come, too—Cole would trust the CR's longtime foreman with anything. But Cole couldn't ride off to the CR right now. He didn't dare leave. And Justin couldn't stay overnight.

They both had to be tucked into their little beds at Pa's home. He noticed he'd made a fist and had his teeth clenched tight together. The rules of Pa's last will and testament were grinding hard on his temper.

"Cole, listen to me." Mel gripped his forearm and drew his attention as she went from kneeling to sitting all the way down on the tunnel floor. "I know you talked about Don Bautista de Val's wife being behind all the trouble that's come to the Bodens, and that she hates you for giving shelter to her husband's illegitimate son and grandson. Or that it pricked her pride that you Bodens got to keep your land while they lost theirs. But maybe it's a lot simpler than that. Maybe somehow word got to her that there was another big strike in the Boden mines. Maybe she wants the gold. Dantalion was paid to hire help, but maybe getting rid of you isn't quite so personal as we figured."

"Not much more personal than premeditated murder."

"It's personal if she hates you and wants to run you off out of spite. But it's not so personal if she's heard tales of gold and wants it for herself. Then it's just plain old greed. It's about money, and she wouldn't care who she had to hurt to get it. The fact that it's the Bodens and she might have an old grudge against you, might have even hired a man to hurt you long ago, would have been a bonus . . . if she's even interested in you at all. But first and foremost it might just be a woman who's got gold fever and is too old to go digging for it herself. Maybe she desperately needs the money."

"Ramone made it sound like de Val was a powerful man who lived a rich life. There was no sign he'd been hurting for money."

"Ramone wasn't allowed anywhere near the account books." Mel shook her head impatiently, straightened and shoved herself to her feet. "We're making things up. That's a waste of time. What do we do with this gold?"

"We can't just leave it here. I've got a sturdy safe in the office, and no one has the combination but me. We can move it all up there tonight."

"That's well and good, but what if there are ten piles like this one and our villain makes off with the rest of it overnight? I've got no wish to see a greedy man get away with murder and thousands of dollars' worth of gold."

Pounding footsteps and racket on the ladder—which sounded like someone sliding rather than climbing—captured Cole's attention. He figured out who it was before his brother-in-law made his entrance. Heath was a man comfortable on a ladder.

"Gold, hidden tunnels—this is getting interesting." Heath's blue eyes flashed wildly, rivaling the nearby lantern with their brightness.

"This mess is making a madman out of you, Kincaid."

Heath raised one shoulder in a shrug and grinned. "What do you need me to do?"

"If it were anyone else, I might think you're excited about striking it rich, crazed with gold fever."

"Nope. I do like exploring these caves, though." Heath peered at the tunnels leading off in all directions. "Can I follow one just to see where it ends up?"

"We thought we oughta do that together," Cole said.

"Why?"

Cole glowered at him. "In case it leads to some murderer who doesn't want us taking his gold."

"That's a good point."

"Now, what I think we ought to do is have the men haul

this gold out of here and put it in the safe in my office. That safe could withstand a direct dynamite blast." Cole turned to Mel. "Since it looks like all the men who died are in on this, plus more, this gold must've come from the mines I leased you, Mel, and those from the JB Ranch. So this gold is yours to be divided evenly among your men."

"All those cuts," Mel said quietly, "and still it'll make us all rich."

"Don't forget, the lease agreement means we Bodens get one of those cuts. And we might find a stack of gold like this behind a wall in every one of the five mines you're digging in. It'll be a new meaning for the word *rich* for all of you."

Mel frowned. "I reckon if our cowhands get rich, they'll all up and quit, and Pa will be hunting new hired men. He's not gonna be real happy with you, Boden."

Cole smiled. "Maybe he can talk you and Walt into staying on. Maybe he can talk you both into chipping in your gold to pay top wages and attract top hands." Then to Heath, he said, "I'm not sure why, Heath, but until you came I was just lining up nothing but problems, figured we should hunt all these tunnels right now, guard the entrances and post a watch on the mines, besides hauling gold as fast as we can. That's work for about three times more men than we have. Now I think we should just carry this one stack of gold up to my safe and call it a night."

Walt's voice echoed from above, his boots clattering as he descended the ladder. Cole heard men coming from behind him. When the old man came in, he had a stack of burlap bags under one arm. He went straight for the gold and began packing the bags. The three men from the JB Ranch followed him. Walt filled each bag so it wouldn't be too heavy to carry up the ladder. Each man grabbed a bag and started the climb back up.

"I've decided to split this gold between all of you." Cole

hoped that would stop any of the men from turning loco and trying to steal it. It did stop them all in their tracks. Even Walt.

"A strike was found in these mines, and the reason men were killed was so that one of their partners could take it all. That means even though it was stacked here behind Mel's mine, it almost for sure came from all your mines. So it's to be divided between you. But because whoever did this might still be around, we'll put it in my safe for now. You men will need to be on your guard through the night. Whoever hid this gold might find out we've got the fortune and attack again."

"I'm going down these tunnels," Heath said. "If there are more stashes like this one, we can get most of them tonight and take a lot of wealth out of a killer's hands. Which suits me fine. Go on up and lock that gold away, then get back here. We may need to make more trips. I'm thinking greedy men like these folks might keep their own piles. Maybe we'll find five like this. All to be divided between the Blake hands, with the Bodens getting their ten percent. Move fast, men, and we might not have such a late night."

Heath took up a lantern and went hurrying down one of the tunnels. Cole almost grabbed him to keep him from going off alone.

Walt shoved a bag of gold in Cole's hands, then another in Mel's, and cleared up the pile in a bag for himself. "Let's go. Heath's a tough man, but he shouldn't be down here alone a second longer than necessary. Besides, maybe he'll come upon more gold by the time we get back."

The men started up the ladder, Walt behind them, followed by Mel. Despite some powerful instincts to stay to protect Heath, Cole went up, too. They hustled up the slope like their tails were on fire. Cole looked around in the late afternoon shadows, wondering if anyone had noticed them. He didn't see a single person.

It was just before most men quit their day's work, so they were all digging away. Murray had left a note at his desk that he had to run to town for supplies. Even he didn't witness them come in with their weighed-down burlap bags. They tossed the bags into the safe, grabbed a new stack of burlap, and headed back.

They found Heath out front of the mine. Dusk was fading to dark now and wrapping night around the mountains.

"I didn't see any more, but I did find that the tunnels don't go too far. They just connect all the mines, and it looks like at least two more."

"We need to find out who those two mines belong to. They might be the ones behind this."

"We can't do any more tonight, Cole. I reckon whoever's been down there has seen what we're doing and has hightailed it. We sure can't track them in the dark."

Again Cole felt the pressure of needing to head home every night. It was frustrating enough that he'd've liked to hunt Pa up and do some hollering about how much harder he'd made things. But for now, Cole didn't have much choice. "All you men be on the lookout, maybe sleep in the same cabin. I'll be here at first light to figure out who's behind this, but we have to quit for the night."

Because Cole had to sleep at home at night to obey his papa.

The three cowhands headed off.

Walt waited until they were beyond hearing distance. "Cole, I want you and Heath to take Mel back to your place again."

"Uncle Walt, I'm perfectly safe. I don't—"

"If anyone involved in this treachery," Walt said, cutting her off, "goes looking around in those tunnels, they're gonna find that hidden door busted open, and it leads into your mine, Mel. If someone's looking for gold, they'll come to you first. I want you away from here. Because I'm gonna set a trap." He sounded coldly furious. "I *want* someone to come a-huntin' you, but I can't do that if I don't know you're safe. Please go. I hope they come, and by tomorrow morning this'll all be cleared up and we can go home and back to working above ground."

Mel nodded and gave her uncle a hug.

Heath leaned close to Cole. "I'll get the horses saddled." He strode up the hill.

When Mel was done with her goodbyes, Cole had her go first up the hill.

She glanced back at him. "I didn't mean to end up needing extra protection every night."

"I feel a lot better with you at the CR rather than here. And if your uncle's worried, then sure as certain I'm worried, too." Then he thought of Walt again. "He said he hoped to have this cleared up by morning." Cole's shoulders slouched as he walked. "I sure hope he's right, but I'm afraid it's not gonna be that easy."

Mel slowed until he caught up, and they went up to the stable side by side.

"The house is prepared, Señora de Val." Tohu gave her his hand to assist her descent from the carriage.

Señora de Val. Hattie controlled a snort. Señora Lauressa de Val was a fancy name for a little girl born Hattie June Hoggins from the Tennessee hills. But since childhood she could sing, loved drawing attention to herself, and never missed a chance to act in the town plays her rough little mountain village put on.

Hattie June ran off with an acting troupe and developed a knack for imitating anyone she met along the way. She and the troupe had made decent money—and not all with their acting. They were known to pick pockets and slip in and out of houses, making away with the silver.

Then she met a rich old man who never saw her coming.

She passed herself off as Spanish royalty—the displaced Countess Lauressa brought low and forced to live among commoners. Bautista believed it from her first word.

Of course, her first words had been delivered with a perfect accent while she wore a revealing dress. He'd wanted to believe.

She'd played him beautifully and made a brilliant marriage, and her friends from the troupe had come along quietly. She'd funneled money to them for years as they conspired together and lived high off de Val's wealth.

But even after years of passing herself as the poor but royal Countess Lauressa, Hattie never forgot her real name and her harsh start in life. Who she had become was much more enjoyable when she remembered where she'd come from.

Tohu didn't know, but only a few still living did. Her old friends from the troupe. She couldn't wait to see them again.

The carriage had pulled under a covered doorway, and Hattie hurried inside so no one saw her. Once in, she eased back her lace *mantilla*, leaving Tohu to unload her belongings.

The house was small, too small. She was used to better. But she couldn't hope for better until she made her presence known.

Tohu came in with a cold drink. Not that hard in New Mexico Territory in February.

"I'm home at last." Hattie smiled. Though it wasn't the home she planned to have.

"I have heard from those you sent for. They will be here soon and our plans will be finalized."

Hattie went rigid, as if the chill wind had frozen her in place. "Our plans?"

With only the faintest wince as he recognized his mistake, Tohu said, "Your plans, señora. Of course yours."

That gave her grim satisfaction. As much as he was her trusted confidant, she didn't consider him her equal in this. Without Dantalion she had no equal—well, one other. And the Suddlers had been with her from the start and had always been loyal and willing to do anything for gold. It was a kind of loyalty she understood.

She went to the window and looked out, careful not to reveal herself. While there were few people around, it wouldn't do for her to be recognized. Not yet.

The time for that was coming.

22

Mel wasn't surprised when Cole caught up to her the next morning before she'd ridden even a mile.

Well, riding together was wise. Annoying but wise.

Wearing a sharp black suit like always, she decided to torment him by making him talk about things she knew he'd rather avoid.

"Good morning."

He narrowed his eyes but didn't lecture her about trying to ride out to the mines alone. "Good morning."

"Tell me more about your grandparents."

He groaned so quietly she didn't think she was meant to hear it.

"I remember your grandmother visiting." To goad him more, she added, "I remember she was really awful to your ma . . . and my ma too, now that I think of it."

"Ma and I . . ." Cole's voice faded.

Mel was suddenly disgusted with herself. Yes, Cole had no business kissing her, but that was no excuse for her to be unkind. "Stop. I shouldn't have asked. I understand your divided loyalties." Truthfully she didn't understand them at all. Still, he had them all the same, even if the befuddled man didn't know what to do about it.

Which meant her understanding was based on her thinking him a half-wit.

"I have loved Veronica from nearly my earliest memory. The few vague memories of my life back east don't even seem real, like stories I was told more than events I lived through. But I remember how fast I fell in love with her." Cole looked at her in the first blush of dawn. "Have I ever told you how my grandmother used to dress me up in velvet short pants, and that I had ringlets in my hair?"

That startled a laugh out of Mel, and just when she'd been wondering if she would ever smile again. "Ringlets?"

"Yep. Grandmother Bradford had a painting done of me. Pa sure didn't tote any clothes of that sort along on the wagon train we drove west. Yet Grandmother had that painting up in her bedroom, in a place of honor. The suit was light blue velvet, and I had lace at my wrists and neck. I was in all ways a fine, wealthy young gentleman. I mentioned it to Pa. He told me how he'd cut each ringlet off, one at a time. He kidnapped me from Boston, or as good as did. He was afraid if he faced the Bradfords directly, they had enough influence to be named my guardians. Once he realized that, he made a lot of quiet plans. Then the first chance he got that'd give him a good head start, he took me, dressed me in rugged clothes and cut my hair, and we jumped on a train to Erie, Pennsylvania."

Mel nodded. "I've heard of Pennsylvania."

"From Erie we took a boat ride down to St. Louis. We got off the boat and rode west for days until we caught up with a wagon train. Pa and me in a covered wagon, pulled by a team of mules. I rode a horse sitting up in front of Pa, and we saw wild land and slept on the trail. It was about the finest time a boy ever had."

"A great adventure," Mel said.

"Pa had hired men and outfitted wagons with all we'd need, then sent them off when the wagon train started off. He wanted it to be a long way from Boston when we joined it. Pa said he lost himself in grief after my mother passed, and my grandparents had taken over raising me. I remember Pa being lonely but enjoying time with him and wanting more. Once we left Boston, all I could see was that finally I could spend time with him. And at the end of our adventure, Veronica was waiting, who always told me she fell in love with me before she did Pa."

Mel watched his fond smile and wondered how he could think he'd be happier in a big, dirty, dangerous city, alone. When he loved his family so deeply and fit so perfectly in his saddle.

When she'd thought of him as a half-wit, she might have been generous. A quarter at best.

"You aren't happy here in the West because you miss the busy city life. In Boston you missed your family and so weren't happy there, either. You're a confused man, Cole Boden. If you've been craving action and excitement, there's been enough around here to cure you, I'd think."

"The thing is, Mel, I feel torn inside. I love both places."

Mel saw his hands tighten on the reins, and his horse edged sideways until Mel's leg nearly bumped Cole's. He turned to her, and blast it all, she wanted to be furious with him, but instead she saw his confusion. A brilliant mind twisted up with two different lives, and he loved both of them.

"I wish I could show you Boston and New York City. There are wonderful things in both places that you'd love. The ocean is beyond imagination, the size of it. Big ships sail into Boston Harbor loaded with people and cargo from all over the world. And the history of our country really comes to life back there where people have family who fought in the Revolution."

"I have to admit, that all sounds interesting. I can well imagine you loved seeing such things." Her response must've pleased him because the worst of the conflict eased from his expression.

Cole reached up a gloved hand and drew a finger down the side of her face from temple to chin. "Thanks, Mel. I think you're right. You would like it. My whole family would. Pa knows what it's like—he lived there—but he won't talk about it. I think he's . . . I don't know, just hoping I'll forget. Hoping that if we avoid discussing my years in the city, it'll somehow just fade away as if it never happened."

"Your pa's a wise man. He must know better than that."

With a nod, Cole said, "You're right, he is wise. But he doesn't know how to handle this."

"Is that what's behind his will with his insisting all three of you live at home? And that made Sadie move home too, though he did it because of you mainly."

Cole looked down at his hands a while. When he finally looked up, Mel saw his eyes and realized the sky was lightening. While his eyes had looked almost black in the early morning darkness, the rising sun made them shine blue now.

"I love my pa, Mel. I do. In some ways I felt like I was closer to him than Justin and Sadie, mostly because we were such a good team on the trip west. I didn't realize it then, but he was worried about my grandparents coming and stealing me away. So Pa stayed close at hand during my growing-up years."

Cole smiled; clearly his memories were happy ones. "But I was different from him, too. He'd talk sometimes about the blue velvet suit and the ringlets. He used to tell a story about Grandmother slapping my hands when I spilled my tea on the lacy cuffs of my shirt."

Mel couldn't control a snort.

Cole laughed. "That happened, the hand-slapping incident,

when I was four. That's when Pa decided to take me and run before they ruined me."

"Smart man."

"But what Pa couldn't ever make peace with was that some of the things from the city are comfortable to me. He liked to blame the influence of the Bradfords, but I think it was my own mother. There's a lot of her in me. I was always better at books than Justin. He's smart as a whip, but he just didn't take to books. Instead he liked being outside and working with his hands, even when a little tyke. I was neat as a child. Justin and I shared a room, and we were always fighting about him tossing his dirty clothes here and there. We were just different. And Pa didn't think it was me; he thought it was the Bradfords."

"What does that have to do with his will?"

"As close as I was with Pa growing up, there's a gap between us that we never quite closed. When Frank Chastain was dying, shot because of the ranch, he forced Ma and Pa to marry. They were heading that way, Pa says, but they weren't there yet. They hadn't known each other very long. That did something to Pa. It dug deep into him the idea that he gained this land with Frank Chastain's blood. Pa considered it a legacy that had to be preserved. After all, Grandpa Chastain paid for it with his life. The ranch was to be handed down through the generations, held close to everyone's hearts. Seeing me move back east, then finally come home but want my own house away from the ranch, he thinks he never explained well enough the cost of this land."

"But you do know the cost, don't you?"

"Of course I do. But that doesn't mean I can't have my own home." Cole quit talking and looked into Mel's eyes. The sun was over the horizon now, and they sat unmoving, side by side.

The trail to the mine was a winding one that mainly followed open rangeland. All along these fertile valleys, hills rose, covered with aspens, their branches bare as they awaited the coming spring.

The day was fine. A light breeze swayed the dried winter grass as if God himself swept a hand over the bowing and waving brown stalks. With each mile they rode, the hills grew higher, building toward the mountains.

"Mel, I . . . I know I hurt you that night in the library. My words were clumsy and stupid. A man doesn't kiss a woman as fine as you unless his intentions are honorable."

Shielding her heart against what came next, whatever stupid reason he would give for leaning closer, looking deeper, she gathered her self-control to straighten away from him and ride on.

Then his lips touched hers, and somehow she'd leaned closer instead of away.

"You know why we—"

"Cole, Mel, hold up." Heath's shout cut off whatever Cole intended to say.

They backed their horses apart and turned to see Heath coming around a bend in the valley. A thicket of shrubs concealed his clear view of them, and Mel hoped that meant Heath had seen the horses but not the riders.

"Before he gets here, Cole, I want this to be clear. You're not to kiss me again. We are drawn to each other, there's no sense pretending otherwise, but right now you're a man who doesn't know his own mind. And there's no place for a woman in your life until you've figured things out. Until you decide if you can be satisfied with hard, honest work at the mine and a family surrounding you with love, or if you want a life that will take you far from all of that." Mel remembered how he'd described his grandfather. "A life that will lead to more wealth so you can keep score with money you don't need."

"I just need time. Time to adjust to life back here or find

out I can't." He gave Mel a lonely look, sad and tinged with frustration. "And it's not fair to any woman to get involved."

She heard what he didn't say. A woman he'd find an embarrassment back east. That was what hurt. Because if he truly cared for her, he'd ask her to be part of his life whatever it held. If her eyes burned a bit, she blamed it on the rising sun and dashed a sleeve across her face to make sure any tears caused by the sun didn't fall.

"Especially a woman who l-loves . . ." Her voice broke. She cleared her throat and went on, "Who loves her life as it is."

The burn didn't go away. Mel wanted to have the last word, then end this conversation before she did something as stupid as cry. "If Uncle Walt can't be convinced to let me stay at the mines, then I'll go home to sleep. It's a long ride, but some of the Blake hands will ride over with me to make sure it's safe. And I'll thank you to keep your hands and your kisses to yourself."

Mel glanced back to see Justin come around the same bend Heath had just emerged from, riding hard and closing the distance between them.

"Remember this too, Cole," Mel said. "When you speak of a legacy that goes with this land, you're talking about property and money and gold. But a true family legacy like the Bodens have is about a lot more than that. It's a birthright." She glanced at the approaching riders and hurried to make her point. "The Boden birthright is *love*, Cole. It's not the blood soaked into the soil of the Cimarron Ranch that makes it precious. It's the love your grandfather had that made him give his last thoughts to caring for his daughter, for giving his blessing to your pa. That's a legacy God would want you to claim. No greater love. While you're deciding what world you belong in, make sure you're giving God a voice, and make sure your decision isn't all about your own happiness, but also about the happiness of those who love you with all their hearts—your family."

Justin and Heath caught up.

Justin slapped Cole on the shoulder harder than he should if he was being playful. "What are you thinking setting off ahead of us? We need to stick together when there are men out here looking for a chance to pick off a Boden."

"Mel might be in danger too, Cole. Next time wait for us." Heath made it sound like a direct order. It wasn't the first time it struck Mel that Heath, for being a former cowhand of the Bodens who'd only recently married Sadie, didn't act like he worried one bit about what his former bosses thought of him.

It'd been late when they got to the CR last night, and Justin had already gone to bed. Now the men did some talking between them about what Señora de Val's role was and how in heaven's name she could have ever crossed paths with the Bradfords.

It suited Mel just fine to listen without comment. She was sick as could be of riding alone with that low-down worm Cole Boden.

23

Cole crawled down into a hole in the ground just like the biggest worm in the world.

Not only was he completely dishonorable in the way he'd treated Mel, but he'd also insulted her. Worst of all, he'd hurt her. He thought she might've been fighting tears, and he had never, not once in his whole life, seen Mel cry.

Well, maybe a couple of times. He had a vague memory of her when she and Justin were both still in diapers. Justin had enjoyed stealing toys from her. There'd been some crying then.

But it took a low-down worm to get salt water out of such a strong woman. He'd understand completely if she never forgave him.

He almost wished she'd just punch him right in the nose. He deserved it, and it might make things better between them. Instead she'd ridden in silence the rest of the way to the mines. Once there, Mel worked with Justin, Heath, and him putting the horses up. Through it all she acted like nothing had happened. And although quieter than usual, mostly she was her normal, hardworking, easygoing self.

Even so, he'd made a mess of things. Mel was never going to be his friend again in the way she'd been. And that was a loss that made him wish for something as simple as a fist in the face.

Justin and Heath split off from them to look for Walt in his mine, promising to meet them in the tunnels below. Justin hadn't even climbed down into one of the pits yet, let alone wandered down the tunnels.

Cole and Mel walked to her mine entrance, went in and climbed down. He wormed his way to the bottom of the ladder, and they went looking for Walt from this direction. Between the four of them, they'd hunt him down. They hadn't gone far before he came walking toward them, grumbling.

"Trouble?" Cole asked as Mel came up behind him.

"Bill Suddler's cleared out," Walt said. "I followed a few of these passageways last night and they're all short connections between the five mines the Blake hands leased and two others. When I went back to it this morning, I followed the first one I didn't know to Suddler's claim. I followed that tunnel all the way up and checked his cabin, too. He kept his horse stabled by his cabin and it's gone, as well."

Cole pictured Bill Suddler. He'd heard his brother call him Bull a couple of times and it fit. A man of solid muscle with a temper that made everyone keep their distance most of the time. Bill had been leasing a mine for a few years now, and just because a man wasn't sociable didn't make him a murderer. "You made it to the ends of all the tunnels?" he asked.

Walt shook his head. "Almost. I've got one more tunnel to follow. But I already know where it'll lead. Sam Suddler's horse is missing, too. Looks to me like the brothers maybe took off together."

"The Suddlers were here a long time," Cole said. "They kept

to themselves for the most part. Not a friendly pair. But hard workers who've never been troublemakers."

"How long is a long time, Cole?" Walt asked. "About as long as these other six?"

While Cole would need to check his files to be sure, he'd done some studying. "I'd say about exactly as long as the other six."

"Calling them hard workers is right, for all the tunneling they've done. Of course, they had six men working with them." Walt glanced back the way he'd come. "You might have to change your mind about 'em being troublemakers." He gave a small jerk of his chin. "Now let's go track down some cold-blooded murderers."

"Cole, get back up here."

Justin was always shouting about something.

"It's the sheriff and it's important. Get up here now."

"Walt, wait a minute. Come back."

Walt glared at him, obviously angry at the interruption. He shook his head in disgust and stormed for the pit and the way outside to where Justin's yelling came from.

Mel whispered, "Uncle Walt must be sure there's no danger or he'd never let his temper show."

"So when he's cranky, you're safe?"

Mel's eyes sparked, but even her good humor wasn't real lively at the moment. "It's when he gets real quiet that you know you're in trouble."

"Cole, let's go." Walt's voice sounded far away, so they'd dawdled long enough. "We got work to do, Mel. Hurry up."

Catching up was no small trick. Finally, Cole caught up with him about the same time he stepped out into the sunlight, Mel right behind him. Justin and Heath stood beside the sheriff. Justin had his arms crossed, looking impatient.

The sheriff's expression brought Cole to full alert. "What is it?"

Sheriff Joe said, "Remember that wanted poster you found on top of Skull Mesa, Mel?"

Mel nodded. "Angie found it, but I was there. It was a picture of the man who shot Cole. Only he went by Dantalion here. The name on that poster was different." She thought for a second. "Web Dunham."

"Yep, and he's wanted all right. I reported him dead and they're sending the reward money. You, Cole, and I got more than we bargained for."

"More money?" Cole asked.

"Nope, more information. He wasn't well-known but he managed to run afoul of the law years ago. For murder. He was arrested, yet he escaped and was never seen again. Until you Bodens brought him in draped over his saddle."

Mel said, "Do you reckon he carried that wanted poster around with him out of some kind of . . . pride?"

"Not something a normal man would be proud of, but then he's not a normal man."

"Dantalion had a lot of secrets and was good at keeping them," Justin said.

"Ain't he just." The sheriff tugged off his gloves and pulled a packet of papers from a saddlebag. "He ran with these men, but like I said, he wasn't well-known. Some of his friends weren't so careful, caused trouble up and down the Mississippi for a whole passel of years." Sheriff Joe passed around the papers.

The one Cole got showed a picture of Sam Suddler. "This poster calls him Snake Smith."

"Yep, a mighty shifty man. Snake is a fitting name for him. Known to run with his brother, Bull. He's in this stack, too."

"Bill and Sam Suddler, not Smith," Cole said as he studied the posters. Cole quickly explained how the Suddler brothers looked to be involved with all that'd gone wrong at the mine.

Nodding, the sheriff said, "Snake did what little thinkin' the two of 'em did. Bull was the brawn one. They and some others were called the Natchez Gang for a while. They ran with Arizona Watts and the hired man you called Windy."

Justin and Cole exchanged a grim look at the mention of two of the three men who'd kidnapped Angie. The Bodens had nurtured vipers. They'd hired those men, who'd repaid their trust by taking Angie in an attempt to lure the Bodens into a trap to kill them.

"It was always speculated that they acted a lot smarter'n they looked. Dantalion was known around the Natchez area and later along the Mississippi, and the Suddlers were in the same area at the time. Some folks figured Dantalion was the brains of the outfit, but he slipped up and got caught, which was how he got his face on a wanted poster. Except the proof on him was mighty slim, and when he escaped jail, the lack of a long list of old crimes might've made folks give up the hunt a bit easier. He was a sly one. I reckon he shot Frank Chastain, then invented a new name and headed east. That's when he did all his damage along the Natchez Trace."

Cole thought of his grandfather and his few long-distant memories of a fine old man.

Sheriff Joe pointed to the poster of Bull. "This your Bill Suddler?"

"That's him," Cole said. "I even heard Sam call him Bull."

"This wanted poster came from San Francisco. I reckon they hightailed it from back in Mississippi as far from the War

Between the States as they could. Too busy robbing folks to stand up and fight for their country, bunch of cowards. This California poster goes back over ten years. Five years ago the Suddlers and some friends turned up and leased claims on your ranch. What are the chances they'd come back to the place where they committed an unsolved murder, one involving an important man? Unless they had a real good reason to come back . . ."

"There was no talk of these men being around back in Grandfather Chastain's day, is there?" Justin asked.

Cole studied the much-younger picture of Suddler. He stared at the man who'd worked for him for years, who'd paid his lease faithfully and never acted like anything but a typical miner.

"They seemed honest." Cole's jaw clenched. "Could they have used this as a base to rob stagecoaches, trains, or banks without you knowing there were desperados working the area?"

"Maybe they'd gone straight." Joe sounded doubtful. "Then Dantalion came here and dragged them into his plot against you."

"His plot," Heath said. "That didn't begin until the avalanche was sent down on Chance just a few months ago."

Walt nodded at the mines. "Well, they've been at this thing longer than a few months. Those tunnels took years of work to dig out."

"A long game." Cole whispered the words. "We've said it many times. Whoever's behind this has worked-out plan. Who finds gold like they did and keeps digging, keeps working, and doesn't spend it? I can see staying quiet for a while, but these men were at it for years."

"If they made a decent strike," Heath said, "and they were all in on it, maybe it was easy to keep digging. So long as it was secret, they could hoard their wealth."

"Don't forget, their plan isn't just to get your gold," Mel reminded them all. "Their plan is to get the whole mine in their names. And to do that, they need to claim the Cimarron Ranch."

The quiet, cool breeze was the only sound for a time.

Finally, Justin said, "We still don't know who's behind it, but I think we at least know what's going on. We've been thinking they want the ranch, and they do, but only so they can get the mine. This has been about gold all along."

"Comes down to greed most times," Joe said and shook his head in disgust. "Take something from an honest man when they could earn their own."

"But who's behind it?" Mel asked. "Dantalion had a plan to kill every one of you Bodens."

"Yep, Heath took the list off his body after he shot him." The memory still stirred Cole's anger.

"They've attacked your parents and your women," Mel went on. "Who's responsible?"

Cole lifted his enraged eyes to meet Mel's. "We know we're looking for someone pure evil. I need to get back to town and see if Ramone has figured out what's in that note."

"That's the other thing I wanted to tell you. Ramone's gone."

"*What?*" Cole's temper sounded ready to erupt.

"His cabin door was standing wide open. I saw that and went right in." The sheriff reached for his saddlebag again. "Is this the note you left him?"

"That's it."

The sheriff offered it to Cole.

"And there's no translation, no extra letter along with it?" Cole asked.

The sheriff held a second slip of paper. "He left you this."

"Let's see what that mangy coyote had to say before he ran away—again." Cole snatched the paper and held it up.

Silence stretched on as if Cole were reading a long letter. Only it was just a small bit of paper so there couldn't be much.

"What is it, Cole? Did he tell you something about the note?" Mel prompted.

Cole crushed the paper into a ball and hurled it to the ground. "All it says is, 'She's coming.'"

24

The sheriff rode back toward Skull Gulch.

The rest of them—Justin, Heath, Walt, Mel, and Cole—went down into the mines together. Walt led them a ways before stopping at a fork in the tunnel.

"I want you two to go that way and . . ." Walt went on to give detailed directions that'd bring Justin and Heath up through Bill's cave. He finished with "I haven't searched Bill's mine thoroughly, so have a care. Cole, Mel, and I will head for Sam's claim. That's the last one to be explored."

Justin and Heath headed off to where they'd been told while Cole and Mel followed Walt.

Walt stopped when the tunnel dead-ended in a large cave, clearly well battered by a pickax.

Mel asked, "What all else is down here? They've been digging gold out of this mountain for years now, haven't they?"

"Yep," Cole answered. He stared at the wall before him as if ready to smash it open if they couldn't find another way. "We found a pile of gold yesterday, but they may have already hauled away a lot more than that."

Walt stepped up to the wall. "Look at this rock. It's been chiseled out and is really noticeable from this side, but remember what it looked like from the other side?"

"It wasn't near this obvious. The thin crack was barely noticeable." Cole sure hadn't seen it until it'd been pointed out to him.

"Whoever did this was good, but they didn't take the time to be careful from this side. Look down here—there's a lever. You step on it and it swings open." Walt pointed at the ceiling, where ropes and pulleys ran down to the lever. "Once you know what to look for, you can open these from both sides." He used his boot to step down on the lever, and the stone door swung toward them. "I'll bet we find a scattered pile of rocks that covers the lever on the other side."

Cole was impressed. He gestured through the door to Mel.

As she walked into the cave, Cole saw the toe of her boot catch a thin wire. Something snapped overhead. A rock pelted him on the back. He looked up. The whole roof began crumbling.

"Run, Mel!" He shoved her forward. "Climb! Get out! It's a trap!"

"Can you get the door, Chance? My hands are full." Ronnie lifted the tray with food for Mrs. Finn.

Though the woman was getting stronger, she was a long way from being ready to be left here alone. Since no one came to their house, Chance hoped this might be the doctor bringing word of a nurse who could be hired.

He swung the door open to see Dr. Radcliffe.

Then Chance's eyes lowered to the knife at the doctor's throat.

"Step away from the door slowly. Get your hands where I can see 'em." A man stood behind the doctor, glaring at Chance with cold, hungry eyes. Skinny, with filthy hands, a curve of black under every fingernail. But the knife at the doctor's neck was as steady as the stare of a dead man.

"I was a long time finding you, Boden. But I knew you hadn't gone back. I'd have gotten word. And I knew this doctor was yours. So I waited and he led me right to you." The outlaw edged Dr. Radcliffe forward, no sudden moves. The knife was pressed hard against the biggest vein in a man's throat. One slit, only one, and the doctor would bleed to death, no matter how fast they got him help.

Chance didn't have a gun ready. He was disgusted with himself. He'd let down his guard, and now he had a houseful of people who'd pay with their lives.

He'd been praying hard his whole life and harder lately, what with the trouble back home and his slow-healing leg that kept him from getting back to the CR so he could help.

That was nothing compared to how he prayed now.

Ronnie . . . God, protect her.

These outlaws had marked the whole family for death, and Chance knew this man intended to kill both him and Ronnie. He was too ruthless to leave witnesses.

For her part, Ronnie was a cautious woman, always smart and savvy when it came to dealing with trouble. She'd grown up on the frontier and had the strength to survive. But right now she was tending a sick woman and counting on Chance to keep her safe.

God, please don't let me fail her. . . .

"The whole cave's coming down!" Cole and Walt charged toward the ladder. "Mel, up the ladder. Go! We're right behind you."

More rocks rumbled down from the mine roof.

A pace ahead of them, Mel grabbed at the ladder and rushed up. Cole stepped aside to force the older man to go first, but Walt rammed into him, pushing him forward. There was no time for a wrestling match, so Cole scrambled up the ladder, his fingers dodging Mel's bootheels. The sides of the pit shuddered.

Metal groaned as the ladder tore loose from a mooring just as Cole's hand reached for the one above it.

Cole clawed his way past the broken spot, looked down and saw the other side of the ladder pull away from the wall while bearing Walt's full weight.

Wrenching his knee around a ladder rung, Cole dropped down as far as he could reach and snagged the back of Walt's shirt. Jerking Walt past the broken spot, Cole began dragging him up when a chunk of granite smashed into his left hand. A shout of pain ripped loose. The stone knocked his hand clean off the ladder.

Walt's strong hand slammed into his back and held him pinned against the wall until he could force his bleeding hand to catch hold again. The ladder gave way before his next step.

Plummeting down, the ladder tore free at every place it was pegged to the stone. Cole bounced off the sides of the pit until he landed with a sickening thud.

Cole looked up and saw the pit caving in, blocking the way out. The room behind collapsed. He found Walt beside him. The old man was moving. Cole helped Walt to a corner as more rocks rained down around them.

Finally the worst of the falling rocks seemed to be over. They lay in pitch-darkness under thousands of tons of rock. It would take years to dig them out.

If they ever could.

A line of blood traced its way down Dr. Radcliffe's neck as his captor kicked the door shut behind him. The gleaming knife never wavered.

One second of distraction, one moment when he could attack, that was all Chance needed. Chance watched every flicker of the outlaw's expression.

Where was Ronnie? She knew someone had knocked on the door. The doctor would have come straight back to see his patient. He wouldn't have slammed the door so hard.

But one more fraction of an inch with that knife and Dr. Radcliffe's life was over.

A high-pitched scream sounded from the street, then something slammed hard against the door.

The desperado twisted around to see if someone was behind him.

Doc Radcliffe shoved at his captor's arm and let his legs go out from under him.

The knife was knocked free of his hand and went flying, but with lightning moves the outlaw's empty hand swept down and drew his gun and smashed it over Doc Radcliffe's head.

The doctor collapsed, unconscious, as the outlaw brought his gun around.

Cole struggled to his feet. "Walt, are you all right?"

Suddenly, like the presence of God, there was light. Cole was a moment figuring it, but Walt wore one of those head lamps and he'd gotten it lit. As if that made the rest of his senses work, Cole heard the mountain rumbling around him. Was the cave-in not over? Would this tiny pocket they were trapped in get swallowed up?

Walt nodded and stood slowly. He was enough shorter than Cole that he could stand up straight but just barely. He shined the light all around.

"We don't dare burn that for long," Cole told him. "Sometimes these cave-ins can cut off all the air, and fire will burn what little there is."

Walt's head lamp swept across a dark corner of the room that had been hidden behind the secret door.

"Wait." Cole grabbed Walt's arm. "Go back. Point the light where you just had it."

Walt turned his head, then steadied the light on the bit of blackness in the corner. "Ain't no rocks there."

"Maybe we can get through—get back to the tunnels and find another way out."

"Maybe," Walt said, "but all that rumbling probably means a whole lot more than just this area collapsed."

Cole started for the corner, praying for all he was worth. Behind him, Walt said, "I wonder if your brothers got out."

Cole staggered to a stop and, for a second, couldn't go on. He wasn't sure if he *wanted* to go on. What if he'd lost Justin? What if he'd lost Heath? What if he lost . . . "I pray Mel got out all right. The mine could have come down right on her head."

"Keep moving, Cole." The razor-sharp tone of Walt's voice, as if looking for someone to kill, cut at Cole's ears. "Whoever did this is playing a long game—that's what you said, right? Well, they'd better start huntin' for a hole." Walt's intentions were clear as day. He was going after them. And if Mel was harmed in any way, then even the deepest of holes wouldn't save them.

Cole turned back to have the light burn directly into his eyes. "A mighty long game."

"Way I see it, they just lined things up so all the menfolk are trapped, maybe dead. Your folks are long gone. That leaves your women back at the CR with few men to protect them." He paused and let out a sigh. "Keep moving. We've got a sight more to do than just get ourselves out of this pit of death."

Chance ducked low, his leg nearly useless from the tearing pain. He hurled himself at the outlaw.

The gun fired, but the bullet passed over Chance's stretched-out body. Chance tackled the man and sent him slamming back into the closed door.

The gun was still in the outlaw's hand. Chance grappled with him and caught his wrist, shoving with all his strength to point the gun away. It fired and fired again into the ceiling.

Chance plowed a fist into the man's belly, then with a wiry twist the outlaw rolled and was on top of Chance. The gun came down. Chance still held on to his wrist. That grip was the difference between life and death.

Chance rammed an iron fist into the man's face, then punched his stomach again. But weakened by his long recovery, Chance felt himself losing the battle as the gun lowered, inching down to aim right at Chance's head.

Something struck the outlaw's side and knocked him away. The gun went flying. The man landed near where his knife lay. He quickly came back up with the knife in his hand.

Stones poured down around Mel's head, the entrance collapsing to nothing in front of her. She dived for the light, landed on her shoulder, and tumbled out onto the ground.

As she whirled back to find Cole and Uncle Walt, grit and gravel blasted out and knocked her onto her backside. The entrance vanished under tons of crushing rock.

"Cole!" Her scream turned into a choke as she swallowed a lungful of dust and dirt. "Uncle Walt!" She coughed and gagged.

Soon men raced to her side and took her away. "Cole's in there. And Uncle Walt. They didn't make it out. . . ."

"The whole mountain collapsed!" someone shouted.

She swiped at the grit in her eyes and saw entrance after entrance puffing with the same cloud of dust right in front of her.

All those men, every one of them, trapped, maybe dead.

She thought of the tunnels, and her eyes went from mine to mine. If even one of those specially dug pits had stayed open . . . and that was when she realized what she was seeing.

"You're dead, Boden. Your wife and family, too. We're not giving up until all of you are finished." The outlaw laughed as he charged, his knife drawn.

"Chance!" Ronnie swung her arm forward.

A poker from the fireplace sailed through the air straight toward him. He caught it, pulled back, and swung it at the outlaw. It hit the man in the shoulder, causing him to stagger backward. A second later, he'd regained his footing and was closing the last remaining distance between them. He raised the knife and brought it down straight for Chance's heart.

Chance grabbed the poker, wielding it like a sword, and parried the knife. The man ducked, reaching for the poker while lunging with the knife. Chance threw himself sideways, swinging wildly at the attacker.

Expecting the man to charge again, instead he stumbled backward. Chance used the opportunity to dive at the man's knife hand. As they collided, he saw Finn clinging to the outlaw's legs. The boy rolled aside, and Chance realized he'd tackled the man, disrupting the attack.

Gunfire echoed in the room. Chance spun around to face the new threat. There was no guarantee that the man was alone. Chance's leg threatened to give out, but he fought through the pain and tightened his grip on the poker . . . and met Ronnie's eyes behind the muzzle of a smoking pistol aimed at the ceiling.

"That was a warning shot." Her voice sounded furious, deadly. "The next bullet is aimed straight for your heart."

The wrench of pure love Chance felt at that moment almost brought him to his knees. Or maybe the pain in his leg did, but either way he'd never been so proud to be married to this woman.

The man lowered the knife, his eyes shifting as he looked for an escape route.

"Drop it! Right now." She lowered the gun slightly. "I don't want to kill anyone, but I'd put a bullet through both your knees without a moment's hesitation. You'll spend the rest of your life in prison with both legs amputated. You and your cronies almost cost my husband his leg, and I'd do the same to you without losing any sleep."

Somehow that rang so true that the man dropped the knife.

Finn rushed over and scooped up the knife, then got well back. Meanwhile, Ronnie's aim never wavered.

The doctor moaned as he stirred on the floor.

"Run for the sheriff, Finn." Chance grabbed a long cloth that was draped over a table and used it to tie the outlaw's hands together. By then the doctor was on his feet, looking dazed but otherwise all right.

The doc pushed a chair around, and Chance sat the man down. Then, with help from his intrepid little wife, he found some rope in the kitchen, meant for hanging clothes out to dry, and bound the man tight to the chair.

Chance turned to Ronnie, who meant more to him than his own life, and took two steps to close the gap between them. "You saved me, Ronnie, all those years ago when you agreed to become my wife. You gave my life meaning. You gave me and Cole the family we so desperately needed. You saved me then, and now you saved me again." He dragged her into his arms and kissed her with all the love and passion in his heart.

"You heard what he said, Chance. 'You're finished, you and your wife and family.' What did he mean by that?"

Chance heard it but hadn't had a second to wonder what it might mean. "We have to warn them."

But Finn was gone. Were there more men out there, waiting to crash into this house?

"I'll send a wire." Chance took one stride toward the door when his leg gave a sickening throb and he fell over, landing hard on the floor. He looked up at Ronnie. "The time for coddling this leg is over. We've got to get home, and I'll crawl to the train station if I have to."

Ronnie's eyes flashed with fire. "You won't have to, Chance."

"We've got to get them out." Mel as good as threw herself at the pile of rocks that blocked the entrance to the mine where Cole and Uncle Walt were trapped.

A firm hand on Mel's shoulder whirled her around. She looked right into the eyes of Gully, the man in charge of the Boden mines.

"Cole's told me all that's been going on with the Bodens, Mel. He also told me about the Suddlers and their running off this morning."

"We've no time to talk," Mel said. "We need to start digging."

"Stop!" Gully reached over and shook her until her teeth rattled. "Listen to me, Mel. I said Cole told me everything."

"What are you talking about?"

"He told me about the attacks on the Boden family, that there's someone out there trying to kill every single one of 'em."

What he was saying jolted something in her head that almost made her sensible again. Even so, she wanted to tear his arm away and get to digging. "Fine, he told you. Now let's get to work."

The old man shook her again. "Miss Melanie, you're not thinking this through."

"Of course I am. Please get out of my way."

"If this mine was rigged to collapse, then there's a good chance Cole is dead."

"No!" It felt like her heart was ripped in half just hearing the words.

"What's more, Justin Boden and Heath Kincaid were in there. They may be dead, too."

Mel almost dropped to her knees as she realized every Boden man living at the ranch had just been trapped in a cave-in. "Why are we wasting time talking? I know they're in terrible danger. I know they might be dead."

"I'm not wasting time. I'm telling you that if someone's out to kill the Bodens, they'll never have a better chance to do it than right now. All that's left is to clean up a few defenseless women. We need to dig, and they need the muscles of every man on this place."

Mel nodded, knowing the men were already digging—the ones down here now, with others coming from all parts of the mountain. "Ride to the Boden Ranch and alert all the hands that an attack could be coming at any time. We've got to make sure Sadie and Angie Boden live through this day or those filthy outlaws will win. Hurry!"

"I saw the mine cave in with my own eyes," Bull Suddler said.

"Both Boden sons were in there," Snake went on, "besides the man who married the Boden daughter. We wiped out most of the family today, Hattie."

A cold chill of victory rushed up Hattie's spine. She'd ordered the trip wire as soon as she'd heard the Bodens had men working her mines. She'd hated the owners of the Cimarron from the day she'd met old man Chastain. Then she'd followed the rest of the family through the years after the old Don had gone back to Mexico with his tail between his legs and dragged her with him.

The Bodens had given a job to the son her worthless husband had left behind—a slap in her face. Now they were dead. She couldn't help but smile at the thought.

"And the parents are in Denver still." She'd known Veronica Boden, Veronica Chastain back then. Young and slender. Carefree and pampered, with her whole life ahead of her. Not trapped in a loveless marriage to a vile old codger with a wandering eye. Veronica had grown into a young beauty while Hattie had one baby after another and still couldn't keep her lecherous husband at home. "That leaves the daughter and daughter-in-law alone at the ranch. We must move quickly." Hattie was savoring the next step in her plan.

"Hattie, we're rich. Too bad old Web didn't live to see it. Windy and Arizona gone, too. Locked up. I don't mind not splitting the gold so many ways, though. We're rich, old girl," Snake gloated.

Snake enjoyed not treating her with respect. He'd been with her a long time and remembered the devious and talented Tennessee mountain girl she'd once been. It was hard to put on airs with Snake and Bull. But she despised men in general, and most certainly despised a man taking charge of her life in any way.

The hatred it kindled in her made her itch to shoot Snake down where he stood.

How she wished it was Web, or rather Dantalion . . . that's the character Web had become. Planned since the first sight of Bautista, Hattie had turned herself into an exiled Spanish countess. And Web became the polished, ruthless Dantalion. It was the role Web was born to play.

"Have you gathered the others?" Hattie asked. She thought of her old acting troupe. In many ways that troupe had been her family and now so many were gone.

She'd given Bautista children, but they were as arrogant as he was. Her sons had married women they were unfaithful to. Her daughters all married to adulterers.

Though she'd never expected the boys could be saved with a father such as theirs, she hoped the girls would learn strength from her. Instead they'd grown up to be fine ladies who let themselves be hurt and neglected.

Hattie should have taught them at her knee how a woman could be strong. But the truth was she'd found motherhood unpleasant and was glad to turn them over to nursemaids and governesses. She'd rarely seen them, and when she had, it'd only been noise that irritated her.

With a mental shrug she cast her children's lives aside. They were a poor legacy and she took no pride in any of them. A woman had to take care of herself and that was what she would do now.

Tohu came in. She looked at him. The man didn't know he was Dantalion's son, born to one of Hattie's maids. She'd cast the maid out and kept the boy and had taken some delight in this one child. As he'd grown she saw him develop the cunning of his father. And now he was one of their company but with no idea why.

This would be the legacy of her life. Her power. Her position. Her wealth. She would rule as many as she could and never let a man command her again.

"They're gathered. Those that are here smelled the trace of gold I waved under their noses and they're itchin' to go."

"As am I, Snake. As am I." Two defenseless women . . . as soon as word reached them about the men's deaths, they had to know they were next. A genuine smile bloomed as Hattie imagined them frightened, twisting in the wind while they waited for the end. "It's time." She headed out of the room with Snake at her heels.

Mel galloped into the Boden ranch yard, yelling for John Hightree.

"What's going on?" John charged out of the barn. Three men came from the corral and the bunkhouse. She saw no one else. Three men against how many?

"John, get the men armed. Trouble's coming. I need to warn Sadie." Mel pulled her horse to a halt just inches from the back door of the ranch house. The sudden stop had the horse rearing up until Mel feared it might go over backward. She quickly jumped to the ground and settled the animal before yanking her rifle from the scabbard on her saddle and racing for the door.

John shouted orders behind her. Mel heard him send someone to fetch the men who'd ridden out to tend cattle.

She burst into the ranch house. Standing at the stove, Angie squeaked in surprise. The ladle in her hand flew up in the air, splattering hot soup in an arc.

Sadie rushed into the kitchen. "Mel, what's wrong?"

The words were frozen in her throat. How could she say it? Heath, Justin, Cole, Uncle Walt . . . who knew how many others? She didn't have time to cry. Finally she found her voice again. "Two men just up and left the mine, rode away in the early morning. We now know they were in on the explosions. I'm here . . ."

Dear God, how do I tell them? Please give me the words to say that their husbands might be dead.

She decided to veer away from speaking it. "We're afraid whoever's after the Bodens will know you're home alone"—*because they think they killed Cole, Justin, and Heath*—"and head for the ranch. I'm here to warn you and get us ready. We think they're aiming to come here to attack defenseless women."

She still hadn't told them. Maybe now was not the time. Where were the men? Why weren't they coming? She braced herself, looking for someone to ask.

Then Rosita stepped into the kitchen carrying a rifle. She had a bandolier slung over her shoulder and across her chest. It was filled with bullets. "I will watch from my room. I can see all the way to the woods toward the south and east from there." Her black eyes landed on Sadie. "The rifle over the front door is loaded. There are boxes of cartridges in—"

"I know—I can see in three directions from the upstairs bedroom." Sadie ran for the stairs.

Angie pulled a pistol from the kitchen cupboard and checked the load, even though Mel knew she'd most likely checked it already. Only a fool didn't take care with her gun. Angie headed for the back door, peered out cautiously, then stuck her gun in her apron pocket and lifted the rifle off the hooks over the door. She stepped to the side of the window to get out of the path of a bullet.

"What defenseless women?" Mel muttered.

A gun fired.

It came from the back, outside the door where Angie stood, where John was supposed to be. Mel charged across the room to the back wall, pressing her back against it. She braced herself to look out. The window beside her shattered, the bullet tearing into the wall across from it.

More bullets assaulted the house, the gunfire coming more frequently, closing in on them.

From upstairs, Sadie opened fire.

Mel used Sadie's shots as cover to get herself a look outside. The first thing she saw was two men on the ground, one she recognized as John. He was facedown in the dirt, blood on his head, a few paces from the barn. His rifle was still in his hand. The other man was farther back and lay as still as death.

Mel had known John from the cradle. She turned her grief—already wild because of what happened to the Boden men—to fury.

Four men on horseback, bent low to use their horses to protect them, shot at the house as they galloped at full speed toward the back door.

Cole sucked in his stomach in order to squeeze through the collapsed opening between the mine and the tunnel.

"It's standing." Cole looked back. Walt was shorter than Cole but stouter. He'd made it through the narrow passageway. "I was afraid the whole tunnel would be swallowed up. Let's hope that's the worst of it."

Mel had gotten to the top of the ladder, Cole was almost sure of it. She hadn't fallen down on top of him. Yet the top of the pit was in a cave . . . had it fallen on her? Was she buried up there? Cole felt his gut twist up until he wanted to start punching the walls.

They came to another cave-in. This one blocked the tunnel beyond any hope of progress.

Cole stopped, stuffed the fear deep down, and turned to Walt. "We can't go back. That pit was filled with rock and we're too far down to dig our way out."

Walt looked at the rocks and, disgusted, shook his head. "Well, I'm not gonna sit down and cry. If we can't go back, then we gotta go forward. I think this is close to the next pit where we could maybe climb out. And if that trip wire set off a series of rockslides somehow, this might be a way out—if the whole pit didn't close up on us."

Reaching for a rock, Walt glanced at Cole. "You pay attention to this head lamp. If the flame looks like it's dying, tell me quick and I'll put it out. Until then, let's keep it burning."

Cole felt the weight of the mountain pressing down on him. The thought of trying to dig their way out in the pitch-dark made him wonder if he'd be able to breathe. "I'll let you know."

They started digging, staying high toward the ceiling. No sense digging lower while the rocks overhead fell and filled in any holes they opened.

What about Mel? What about Justin and Heath? What about Sadie and Angie back at home? Soon the sound of rocks getting tossed aside and their heavy breathing caused by so much exertion were too much. Cole needed to think but out loud.

"Justin and Heath were going to Bill's mine. They would have gotten out, don't you think, Walt?" The question sounded like a youngster asking someone to reassure him about something impossible to know.

"I'm hoping, boy." And Walt's answer sounded like a grown-up who wanted it to be true just as much as Cole did. "I'm hoping and praying they watched the cave-in from the surface, and now they're out there digging like madmen."

"Half of the miners digging. The other half would've run for home to protect Sadie and Angie." Cole desperately wanted that to be true. And there were more lives at stake than Sadie's and Angie's. Rosita and John and all the other hired hands, as well. Lots of people were standing in the path of a cruel, greedy woman who'd proved she was willing to kill to get what she wanted.

Cole dug faster, threw stones aside with an almost frantic haste as he thought of his family. His family . . .

It was as if he'd dropped one of the rocks on his head. Cole suddenly figured it out.

He figured out what was behind Pa's will and all the talk of the land being a legacy. He figured out what family meant to him, what he wanted to do with his life, and who he wanted to spend it with.

He understand what Pa meant by the CR being the Bodens' birthright.

And he saw the love of God and the love of an earthly father in a way he never had before.

He dug faster. He had a few things he needed to say to the people he loved the most, and he prayed that each and every one of them was alive and well when he got to the surface.

"Cole, my head lamp just flickered." Walt's voice echoed in the tunnel like the voice of doom.

26

Mel fired and fired again. Sadie rained down a volley of bullets from overhead. Angie had the door open a crack and unloaded her gun at the approaching men. Shots roared from the far end of the house where Rosita was on guard.

Two men fell from their horses. The charge broke off, and the remaining men whirled and raced away. They took cover behind the barn and the bunkhouse. The outlaws were now protected from any shooting coming from the house.

"We have to hold them back until the men get here," Angie shouted.

The shooting stopped. They had a moment to gather their wits.

The men weren't coming.

Mel couldn't tell Angie the truth right now—there wasn't time. No help was coming. Not from the mines, and if John hadn't gotten a man away, then no help could be expected from the other cowpokes.

Though they had plenty of ammunition, they were trapped and with no help in sight. Eventually their attackers would lay siege to the ranch house. They could come in a charge just as they'd already done once. They'd be sheltered behind their horses and force Mel and her friends to waste their lead.

Mel needed to tell Sadie to save her bullets. And to do that she'd have to explain that they were on their own, and why. It made Mel sick to think of it. Sadie losing Heath. Angie losing Justin. Mel losing Cole.

No matter that the man didn't know his own mind and didn't have good intentions for Mel, she felt the draw to him. And she'd been telling herself it was just a physical longing. But now, knowing she might never see him again, she admitted to herself it was much more.

It was love.

She loved the half-wit, and all he wanted was to go to the city and make a living.

Well, she decided she wasn't going to just smile and nod and ask him kindly to make up his mind and decide whether or not he wanted her.

As she reloaded, she vowed to God she'd save the Boden ranch, then go dig that man straight out of the belly of the earth on her own and haul him home, trussed up over her saddle, and marry him. And if he made any stupid remarks about moving back east, she'd lock him up in the cellar until his thinking came around straight.

That was if he refused to cooperate. Maybe he'd come along quietly and her lasso wouldn't be necessary.

Suddenly a heavy wagon came into sight from behind the barn. It charged straight for the house, the horses running at full speed and pulling what looked like a stagecoach of some kind. The man driving the wagon was hidden, the reins passing through an opening in the coach, and the horses blocked any chance of Mel getting a shot off.

From upstairs, with an angle on the coach that missed the team pulling it, Sadie opened fire until she splintered one of the wagon wheels. The coach slewed sideways as the horses veered away.

Mel drew a bead on the cracked wheel and fired. The coach twisted, and the wheel collapsed. The harnesses snapped, scattering the horses in different directions. Tipped onto its side with a loud crash, the coach skidded toward the house. Mel saw the attacking men rush out from behind the barn in the wake of the crash.

The coach finally came to a stop just twenty feet from the back door. The men dove behind it for protection. They popped up and began firing bullets into the house again.

"Hold your fire!" a woman's voice shouted. She stepped out of the barn. The woman hadn't rushed behind the coach or risked her life with the men, who'd attacked the house on horseback.

Mel could see that the woman had arranged for the others to take all the risks.

"I want to talk to Sadie Boden." The woman had a regal way of speaking and a tone that carried across the distance. Mel could imagine her behind a pulpit, or no, most likely on a stage, casting her voice to the farthest seats.

On second thought, there wasn't much about her that brought a preacher to mind.

Long, nearly black hair flowed around her shoulders and arms. She was less than a hundred feet away, but Mel had sharp eyes. She saw the straight line of the woman's nose, the flashing black of her eyes. The woman's face was beautiful, as if it'd been sculpted by the hand of a master artist.

She wore a shawl. Mel was sickened as she realized the shawl was the same color as the scrap of cloth she'd found near her mine entrance.

"Angie, I believe we're finally going to meet Señora Lauressa de Val."

Cole glanced at the head lamp. With regret ripping at every word, he said, "Turn it out. It's dying."

We're dying. God, we're dying down here—please help us.

He said the prayer in silence. As if Walt didn't know.

The light vanished and plunged them into the blackest night of Cole's life.

"Keep digging," Walt said, his voice a steady presence in the darkness.

Cole didn't need to see to lean forward into a wall of rocks and grab one, then another, and toss them out of the way. They worked on, faster now. Maybe they should move slower to conserve air, but Cole thought the difference in how fast the oxygen ran out was a matter of minutes, so what was the point of being cautious?

Sweat ran down Cole's forehead and burned his eyes. A faint ringing in his ears began. He realized he was leaning against the pile of rocks even as he dug. He became unsteady. The air was running out.

Those who wanted his family dead were winning and it made him sick to think of it. Not for himself so much. He knew God and believed eternity was waiting.

But for his family. And Mel. They needed protection. They needed him.

God, we're dying down here. Help us. Protect my family. Protect us all.

A sudden clatter brought his head up. Another avalanche? Running out of air wasn't the only way to die.

❧

A bullet struck the barn only inches from the evil woman's head, and she ducked back into the barn. Sadie, firing from upstairs.

The woman shouted, "I'll give you a chance to ride away. Put down your guns and you can live. But you leave the Cimarron Ranch now, as soon as you can saddle a horse, and you never come back."

"This is Boden land." Sadie's voice cut through the February breeze. "You have no claim on it, de Val. If you want it, you'll have to kill every one of us. And not just those of us here, but my brothers and husband, my parents, too."

"Your brothers and husband are dead, Sadie Kincaid." The arrogance in the woman's voice rang with truth. "They're dead and buried in the mines. We saw a rider come in from there before we attacked. So a messenger got through with the news. Ask if it isn't true. I'll wait."

Angie turned, her eyes wide. She looked at Mel, and the truth must have shown because the color leeched from Angie's face. She sagged back against the kitchen wall, and the gun dropped with a dull thud to the floor.

"Justin? He's dead . . . in the mines." Angie's hands came up to cover her mouth as if to stop the words, as if the truth could be denied if she held them in.

Sadie rushed through the door. She saw Angie first, but then her horrified gaze moved to Mel. There was nothing to do but tell it straight. "A trap was set in the mines. I tripped it. The pit we were in collapsed. I was ahead and got out, but Cole, Justin, Heath, Uncle Walt, and anyone else who was down in the mine were trapped. We watched from outside, and no one came out. I don't know if they're dead. Men are digging right now. With all of them stuck, your enemies would never have a better chance of attacking the rest of the family. I came running home to warn you."

"No, not *mis niños*. No . . ."

Movement through a doorway drew Mel's attention. Rosita stood, tears running down her cheeks. Her hands turned white from their death grip on her rifle.

Another man appeared from behind the bunkhouse on the southeast side of the backyard, his rifle leveled. One appeared on the southwest and another from behind the barn. An armed man still hid behind the coach, ready to fire.

"If you want to live, you will come out now," the woman shouted. "Otherwise your entire family is as good as dead. I have men even now in Denver after your parents, but they may yet survive. I'll allow you to ride to town and board the train to Denver to be with them. So long as your family stays away, they'll live."

Sadie said, "She's a fool. My father would never turn his back on this ranch."

"She knows that," Mel replied, keeping her voice low. "She wants us to step out from behind these walls so she can finish her murderous work."

The woman yelled at them again from the barn. "If you don't lay down your guns and walk out of that house on your own, we'll have to burn you out. You got five minutes to decide which it'll be."

27

Cole pushed hard against the rock in front of him, thinking it might be rolling, working to shove it aside and preparing to do this over and over to keep the whole mountain from coming down on their heads. And all while feeling dizzy from the thin air.

"Cole, is that you?"

Someone's voice . . . coming through solid rock?

Wait! Cole forced his heavy eyelids open and saw light. "Justin, is that you?" Not solid rock at all. "Justin, you're alive!"

"Step back—I'm going to shove a big rock your way. We've got a pile over here we're digging through."

Cole looked at Walt and saw the old man smiling. With a jolt, Cole realized he could see the man, thanks to light passing through a hole in the rock wall.

Walt caught Cole's arm and drew him aside. It seemed odd to Cole that it was so hard for him to lift his feet, to think clearly enough to move. Lack of air maybe. The only thing clear was his profound relief to hear his brother's voice on the other side of the rock wall. Which reminded Cole. "Is Heath with you, Justin? Is he all right?"

"I'm here, Cole!" Heath shouted back.

More rocks tumbled down in front of Cole as the small circle of light grew larger with every second. Cole's head cleared some, and he believed it was due to his breathing better.

As his thoughts became ordered again, all the danger flooded back in. "Mel, did she make it out?"

There was a long silence. Cole could almost see them bracing themselves to give him terrible news.

Finally, Justin said, "We don't know. We're digging through this rock wall because we're trapped. We were hoping that on the other side we could find a way out of here."

"We can leave the house through the back bedroom window," Rosita said, "and escape into the woods."

"No." Sadie's voice echoed with defiance. "I won't be driven out of this house by that woman."

"You will if she sets it on fire." Rosita came to the door beside Angie and peered out.

Angie bent and picked up her rifle, still ashen, tears threatening to spill over. But her hands were steady, her jaw firm with determination. "They're not going to kill my husband and run me out of this house. Besides, if they want the place so badly, I doubt they'd just set it ablaze. I think she's bluffing."

Which brought Sadie to the window next to Mel. She was careful to stay off to the side. "Lauressa," she called out, "you are out of your mind if you think you can just take over this ranch. There are laws. Even if you kill each and every Boden, there's the sheriff to face. There are neighbors too, along with the governor. This is a settled land, and you'll not get away with this. You'll be taken prisoner and hung for murder. Leave now and we'll run for the mine to see if my brothers and husband can be saved. You can still get away."

Scoffing laughter came from the barn. "Have you not noticed that all the big land grants have been taken over? This is all part of the plan. There will be a minor fuss, but few will speak up against me and many will take my side. I have the papers from the old land grant. Chastain and my husband divided it in half, but in truth they both owned half of the whole. This side was half mine, just as the side we lived on was half yours. I can prove ownership."

"That's what the note meant, the land we stole from Mexico? The note found on Grandfather Chastain when he was shot, and the note left where the avalanche was set to kill my father."

"Yes, I told Dantalion the words to write."

"Dantalion." The contempt in Sadie's voice could have shattered glass. "He killed my grandfather. He did his best to kill the rest of us. And he failed, just like you'll fail. Just like you'll hang if a single Boden dies."

Lauressa laughed boisterously. "'*This is a warning. Clear out of this land you stole from Mexico*.' I didn't want to reveal myself then," she said, getting her laughter under control, "so I wrote 'Mexico' just to confuse things, to distract you from the land you stole from the house of de Val. None of you gave it a thought, even though you'd stolen this land from my family only a few years before."

Mel stood across the window from Sadie. Their eyes met. "She's raving mad."

"I don't know if she's mad," Sadie whispered. "She's very organized for a lunatic. I think she's just so arrogant, she thinks that whatever she wants, she gets."

Mel nodded. "Whatever she is, she's not going to give up."
"Men," Lauressa's voice rang out, "light a torch."

❧

Cole couldn't speak, so he turned his attention back to the rock wall. It was a long, hard struggle, but finally the space was large enough.

"We're coming through," Justin said.

"No, wait." Walt's voice cracked like a whip. "We'll go through to your side."

"But there's no way out of here," Heath said.

Walt said, "There's air on your side, and there's precious little of it on ours."

"Well, it's gotta be coming in from somewhere," Cole reminded everyone.

"Then come on through this way," Heath agreed. "If there's air, there's an opening. We'll find where it is and make it larger."

"Go, Walt."

Walt didn't argue with Cole. Without hesitation, he slid through the opening, and mighty spry for an older man.

Cole followed him. The opening was head-high and not much bigger around than Cole was. He reached his hands through and felt someone grab them. Justin.

One hard yank and he was through. Justin and Heath helped him to his feet.

Walt had already relit his head lamp and was starting down the tunnel. "We've passed six openings, all the tunnels collapsed. Whoever set that trip wire did some hard work to make them all fall in at once."

"Who has that kind of skill?" Cole didn't think of any of his men as engineers or even particularly studious, and it would take a lot of learning to figure out how to cause a series of rockslides to be set off together.

“They arranged it like dominoes,” Heath said. “Someone had training, that’s for certain. Have you got any miners who’ve been to war? Soldiers are often called on to dig trenches and tunnels.”

“Come after me,” Walt snapped. “Spread out and check the same places I’ve been. Remember those fine cracks in that first door? Maybe there’s something like that down here letting in air.”

Cole and his brothers were already doing so, but it might make Walt feel better to yell at people, so Cole didn’t object.

“None of the miners I know of had war service or any kind of special training. But they know all about tunnels and how to shore ’em up. And if they understand how to brace a tunnel, they also know how to cave one in.”

“True, but you don’t know the backgrounds of all your men,” Justin said, running a hand along the tunnel wall. He took off his head lamp and looked between the flame and the wall. “Maybe if there’s a tiny current, I can see the light jump.”

“Cole, get over here.” Heath dropped to his knees on the right side of the tunnel. He had no lantern. “Justin, Walt, get back here with the light.”

Justin got there before Cole, and all three of them saw Justin’s lantern dance.

“Look at this, will you?” Heath drew a finger along a line Cole couldn’t see. “It’s a seam, much like the one we found in that first tunnel.”

“Another tunnel? You think maybe there’s another man mixed up in this?”

“You had six men die, Cole,” Justin said, “and two others run off—the Suddler brothers. But we always knew there were three.”

Heath looked up at Walt. "You found the levers to trip these openings. Can you find a lever for this one?"

"That's so low to the ground, a man would have to crawl on his belly to get through it." Walt began searching along the base of the tunnel wall to where the seam was.

"Who has a mine here, Cole? All five of those mines along with the Suddlers were one after another in a row along the bottom of the mountain. We're right in the middle of that row. There's not room for another mine."

And then it clicked, as if the whole tunnel were flooded with light. "Not down on this level, but remember, we have mines higher up."

"Do you know where we are well enough to know who's got a mine directly overhead?"

Walt did something that made a grating sound and the slab of rock tipped, then fell backward into another tunnel.

"I do indeed know who owns it. And it's a man who knows mining better than I do."

Cole slid through the opening and stood to face Murray Elliot, his gun drawn and aimed at Cole's heart.

"Before you light that torch, Lauressa," Mel roared, "I need to know why you want this land. You're from a wealthy family in Mexico. And the rumors I heard said you're from the royal family in Spain. What do you want with a New Mexico Territory ranch far from your fine friends and fancy food and clothes?" She caught Sadie's eye and whispered, "We have to keep her talking, and she seems to like to boast."

"What good will that do if no help's coming?" Sadie sounded near despair. She'd talked tough to Lauressa, though Mel could see that was only for show. "Pa left us this land, left it as the legacy of our grandfather. I'm the only one here with Boden blood, and if we can't stop her, I'll lose the ranch and the house. That'll end the work of three generations."

Angie interrupted their whispering. "I'm going to keep watch from upstairs." She left the room, and Mel was afraid the woman was hunting for a corner where she could have a good cry.

That was fine so long as it didn't interfere with her aim.

"I have hated every hour I've spent in that hot, ugly city!" Lauressa shouted, her voice shrill and edged with fury. "I tried to get Bautista to stay here and fight for this home, but in his arrogance he turned his back on it and rode away. I had no choice but to go along with that foul old man."

"But we heard you were in a mansion, surrounded by comfort and wealth. Why would you prefer to come back here?" Mel dropped her voice again. "It's a good thing Rosita's father was obsessed with tracking down Ramone when he thought he'd killed Frank Chastain. At least we know a little about Lauressa's life."

Mel looked over her shoulder at Rosita.

"My father knew more about the old Don than any man alive." Rosita nodded her head with pride. "Though he was sure Ramone had killed Frank, Ramone lived on under de Val's protection. Papa could see no way to make Ramone come back for trial. But he tried; he went down there and hunted and pried into de Val's business, hoping to find a way to snatch Ramone away. You are right, Mel. The de Vals were rich and important. They had connections all the way to the Mexican president. And now it seems that is not enough for her." Rosita gave a snort of contempt and left to go stand guard from another window.

"I wanted to come home." Lauressa's anguished words

echoed across the yard. "I am an American and I wanted my own country."

"An American?" Mel glanced at Sadie.

Sadie shrugged. "You're not an American. You're a countess of some kind—from Spain." Mel wracked her brain trying to remember what she'd heard on the rare occasion when Ma had talked of Don and Señora de Val.

"I'm Hattie June Hoggins. I grew up in the Appalachian Mountains of Tennessee."

"What?" Sadie looked cautiously out the window despite the threat of gunfire.

Mel couldn't resist peeking either. Lauressa stood, hands on her hips, just outside the door of the barn. A place to hide close at hand, the coward.

"John!" Sadie gasped and slumped out of the window frame against the wall. She gripped her rifle with both hands, the barrel aimed at the ceiling.

"He went down in the first volley of gunfire, Sadie. I'm so sorry. He was like that by the time I got to the window."

"I didn't see him from upstairs. That watering trough blocked my view. We've got to get out there." Sadie's voice rose in a mix of determination and panic. She straightened away from the wall.

"No." Mel grabbed her wrist so hard it would leave a bruise. "You know we can't. If he's alive, we have to stay alive to help him. And if he's dead, it would break his heart to think his last act led to you exposing yourself and dying. No, you're not going out there."

Sadie closed her eyes and leaned back. "You're right. I wouldn't even get across the yard alive. You're right. You're right." She said it several times quietly as if trying to convince herself.

"I fooled that blackhearted betrayer Bautista and his whole family, his whole *country* for all these years. They treated me as a countess, and well I earned it for putting up with them. I savored each moment they treated me like royalty, all while I sneered at their foolishness. Dantalion and I, along with the Suddlers and others, we all fooled them. Yes, others you foolish Bodens know nothing about even yet."

"Who else?" Sadie asked Mel. "We have more people set to betray us?"

"We were part of an acting troupe. We made a decent living. We came into Santa Fe one day long ago to find the Don lording it over everyone, pouring out his gold coins as if they were water. Before he saw us we hatched our plan."

"So Hattie June became Countess Lauressa, the long-lost third cousin of the royal family from Spain!" Mel shouted her guess. "That's really talented acting, Hattie June. And you managed to play this role all those years?"

Though it pained Mel to admit it, it honestly was good acting. Hattie was mighty gifted for a murderous liar.

"Yes. I was young then, even though I'd already been with the troupe for a couple of years. We spied on Bautista and saw that he favored very young women, so I shaved a few years off my age. Dantalion and I had everything we needed. We had costumes. They weren't fine like a countess should wear, but then I was down on my luck so it suited the role I was playing. We knew how to speak Spanish. I even had an accent for a peasant and another one for an aristocrat learned for the parts we played. I threw myself on the old Don's mercy. We were married before we'd known each other a month. Shortly after that my husband got the land grant. He'd been angling for it for years, but the governor would never agree to it. I think he liked keeping Bautista dangling."

"You got the land grant because you happened to be riding with my grandfather Chastain," Sadie snapped, "and Grandfather saved a life while you and your cowardly husband stayed safely away. Then your husband used his influence through lies and deceit to act as if he'd been part of the rescue and that gained him part of the reward given to my grandfather."

Mel shook her head. "Don't make her any madder than she is already."

A shriek of laughter sounded from outside. "Ah, the cowardly old Don. I do wish he was alive to hear a slip of a girl say such a thing. How often I said it in my thoughts. You're right. Ramone grew up to be a coward in his father's image. And Ramone's son Alonzo was as bad as the both of them. Bautista covered up his cowardice by being cruel to those under his power."

"Including you, Hattie June?" Mel felt little compassion for the woman. Whatever fires had forged her, she was now evil. Through her scheming, men had died. But just how cruel was Bautista to her? It might explain her erratic behavior. Had cruelty at the hands of the Don driven her mad?

"Of course including me. All men raise a fist to their women. My father to my mother. My husband to me. My daughters' husbands are the same."

Mel looked at Sadie. Both frowned.

"Blast it," Sadie whispered. "I almost feel sorry for her. No wonder she's so twisted up with greed and vengeance."

Mel jerked one shoulder in a shrug. "She may have a really good reason why she's twisted up, but that doesn't make her straight. Fact is she's a dangerous woman, and I doubt our sympathy will make her cheer up and go back home."

"True."

A shot rang out.

"It's from upstairs. Angie."

"You killed my husband. You deserve to die."

Mel and Sadie peeked out the window to see Lauressa-Hattie holding her arm, lying flat on the ground. Another shot rang out. Hattie rolled and scrambled, dodging the bullet. Blood shone between her fingers as she threw herself sideways behind the barn door.

The men behind the overturned coach opened fire at the upstairs window.

Angie quit shooting and yelled, "I'm fine. They missed." Her voice sounded grief-stricken as she added, "So did I."

A scream of rage from the barn nearly cut Mel's ears. The men stopped firing.

"You'll die for that!" Hattie shrieked. "Every single person in that house will die."

Mel snorted. "As if she wasn't planning on that anyway."

"Stay out!" Murray cocked his gun.

"Cole, who's there?" Justin shouted.

"Don't come in, Justin! Murray has a gun on me."

"Murray?" Justin's voice dropped, yet Cole heard muttering between him, Heath, and Walt.

"Stay out or your brother dies." Murray's eyes were sharp as he stared at Cole. "Get your hands where I can see 'em."

Cole raised his arms slowly. "Murray, what's going on?" Speaking slowly, with Cole's mind taking in the shocking scene playing out right before his eyes, a few pieces of the puzzle fell into place.

"What's going on?" Murray repeated. "That's a question about as stupid as you are, Boden."

Murray had a lantern burning. He must've lit it just as Cole came through the opening, because this space was in pure darkness when they'd gotten the little door open.

"You're behind the killing?"

"Finally figuring that out, are you? Well, aren't you just the genius college boy. They said you were smart, which is why you got to come home and run me out of my job." Murray's gun barrel started to tremble.

Considering all the planning it had taken to set those explosions and cover up the deaths of the miners, Cole figured Murray to be very smart. But the shaking hand showed a man not used to face-to-face violence, which meant Murray hadn't done the dirty work himself—he'd ordered it done. It was the work of the Suddlers.

"You did all of this because I took your job?" Cole heard rustling from behind him. Down low. Justin would be getting in place to launch himself through the narrow opening, but first he'd wait and listen and pick the right moment.

It was up to Cole to create a diversion that would give Justin a chance to make his move. And Cole planned to make it a big enough diversion that if the gun went off, it'd be aimed at him and no one else.

Murray said, "Another stupid question, Boden. I had all of this done before you even got home. I found a nice strike of gold and I didn't see a single reason to share ten percent of it with a rich family who'd done none of the mining. So I started bringing men in. Men I've known a long time and was sure I could trust. Instead of paying, we kept it all. Hid it down here and moved it out in small amounts no one would notice. Besides, it was a sizable strike and I didn't want another gold rush. It makes mining too dangerous when men mad with gold fever come rushing in. They're followed by riffraff, the scum of the earth."

"You mean they're followed by thieves? Like you?" Cole hoped to goad Murray into losing his temper and letting his aim waver.

"Nope." Murray smiled proudly. "Thieves who're about half as smart as me."

"I pay you good wages, Murray. Very good wages. Why isn't that enough?"

"Because my loyalty lies elsewhere." Murray's voice rang with something theatrical.

It struck Cole as feigned, as if being used for dramatic effect. Every word he said had been delivered with stylish flair.

"Where does your loyalty lie? You've been here for years. You have no family. You rarely, if ever, travel or take a day off. This mine is your whole life."

Murray's smile turned to a sneer. "My loyalty lies with my brother."

Cole shook his head. "Then why isn't he here, or you there?"

"Because my brother Web is dead. Web Dunham Elliot. You knew him as Dantalion."

A sharp inhale of breath came out as a gasp. Cole remembered the wanted poster for Web Dunham, Dantalion's identity while he committed his crimes along the Natchez Trace. He looked into Murray's eyes and knew it was the truth. "I never saw your brother. Maybe once from a distance, and I reckon I know what he looked like from seeing the wanted poster. But I can see the grief. You know we didn't kill him. We tried to bring him in, but he was killed in a fall while trying to escape."

"He's dead, Boden, and I lay that right at your feet."

"He *shot* me." Cole made a fist and was tempted to lunge at this coyote. "What's more, I never shot back, and we tried to bring him in alive. I doubt you or your brother would've been so decent."

"The two of us, along with some other old friends, had plans that were working fine until you came home, Boden. We were making a nice living off the mines. Mostly letting others do the work for us and taking a cut. Just like you do."

"There's a little difference—we own this land."

"Ha, a gift from the Mexican president. This land is yours because of powerful connections. Well, I had some connections, too. It got me this job, and we were content for years."

"And then I took over." It made sense to Cole now. "And suddenly it was a lot harder to steal gold from this place."

"We managed to sneak a nice pile out, but yes, it was a lot harder."

"So you started hatching your plan because I came home." Cole's gut twisted. All that had happened was because he'd returned.

When he thought of how he'd wondered about staying, and now to find out that if he'd just left, Murray would have continued quietly skimming gold from a few mines and nothing more would have happened.

Pa wouldn't have been hurt. Cole wouldn't have been shot. Angie wouldn't have been kidnapped.

Then Cole thought more about it. Pa wouldn't have sprung that will on them. Sadie wouldn't have quit at the orphanage. She wouldn't have noticed Heath, a wandering cowhand. Heath would've moved on, and the two wouldn't be married. Sister Margaret wouldn't have been shorthanded and sent for her niece.

Justin wouldn't now have a wife he loved with all his heart.

And Cole wouldn't have discovered how Melanie Blake welcomed his embrace.

Cole couldn't regret one moment of being here. He remembered what they'd learned. "You partnered with Dantalion, your brother, and another old friend, Lauressa de Val. More family of yours?"

Murray's teeth flashed in a broad smile. "Lauressa, ah, what a talented actress she is. Not blood kin, but she's like a sister to me. Her real name is Hattie June. She's from Tennessee. She's got a fine fake Spanish accent. Add that to her dark hair and eyes and she made a perfect long-lost Spanish countess. She used that to snag de Val into marriage. But he turned out to be a miserable husband, a low-down adulterous varmint. It was a lucky twist that put Ramone close to Chastain when Web killed him. We all loved that one of the Don's by-blows got blamed. It gave Hattie real pleasure to steal money from de Val all these years and send it on to us. Then he died and she found out he was penniless. He'd spent it all—except for the money he'd left to his children. And he was generous to all of them, those born to Hattie and those born on the wrong side of the blankets.

"He left Hattie with the house and a pittance. She was mighty deep in a hole from her spending before she finally admitted she wasn't going to get her hands on de Val's money. If she'd gotten it, we might have been content. We could have all lived in de Val's huge hacienda. With Boden gold coming in steady, we could have made it work. But I lost free run of this place, and Hattie had always wanted to come home. She hated that she was dragged away while you Bodens held on to a ranch as much hers as yours. Back then, Web almost drove the Chastains off by killing old Frank, but Veronica married your pa and hung on."

"Hattie arranged for Grandfather's murder from Mexico," Cole said, "and Dantalion killed him. But was he alone? Ramone said a couple of other men were shot."

"Yep, the Suddlers were four brothers back then. Chastain killed two of them. They've been burning for revenge ever since."

"Who else was in your crew? Arizona Watts?"

"Yep. Watts was the best cowpoke of any of us."

"So you went east and worked along the Natchez Trace."

Murray nodded. "Hattie was good at taking care of herself so we didn't worry about her. The pickings were good in

Mississippi, but after a few years, there were too many wanted posters. We headed west when the war broke out and laid up in San Francisco for a while. I did some gold mining out there too, and we started a smaller version of this. I'd own the mine and learn about the nearby miners, then pass the word along if any of them were riding out with gold in their saddlebags so my friends could rob 'em.

"Then we heard about gold in New Mexico. Right near where Hattie had lived all those years ago. We got here and realized it was on the land she still swore she owned. Web had stayed in touch with Hattie and let her know. I knew mining, so we hatched a plot to work things like we did in San Francisco. Sure enough, I found a little gold, which I snuck out of the mine rather than pay you Bodens. That was when we came up with our plan to get it all back. Before long I worked my way up to managing the mines."

"And that plot included killing every Boden?"

"I didn't want a killing spree. That's the kind of thing that gets the law's attention. We thought we might take over by killing your pa only. I figured you'd head east. Your sister is a weakling and would probably go along with you, your ma, too. Justin, well, I always figured he'd stick. But I hoped you'd leave, maybe take the women, and Justin would be standing alone fighting for a ranch that no longer had a family to go with it. That'd make him easy pickins, especially with my men signed on as cowhands and miners right on your property."

"So Pa's death looks like an accident and maybe you can arrange the same kind of thing for Justin. But then Sadie got married. Pa was rude enough he refused to die. Then Justin got married. No one was going anywhere, and your list of people to kill grew by the day. No way to murder that many folks and hope to get away with it."

"Until today. Today is my chance."

"Three Boden men in one awful mining accident."

"Yep, and Hattie and her men are riding onto the CR right now. She's gonna take back what should have been hers in the first place. And leave you buried so deep in this mine, no one'll dig you out to see the bullet hole in your chest."

Like an alarm bell ringing in the back of Cole's head, he realized that despite the gun aimed at his heart, despite his brothers trapped behind him, despite his sister and Angie and Mel facing death . . . despite all of that, finding Murray down here meant one thing, one very important thing.

There *was* a way out. They were *not* buried under tons of rock.

Now all Cole had to do was survive long enough to make Murray sorry he'd ever left the stage, then race home and save the womenfolk.

And he had to do it fast. Or those tough, smart frontierswomen would save themselves and ruin Cole's chance of being a hero.

"We're gonna run out of bullets, Sadie. We can't hold 'em off after that." Mel reduced the stack to reload her pistol, then took more to reload the rifle.

Once ready, she peeked out the window to see what the furiously mad woman attacking them would do next.

"Why is it," she asked the ceiling, "when you really need a man around with some idea about how to rescue a bunch of damsels in distress, they're nowhere to be seen?"

She figured she, Sadie, Angie, and Rosita would just go ahead and save themselves, but a little help would've been nice.

"I got an idea." A man's voice turned Mel and Sadie around. Their guns came up. Mel hesitated a split second and fired.

The stranger saw it coming and jumped out of the room before the gun blasted.

"Hey, don't shoot. I'm here to help."

The man waited. Mel looked at Sadie.

In the silence, the stranger stepped around the corner. He held his hands up, no gun, and stared at them with the wildest blue eyes she'd ever seen . . . except she had seen eyes like that.

"You're related to Heath," Sadie said. "You have to be."

That was it. Those were Heath's eyes exactly.

"Yep." The man stepped farther into the room. "Heath's been writing me some mighty strange letters. I came down to see for myself if the boy needs his big brother to clear up the mess he's gotten himself in."

Sadie smiled. "You're Seth Kincaid. It's nice to meet some of Heath's family."

Seth tapped the brim of his hat. "That's me."

"I'm Sadie. Heath is my husband now."

Seth's grin made his eyes flash. "I reckon that makes you my baby sister."

Mel felt her brows rise nearly to her hairline at the newcomer. A Kincaid. Heath's family lived between here and Denver. He must've decided they weren't going to shoot him because he lowered his hands and pulled his gun with moves as smooth as oil. Seth checked his revolver and tucked the weapon away.

"Seth, I . . . she, the woman behind all this, said Heath is—"

"I heard all of it, Sadie. I've been slippin' around a while so I could get in the back window. And maybe she's right and my brother is . . . gone." Seth sounded bleak when he spoke those words, but then his shoulders squared and his chin came up. "But if ever there was a man on this earth who would keep his head in a cave-in, it's my little brother. He ain't as good as me, but he's mighty close. If there's any way for him to survive, and to save your brothers, he'll do it. He practically grew up in a cavern that's a whole lot more dangerous than the Boden mines."

Mel thought Cole knew his way around underground pretty well. And no one besides Uncle Walt was tougher than Justin. Maybe Seth had the right of it. Mel's hopes rose, but they'd been in the dirt, so she was still plenty worried.

"You can't know how dangerous those mines are," Sadie said. "You just got here."

"You're right about me not knowing your mines, but I know my cavern on the Kincaid Ranch. It's the most exciting and deadly cavern in the world, so your mines aren't a patch on them, no matter what they're like. Trust me, Heath will know what to do."

"You mentioned an idea?" Mel thought if he had one, they'd better go ahead and find out about it. Since they had a lunatic about to kill them all.

Seth's eyes flickered to Mel, and it struck her how much Seth looked like Heath. But there was a notable difference. Heath could smile and get a wild idea now and then, but mostly he was a solid, steady man.

This man looked like he could be a lunatic with just the littlest encouragement.

His eyes went right back to Sadie. "You're not gonna like my idea."

Sadie rubbed a hand over her face. "Heath has told me a lot about you."

"Uh-oh."

Mel cut into their talk. "You have an idea?"

"Brace yourself. Especially you, baby sister."

Somehow Mel didn't doubt for a second that they oughta take his advice, mostly because of the scared way he looked at Sadie. It meant the idea must be wild, and Mel was sorely afraid they were in need of some desperate act to save themselves.

"I scouted around and you are surrounded for a fact. She's got a lot of men—all of 'em seasoned and serious, all watching the house. I snuck up on the bunkhouse thinking to catch them, get 'em out of the fight one by one, yet there were too many for me to chance it. But I couldn't get to the barn, or to the ones just west of the house, or those behind that tipped over the coach—not without stepping out into the open."

All his talk made Mel brace herself all the more, because he didn't just tell them his idea straight out. That struck Mel as a bad sign. She suspected Seth Kincaid didn't believe much in breaking things gently. He seemed more like the bald truth and blunt talk type.

"I had to sneak my way along the ground across an open space between your bunkhouse and the woods. It took some doing."

"Which means," she said, "we're trapped in here unless we make a run for it the same way you came in? That's your idea?"

"Nope." Seth shrugged a shoulder. "I'm not sure how that'll work . . . four women sneaking across that open space."

"So, what should we do?"

"I've thought of how we could slip away."

"I'm not going to abandon this house," Sadie said in a crisp, no-nonsense voice.

"I'm not advising you to *abandon* it. That's not my idea. Exactly." Seth didn't seem too impressed with Sadie and her no-nonsense tone.

"I think if we want to live," Seth said, looking just plain unhappy as he hesitated to say what came next, "we're gonna have to burn it down."

Cole looked past Murray. The cavern they were in was different from the others. There was a desk for one thing, rustic as if maybe it'd been built down here. They could have smuggled in the wood for it a piece at a time. Two drawers, one on either side of the kneehole, were open with papers spilled out onto the floor, as if someone had been packing things up fast.

Was Murray trying to cover his tracks in case they found this cave? Or was he planning to move his secret papers up to the main office building if things came out well?

"You've been living down here?" Cole asked. Besides the desk, chair, and lantern, he saw a small stove and a doorless cupboard stacked with food. A bedframe with a thin mattress sat along one wall. The room wasn't overly large so all the furniture, even small as it was, filled things up.

"I'm a man of business. I've been keeping records and accounts down here. No one notices much after dark. I come here and keep the paper work up to date, talk with my men and arrange shipments of gold small enough they can be carried up by one man."

"And these men come back? They walk out of here with as much gold as they can carry and none of them just keeps walking?"

"Sure we've lost some gold, but the men who work with me are building wealth. They almost all come back because they want more, and I make sure they get a healthy cut of all they find and all they carry away. It's a good business, and my men aren't fools."

"All except the ones you killed."

"I'm not a killer, Boden," Murray sneered. "I'm a businessman. Just like you."

"Not like me. Not at all. And if you order someone killed, you're a killer. No judge is going to pay much attention to that kind of attitude; he'll order the noose for you same as the man who did the killing. And if you haven't killed anyone up until now, you seem plenty eager to change that."

"I'm making a special exception for you, Boden. I'll enjoy doing it, too."

Cole watched every move Murray made, waiting for an opening where Cole stood a chance of closing the distance between them before Murray could fire. Probably six feet, and Murray's boast that he was no killer didn't seem to bother his aim.

"You were planning to hide out down here if things turned ugly for you. You could have come and gone in the dark, lived and slept here and kept on mining for gold. If I was dead and you got lucky with the new man running things, and he wasn't paying close attention, you could keep this going for months, maybe years. Maybe forever."

"It's a decent hideout. Even if they leased out the mine I've had in my name all these years—I'd stay behind the hidden door and dig my gold."

"You've built quite an operation underground. I'm impressed." Cole was sort of impressed, in the sense that it was a very good tunnel. Of course, Murray was a low-down, murderous sidewinder, so he wasn't all that impressed really.

"I was a mining engineer in college."

"College? When did you fit college into your life of crime?"

"I went before I started with the acting troupe. I found working in an office didn't suit me so I joined up with my brother. Even then I handled the money for the group. But then I got the job here and remembered a few things from college. I knew how to look for the right books and study them."

"Why didn't you just take this job honestly? What's wrong with you?"

Murray smiled again and shrugged. "I don't reckon I know what's wrong exactly. I just know I never had more fun than when Web and I were up to something."

A rock smashed through the opening right at Murray's legs. It hit him hard, and he went down. Cole was on him with the speed of a cracking whip.

Sadie's gun swung up and leveled on Seth. "Get out, Kincaid. You're not welcome here."

"Now, baby sister, let me explain."

A bullet whizzed in through the window between Sadie and Mel. It shattered a picture on the wall about a foot from Seth's head. The wall exploded in plaster dust with shards of the lath cutting Seth's face.

He hit the floor. More gunfire from outside blasted away. The back door split and hung by one hinge. It distracted them all from Sadie wanting to shoot Seth.

Return gunfire rang out from upstairs and from the back of the house where Rosita stood guard.

The men sheltered behind the coach continued to rain lead on the house. The back door broke loose and collapsed, leaving them wide open to the outlaws.

Seth stayed flat on the floor, and for a second Mel thought he'd been severely injured, but then he crawled on his belly under the flying lead and came up beside Sadie. He whispered to her. She crossed her arms and didn't even bother shooting at the outlaws. He pulled her aside so that Mel couldn't hear a thing over the roar.

Mel rushed to the back door and fired, mindful of their shrinking stack of ammunition. She was afraid they might make a run at the house.

Over the shots, Mel heard Seth say, "She wants the house. If it's not here, then she's not going to stick around."

Mel got busy again, but at some point Sadie's voice rose to carry over the shootout, and Mel heard her speak the words *Cimarron Legacy*.

Seth kept talking. Sadie poked him in the chest.

Mel kept the varmints outside. She wouldn't have minded some help.

Then Seth smiled in a way that had Mel wondering if he was just the littlest bit touched in the head. Mel wasn't sure what he said next, but Sadie went as pale as milk and sagged back against the wall, her hands clutching her belly.

Mel was glad the house was made of adobe and logs, which stopped the bullets from getting through to Sadie—and held Sadie up or she'd've collapsed to the floor.

Sadie turned to Mel. "Go get Angie and Rosita. We're going out the back."

Seth belly-crawled to the kitchen stove and tossed in logs, getting a fire built up.

"We're leaving?"

"Yep," Sadie said, her eyes wide. "We'll leave right after the house is burning to the point it can't be saved. That'll distract them so they won't notice when we run across that open space. I'll protect myself while my family home's on fire and being overrun by murderers."

"Sadie, no! You can't do that."

Her jaw tight, Sadie said through clenched teeth, "We have to. If we don't, we're all going to die."

Seth crawled back to Sadie's side and pulled her down from where she crouched until she was flat on the floor. "Stay low." He looked up. "Mel, go get Angie and Rosita. Be mindful of the back door, come all the way into the room, get down and move past it. Those men might charge the house any minute. It's time we got out of here." Then to Sadie, he said, "A family's legacy isn't a building. It's blood. It's loyalty and love and faith."

His words sounded strange given the backdrop of gunfire. "If you want a legacy, you have to be alive to hold on to it. And that woman out there, she'll quit if the house catches fire. That's why she hasn't torched the place yet, despite her threats. She thinks this house is the Cimarron Legacy. But you know better. If the house is gone, she'll go, too. With her gone, you live. The baby you're carrying lives."

"Baby?" Mel's eyes locked on Sadie. "What?" Then Mel remembered the way Sadie held her belly.

"Heath wrote about it. If Heath really is d-dead—" Seth choked on the word, then lifted his chin and looked straight in Sadie's eyes—"then your family's legacy is contained right inside you. Those in this house are the legacy. Your child survives. Justin's wife survives. Your parents have a daughter, grandchild, and daughter-in-law to come home to. You can build another house, but *you* can't be replaced. That's the legacy we're fighting to save."

Seth laid a hand on Sadie's shoulder. "You aren't destroying the Cimarron Legacy by starting this fire and running. You're saving it. You'll live to fight another day. There's no glory in dying under this woman's guns in some defiant refusal to abandon your home."

Sadie gave a firm nod of agreement. She went to the hot stove and used a metal poker to knock wood out onto the floor, then shoved it up against the wooden cupboards. She tossed a heap of towels on the burning logs. Then she got a mean look in her eye, reached for a chair, and smashed it against the wall.

She held two pieces of it to the fire leaping up around the towels. When the wood caught, she hurried to the window and threw the pieces at the overturned coach. One hit its roof and bounced off, burning harmlessly on the ground. The other went right into a square opening on the coach, a trapdoor leading to the roof.

A *whoosh* from inside told them Sadie had hit something flammable. Quickly she went to a lantern hanging on the wall and hurled it at the coach. It smashed against the wood and caught fire. Flames crawled and spread, eating at the wood with the vicious hunger of a starving wolf.

"Get ready. Those men are going to come out from cover." Sadie's voice rose with the anguish and rage of what they were doing. "When they do I'm going to shoot every one of them. Then we'll get out of here."

As the flames chewed their way up the walls of the kitchen, the fire grew and spread all over the coach outside. Finally one man leapt up and ran for the barn.

Sadie's gun came up, but rifle fire from the bunkhouse hammered at the window where she stood. Seth tackled her to the floor. The pepper of bullets sent splinters of wood in all directions. Mel opened fire on the bunkhouse, driving the shooter back.

Another man broke from the cover of the coach. Mel aimed and got two rounds off. The man shouted in pain and fell facedown. Hattie and at least two other gunmen fired from the barn.

Mel pressed her back against the wall beside the door, unable to take a shot. Gunfire poured down from upstairs and from the back of the house.

Mel glanced out to see the man she'd shot jump back up. A crimson stain on his pant leg said she'd gotten a bullet in him that left his leg bleeding, though it wasn't enough to stop him. He ran to the safety of the bunkhouse.

Cover fire from the bunkhouse and barn allowed the rest of the men hiding behind the coach to make their escape without a scratch.

Mel watched Sadie crawl to a second lantern hanging on the wall. She tossed it at the burning wall. Seth knocked more logs out of the cookstove, spreading fire around the kitchen.

They were really going to do it—burn down the CR ranch house. But Seth was right. They had to get out, destroy the place themselves, and deny Hattie her prize. Only to lose the house this way felt like the worst kind of defeat. Listening to the crackling of the flames, Mel knew that Cole would be devastated by the destruction of this place so dear to his heart.

Just to be truly involved, Mel ran to a fancy lantern hooked to a stand on the wall by the living room fireplace. She poured a line of kerosene from the fire to the center of the room and watched the flames leap higher.

She would taste the ashes of this day for the rest of her life.

Cole slammed into Murray, but the man whipped his gun around and cracked it against Cole's head.

As he staggered back, tumbling to the floor, Cole hung on doggedly to Murray and dragged him down with him. The gun went off again and again. Cole grappled for it as Murray, with a howl of rage, rolled on top and fought to bring the weapon around to point it at Cole.

Cole felt his back slam into the wall. He felt hands shoving at him. It was Justin trying to get through, but Murray had Cole pinned in front of the opening.

Murray's hand grasped at Cole's throat. Cole threw himself sideways. Murray managed to hang on, however, keeping Justin and the others from entering the room and helping Cole.

His air cut off, Cole gripped Murray's gun hand, then caught his other wrist to try to gain a breath. With no success, he found himself weakening. Slowly, Murray's gun began to descend, lower and lower, aiming for Cole's head.

With his last ounce of strength, Cole arched his back and heaved Murray to the side, spun around, and dove onto him before the pistol came back up. Murray twisted like a snake and pounced on Cole.

Then Heath ripped the gun out of Murray's hand. He grabbed Murray and tore him away. Cole watched as Justin rushed in to take Murray by the lapels of his suit coat and slam a fist into his face. Murray crumpled into a heap.

Cole stumbled as he got to his feet. Walt was there to brace him. "Thanks." He meant it for everyone.

Walt chuckled. "You're welcome," he said and let Cole go.

Cole found that he could stand on his own.

Murray must've faked his collapse because he made a sudden lunge for the opening they'd all come through.

Justin caught the outlaw by the back of his shirt. "This coyote's not gonna admit defeat, is he?"

"Tie him up," Heath said, grabbing a ball of twine from Murray's desk.

Justin used it to bind Murray's hands together tight. "If this was a sturdier rope, I'd say we tie him up and leave him here. We could deal with him later. But if he escapes, he's enough of a sly fox to hide so we never find him."

Heath nodded. "And since he's evil to the bone, we need to keep our eye on him."

"Let's take him with us," Cole said. "But we gotta go now. We have to get to the CR, and fast."

Murray was conscious enough to stumble along beside them, though he had to be goaded to hurry.

Soon they reached the pit. Murray had to be untied to climb. Heath went up first, then Justin and Murray, with Cole right below their prisoner. Walt brought up the rear.

Cole itched to pass Murray's slow-climbing form. Everything in Cole wanted to race up the ladder. They were climbing for what seemed an eternity when Cole remembered that Murray's mine was on a lower level than the other men. They were farther down than he thought.

Without warning, Murray dropped and stomped a heavy boot on Cole's hand, knocking Cole from the ladder. But Cole had learned what a snake this man was. Despite the pain, he hung on to the ladder by the fingertips of his other hand.

Without Cole there to stop Murray's fall, the man plunged down. Walt dodged him too, and a scream of terror cut the air, fading as Murray dropped.

The scream ended with a sickening thud. Walt scampered back down to round up the prisoner.

Cole began descending, thinking to help, but Walt shouted, "Go on up. I can see him and he's dead. Broke his neck. We don't need to worry about our prisoner anymore."

With no time to feel much but relief, Cole started climbing again, doubling his speed now. He reached the surface, with Walt only a few steps behind him.

Emerging into the sunlight, Cole took a few seconds to breathe in the clean air and get the weight of the mountain off his shoulders. He saw Justin and Heath sprinting up the side of the mountain.

Men digging looked up and saw them, and a cheer went up.

The horses. The Cimarron Ranch. Sadie, Angie.

Mel . . .

Cole raced after them, praying he'd get there in time to stop a tragedy.

Smoke billowed out of the broken windows of the ranch house.

"*What are you doing?*" A scream of rage came from outside.

"We're burning it down!" Sadie's voice lifted over the roar of the fire.

Mel had sent Rosita and Angie to the window in the only bedroom downstairs. They could climb out the window and be gone as soon as it was safe to abandon the house.

"I'll destroy this house before I let you have it."

"No! It's mine." Hattie came charging out of the barn.

Seth was ready. He fired steadily at her. The distance was enough that he missed, but he got close enough he stopped her from advancing. She hit the ground and scrambled back inside the barn.

"I can't get out, and you can't get in," Sadie shouted. "When this is done you'll be living on an ash heap, and my pa will come home and bury you under the foundation of the new home he'll build. You'll get nothing."

"Let's go, Sadie." Seth tugged at her arm, but she resisted.

Mel hesitated. "We still have time. I don't want her getting in here in time to put the fire out."

"Well, I don't want us still in here when the roof starts caving in."

"I thought she was supposed to give up when she saw the house burning down."

Seth gave Sadie a strange, confused look. "Uh, no, she's supposed to give up *after* the house burns down."

"That's the same thing," Mel said.

Shaking his head, Seth asked, "You didn't think we were just going to pretend to burn it down, did you?"

"I hoped there was a chance . . ."

"It's gonna burn, baby sister. Hattie won't head out soon enough that we can put out the flames. I'm sorry if I left you any reason to hope."

"Yep, hope is just a waste of time today." Sadie nodded, then looked back out the window.

Mel saw the ceiling of the living room by the fireplace start to break up, sending sparks flying as the fire spread fast toward the kitchen.

"Now, Sadie," Seth called out. "Let's go!"

Mel looked around. Flames were everywhere. Smoke billowed from the rooms Rosita used. She stepped into the hallway that led to the office, the downstairs bedroom, and the stairs to the second floor. Choking smoke poured down from upstairs, and the bannister was on fire. Heat and fumes pressed against them as the flames consumed every section of the house.

Sadie looked at Mel and nodded. "Let's go."

Mel had never seen her friend quite like this. The strength that came with the Boden name was alive and well in her. Mel felt her own upbringing lift her courage.

Despite the fight and the fire and the sickening twist in Mel's stomach to know she'd shot a man, she was still in the fight. But right now the fight meant *retreat*.

The two women rushed to the bedroom with the window that led out the back. Seth was right behind them, with Angie and Rosita already gone.

Mel went through the window, knowing Sadie wouldn't go first.

The dense woods came up close to the house, and Mel ran for cover.

She saw the skirt of Angie's dress vanish around a clump of aspens, heading straight north. Mel had never been in these woods before. They were too crowded with trees to make a proper playground when they were children. She paused, glanced back to see that Sadie was out of the window and Seth was swinging himself through, then turned and slammed into something like rock.

It was Cole.

❧

"I'm going in on foot from here," Chance shouted over the clatter of the racing wagon wheels. He'd been hearing shots for two miles and driving like a madman. He reined in the team, fighting the near-panicked horses to pull the wagon to a halt.

One neighed and reared up so high that Chance thought the critter was going over backward. Instead the horse leapt forward, jerking the wagon nearly in half.

Finn and his ma had stayed with Sister Margaret. Chance wasn't taking a sick woman and a little boy to a gunfight.

Nor his wife, who'd refused to stay in town.

"Stay back." Chance glared at Ronnie. Boy, was that ever an order not apt to work. Unless he moved so fast his feisty wife didn't have time to think—and she was fast thinking.

He jumped off the wagon before it'd rolled to a full stop. His leg sent a stab of pain up his spine all the way to his eyeballs.

He paid it no mind. His rifle in hand, a six-shooter on his hip, he sprinted for home.

He rounded a bend in the trail to see smoke billowing from his house, flames licking out of every window. He heard bullets whizzing from the barn to the house, with return fire being sent right back. His family had to be in the house, and it was burning down around their ears.

"No!" Ronnie raced past him. He didn't have time to wrestle her to the ground and haul her back. With his bum leg he might not even be able to catch her to try such a thing.

He ran on. This was no time for yelling. He didn't want whoever was attacking the ranch to know the cavalry was coming.

There were men in the bunkhouse, and more in the barn. He saw a man lying motionless on the ground and recognized him as one of the CR hands. A wave of grief washed over him. How many others were dead? Were his children among them?

Ronnie went to the back door of the barn and waited. He caught her and saw eyes that burned so bright with rage, his little wife might just set the varmints on fire rather than shoot them.

"Ready?" She grasped the door handle, her pistol drawn and aimed straight up.

"Three of them in the barn." Chance held up three fingers, his voice low. "Two behind the big door on the right, one on the left. I'll take the two on the right."

"The gunfire from the house has stopped." Ronnie's eyes narrowed, and they both considered what that might mean. "Even so, look out for bullets coming from the house."

Chance brought his rifle up. The barn was big; it would be wise to have the best aim possible to hit something on the far side of it, and that meant using the rifle.

"Go!"

"Go!" Cole jerked his head to indicate the east.

Instead, Mel threw herself into his arms. "She said you'd died."

Cole's arms came around her hard. The two staggered when Sadie hit him on the shoulder. "Cole, is Heath with you? What about Justin?"

"We're all fine. Walt too." Cole's eyes went past Sadie, and his brows arched.

Seth walked right past them on his way to Heath. Sadie saw him, gasped, and abandoned Cole for her husband. Mel saw Rosita beaming to find her boys alive and well.

"Hugging time's over." Cole kept his arm around Mel even after he'd said it.

His arms, the life and strength of them, knowing he'd survived—Mel felt a surge of triumph. With Cole and Heath at their side, they were going to finish this thing right now. But where were Justin and Uncle Walt?

Cole added, "We're going to get behind the bunkhouse and clear out those varmints. Then we'll take over the barn and—"

"I just came that way," Seth said, cutting him off. "There's an open stretch and it was all I could do to slip across it on my belly, one inch at a time. We're not all going to cross it unnoticed."

Seth had lost his place by Heath, who had an arm around Sadie. "I'm Seth Kincaid, by the way. It was my idea to burn your house down."

"What?" Cole turned toward the house, not visible through the dense woods. But the acrid smell of smoke hung thick in the air, unmistakable. "That's our house burning?" He glared at Seth, his eyes on fire.

With an incredulous expression, Heath said, "You burned down the Boden house?" He punched Seth hard in the shoulder.

Seth rubbed his shoulder without paying it much attention. "Yep. Figured that loco señora was going to kill everyone in the house just to get her hands on it. Burning it down denied her the house, stopped her from overrunning it and turning the place into a fort."

Cole shook his head as if to clear it of the desire to murder Seth where he stood. "I'm going to wait and kill you later. Right now I need your help stopping these varmints."

Seth grinned. "I'll be around if you've a mind to try."

"We don't need to sneak across." Cole caught Mel by the arm and started heading north. "Justin and Walt are going to create a diversion. We'd better be in place. We can slip through the woods on past the house, then run to the cabin Heath and Sadie live in now. Best take advantage of these outlaws looking elsewhere."

Cole quit talking and snuck along the north side of the house. He ducked into the woods and kept moving. Mel did her best to keep up with him. Seth was on their heels, followed by Heath and Sadie, then Angie and Rosita. Within minutes they reached the end of the clearing, just fifty paces from the forest edge and the first structure.

Heath grumbled, "We're gonna be real close to my house, Seth. Should we pause and turn it into kindling while we're at hand?"

"Better not." Seth didn't sound one bit worried about what anyone thought—or maybe he missed Heath's sarcasm. "The family might need a roof over their heads."

Cole stopped and turned. "Give Justin and Walt a chance to get into place. Rosita, you should stay here with Angie."

"I will fight at your family's side, Cole." Rosita hefted her rifle.

"Yep, I know it, but I need someone here in case they spot us while we're in the open. We're gonna run flat out, and I don't want to have to stop while we're exposed and shoot back."

Rosita glanced at Angie. "We can watch their backs, can't we?"

Mel heaved a sigh of relief. Yep, Angie had gotten to be a good shot, so this was a job she could handle. And she'd been in the middle of the fight back at the house. Yet the sweet woman didn't have a killer bone in her body. For a second she had, when she thought Justin was dead. Now that she saw he was alive, though, Angie seemed to have gone back to her sweet self.

Which didn't mean she couldn't shoot straight.

"Thanks, Rosita." Cole looked from Mel to Heath, then Sadie to Seth. "We wait for the diversion."

They held when everything in Mel wanted to break from cover and run. She knew part of the urgency was the Boden house fire. She still hoped they could get to it and put the fire out, save at least part of it.

Gunfire sounded from the west, from the direction of Skull Mesa.

"That's Justin's Sharps rifle," Cole said. "They're rounding up the outlaws to the west."

More shooting rang out, this time coming from the barn and the bunkhouse but aiming away from the burning ranch house. Hopefully all their eyes were to the west as well as their guns.

"Now move!"

31

Ronnie ripped the door open. Chance dodged around the corner, Ronnie only a pace behind him. They rushed the gunmen on the far side of the barn just as shooting started from the west.

Chance slashed his pistol butt across the back of the outlaw's head while Ronnie swung her rifle with all her strength to knock the man on the left of the doorway. A dull thud sounded and her man crumpled to the ground.

"No!" a woman shouted. She was standing off to the side in the shadows. The woman rushed forward.

Ronnie recognized her.

Señora de Val's rifle came around and fired.

Cole reached the safety of the ramrod's cabin and whirled around to see the rest of his crew gain cover one by one—Mel, Sadie, Heath, and Seth the house-burning polecat.

"There's open space between here and the foreman's house, and more between that cabin and the bunkhouse." Cole looked around the corner and didn't see anyone aiming at him. "I think we got across the open stretch without being seen."

Suddenly the shooting picked up, coming from Justin and Walt. Right when Cole needed them to let up so he could get behind the bunkhouse.

Mel grabbed his arm. "The shooting from the barn is aimed this way."

Chance dove past Ronnie and grabbed the rifle barrel.

Ronnie dropped to the floor just as Lauressa fired. The bullet passed over her head. A second later, Chance jerked it up and aimed at the roof. The long gun fired and fired again while Chance wrestled for it.

Lauressa de Val screamed and fired as one possessed.

Ronnie saw it on the foul woman's face. The condemned soul, the hatred, her inhuman strength—everything about her shouted that she was in league with Satan himself.

Ronnie's strong husband tore the gun free and disarmed her. Lauressa clawed at her holstered pistol, but Chance snatched it away and tossed it across the room. It skidded just inches from Ronnie, who promptly picked it up.

Lauressa shrieked with every breath. Without a gun, she now turned her claws on Chance and raked them across his face.

Ronnie knew her husband well, and hitting a woman, let alone shooting one, went against every fiber of his nature. He'd do it to save someone, but it'd hurt him all the days of his life. She glanced at the man she'd whacked, saw he was unconscious, then strode across the barn and slapped the devil woman across the face so hard it knocked her down.

Ronnie had a feeling she wouldn't be bothered by that for one minute.

"The shooting from the barn has stopped." Looking around, Cole tried to judge if Justin and Walt would be careful enough, their aim tight enough, that they'd be safe getting across about a twenty-foot space between the two buildings.

That was when he saw John. He wanted to start shouting, but that would warn the outlaws he was close by. Pressing his back against the ramrod's cabin, he looked at Mel, then Sadie. "John's out there."

"We saw him," Mel said. "He went down in the first assault. I came riding in from the mine to warn Sadie, and John ran to gather your cowhands while I went into the house. The gunfire started before he got out of the yard."

Cole swallowed hard. "You must've gotten to safety just a few steps ahead of the attack."

Mel gave a slow nod, her golden-brown eyes filled with sadness. "Then I had to go inside and tell Sadie and Angie that their husbands might be dead."

"Sorry you had to bear such hard news."

Mel patted Cole on the arm. "Glad I turned out to be wrong."

"So am I."

"I count five men in the bunkhouse." Cole looked at Heath, who nodded his agreement. He noticed Mel and Seth had nodded, too.

"There's a back door," Cole added, "and no one's shooting that way. We'll head through there and take care of these men, then go after the last of them in the barn."

At that moment a bloodcurdling scream came from the barn.

The screaming grew louder.

Lauressa lunged at Ronnie.

Chance, still wrestling with her, said, "Was that necessary?"

Ronnie shrugged. "How much angrier and noisier can the furiously mad woman get?"

Chance pulled a kerchief from his pocket. "Gag her."

Ronnie enjoyed that. Even more, she enjoyed the silence. She found a length of rope, and soon they had all three outlaws trussed up.

Chance went to the doorway to look at the house, leaning out an inch at a time. "Still shooting coming from the bunkhouse. And also from the west."

"They seem to be shooting at each other. So one of them is on our side and one the other."

"I think Loco Lauressa here was shooting toward the west, so I think that's our family."

"And I think that's Justin's old Sharps rifle." Chance looked again, going out a bit farther. He bellowed with rage. "John's out there! Looks like he's dead."

Ronnie leaned out and gasped. Clutching her stomach, she considered giving Lauressa a nice hard kick. How many more would they find? "We've got to get him out of there." Despite the shootout, she couldn't stop herself from looking again, this time more closely. "I think he's breathing, Chance."

Chance studied his old friend. "It's ten paces to get him, ten paces back." Chance turned back to Ronnie. "Let's swing the barn door open. That'll cut the number of paces in half."

The barn had two large doors on this side, big enough to drive a covered wagon through.

"So you'll be in the middle of a gun battle only for a few paces?" Ronnie looked from John to Chance. "That's the devil's own choice to make."

"The gunfire from the west is aimed at the sky." Cole glanced back, and Mel saw that it was time. "Justin knows I'm ready."

Mel judged the shooting from the bunkhouse. "Five men—that's one apiece and one's wounded. We're ready. Go."

Cole darted across the open space, Mel hard on his heels. The rest were right behind them. Cole stopped at the back door to the bunkhouse, centered in the middle of the long, low building. His eyes met Mel's. She nodded. They'd all made it across. She and Cole got on the far side of the door, with Sadie, Heath, and Seth across from them.

Cole jerked open the door and went in to find five men all facing away from him. "Drop your guns now. We've got a gun on every one of you. One twitch and we fill you all full of lead." His voice was harsh, the kind of tone that made a man freeze in his tracks. Mel had never heard Cole Boden speak that way before.

The five men's guns, all aimed in the wrong direction, dropped. Their hands flew up. There was rope aplenty in the bunkhouse, so Cole, Heath, and Seth got busy tying up the hands and feet of those who'd spend the rest of their lives in jail.

Cole thought of John, turned and looked out the window at him, already grieving.

Chance pushed open the door and listened. The gunfire had stopped from the east and west. The silence was broken only by the crackling and burning of the house, which sent up clouds of smoke. With the door half open, he wasn't visible from the bunkhouse. He poked his head out so those on the west could see him, then pulled back just in case they didn't recognize him from a distance.

"Let's hope the men in the bunkhouse don't expect to shoot at Lauressa and her men. I'm going to get John, Ronnie." Chance eased forward. "I just saw Justin's hat—he waved it."

When the shooting ceased from the bunkhouse, Chance braced himself and ran for it.

Cole saw someone dash out and grab John by the legs. Cole whipped out his gun to stop whoever might be meaning harm when he realized what he'd just seen. He held his fire as Pa dragged John inside the barn.

"Pa? Here? Did I just imagine that because I wish it was true?"

Sadie came to his side. "You saw Pa?"

"Yep, I reckon I did."

Sadie stared at him a second, as if checking for head wounds. "Maybe that's why Lauressa quit shooting. Pa got her."

She hurried to an open window and shouted, "Pa? Are you in the barn? We've got these outlaws tied up in the bunkhouse."

Justin stood from behind a boulder on the west and started in, carrying a rifle aimed upward, but in such a way that he could get it into action fast if more trouble presented itself. Walt was right behind him.

Pa and Ma stepped cautiously out of the barn, Pa limping but looking almighty good. They met in the center of the ranch yard, where Sadie launched herself into her mother's arms and started crying. Cole didn't see how that helped the situation any.

Pa said, "Help me with John. He's still breathing."

The menfolk rushed to the barn, Cole not a bit sorry to leave the tears behind.

Heath beat them all there and dropped to his knees beside the wounded man. "I need clean rags and warm water and—" Heath turned to the door and glared at what was left of the house—"I need a lot of things that are all burned to ashes now."

Rosita came in with her arms loaded. "John's cabin is well supplied with such things." She knelt beside John's outstretched body just as he groaned for the first time.

It put heart into Cole, and everybody stood a bit straighter.

Walt said, "I'm riding for the sheriff. I'll send the doctor out and get more supplies for you all, what with no house to live in." Walt gave the house a look just as the roof collapsed.

"Thanks, Walt. Tell Sheriff Joe to bring a wagon."

Walt left the barn. Galloping hoofbeats sounded from outside within minutes.

Cole saw three more outlaws tied up in the barn. "Lauressa and the Suddler brothers. How many did you get, Justin?"

"There were three men to the west. Not even a fair fight when one of 'em on my side is Walt Blake."

Cole found his first smile in some time. John making a sound sure helped. There was no room by John's side and Cole wasn't half the doctor Heath was, so he turned to his pa. "I expect you'd like some introductions."

Ma was still outside, busy hugging, while Angie and Mel had stayed. Pa nodded. "I know Heath. Understand you married my girl."

"Yep." Heath looked up from his work for just a second and grinned, not one repentant bone in his body over the hasty marriage without Sadie's parents at the ceremony. "I think John's gonna be all right. He's lost a lot of blood but he ain't even shot. Someone must've knocked him over the head and left him there bleeding. Lucky man that these varmints were so busy with their filthy crimes they weren't thorough."

A low hiss came from Señora de Val and drew Cole's attention. Cole had noticed the bloody scratches on Pa's face. Fury blazed in the woman's eyes.

"Pa, you gagged and bound her for a reason, didn't you?" Cole approached her cautiously.

"I think I lost part of my hearing from all her blasted screaming." Then, turning serious, Pa added, "I don't think she's in her right mind."

Crouching by her side, Cole said, "Dantalion is dead. His brother Murray is dead, too. We've finally caught you all, and Hattie June—that is, Countess de Val—I'd like to know something."

"Hattie June, what's that mean?" Pa asked.

Cole told them what Murray had said in the caved-in mine. Heath and Justin had heard it as well from outside the cave, so they added more details.

"She was gone before I ever moved here," Pa said. "But I always heard she was a poor, deposed countess, or some such nonsense."

"She's an actress who passed herself off as a countess to trick de Val into marrying her," Cole said. "What I want to know is how did my grandparents get involved in all this?"

Pa froze. He was already standing still, but Cole could feel the complete end of any motion right down to holding his breath.

Since Hattie June was gagged, Pa had time to shake himself free. "Whatever caused your grandparents to be in those notes, Cole, it doesn't matter now. The real evil came from this woman, and we don't need to fuss over the Bradfords."

Cole, still in a crouched position, turned on his toes to look up at his pa. "I don't want to be shielded from this, Pa. I want the truth." Cole swallowed hard. "If it helps any, I've decided that the CR is where I want to spend my life. Running the mine suits me fine, and I plan to make it my life's work."

"I'm glad to hear that." Pa seemed to stand straighter, as if a weight had been lifted from his shoulders.

"It wouldn't hurt you to herd a cow now and then," Justin muttered.

Cole chuckled. He turned back to their growling, hissing prisoner. Though there was no excuse for it, Cole had a feeling the Don had started with his wandering eye mighty quick after his wedding.

Cole pulled the gag off the phony countess. "How do you know my grandparents, the Bradfords?"

A cruel smile curved Hattie June's lips. Honestly, it was almost worse than the screaming.

"They were greedy people," she said. "They sent a man to Santa Fe hunting for a way to use their money and make it so you didn't have a home to come back to. They came to Web and Murray's attention."

Cole noticed her voice fell into a Mexican accent. Until now, she'd been talking English as if born to it—which she had been.

"They knew I'd want to hear about these people with a grudge against the Bodens, so we made plans to send Murray out to the mines to look around. There were already forces around the governor who'd spent years pushing out the land-grant owners. Dantalion became friends with that group. He'd always been good at ingratiating himself. He explained about the land-grab conspiracy and made up that map to convince the agent your grandparents sent that he was the man who could see to the Bodens being ruined."

A low laugh sent a chill up Cole's spine. Hattie's eyes gleamed with malicious pleasure.

"Then your parents would light a shuck and head on down the trail."

Her voice changed again. Cole could imagine her now as a girl from Tennessee. He wondered if she'd played so many parts for so long that she no longer knew who she really was.

"And if there was no Cimarron Ranch for you to come home to, they figured you'd just stay right with them. Your grandparents were generous and funded us well to make our land grab."

"Did they pay you to kill my family?" Cole asked.

Hattie laughed and said, "Did you not notice that we shot you, Cole? Dantalion died that day, but Watts was with him. And after he escaped jail, he got word to me.

"Are you such a fool, Cole, you think that was your doting grandparents' wish? No, but they died and left their money in our hands. And then Murray made his gold strike and we had his money, too. But all of it had to be played out slowly because my husband couldn't know. He hated America and would never agree to return. Then he did what I'd hoped for years he'd do—he died. Finally, I had the freedom to act on my own." Her laughter grew louder, almost hysterical.

Cole was quick to put the gag back on her, and she tried to bite him. He was grateful she'd been tied up. He rose and looked at Pa, then stepped right up and gave him a hug. The kind of hug a man rarely gives another. "I love you, Pa. I know my grandparents always made your life difficult."

"My life has been fine, Cole. Mighty fine. We can talk more about this later, but it looks to me like we've finally got things settled. Let's go meet my new daughter and have . . ." Pa stopped talking.

"What is it?" Cole slid an arm along Pa's back.

Justin came to his other side. “Is your leg paining you, Pa? Let’s get you . . .” Justin fell as silent as Pa.

“What’s the matter with you two?” Cole looked between them.

Heath said, “I think they both were speaking of plans for the near future that requires the use of your house.”

Pa glared at Heath, then shook his head. “I’d like to spend some time getting to know you better, Heath. Maybe you can find the courage to ask for my permission to court my daughter.”

“Yep, maybe.” Heath barely glanced up from where he still knelt by John, doctoring him. He flashed Pa an unrepentant smile, not sounding one speck worried.

Cole sighed as he led the way outside.

“This woman,” Justin said, drawing Angie’s attention, who turned and threw herself in his arms, “is my wife, Angie.”

“She’d better be,” Pa said, but he looked pleased with her show of affection.

Cole whispered, “She thought Justin was dead. They don’t behave like that all the time.”

Pa nodded, and Angie got ahold of herself—instead of Justin having hold of her—and faced Pa.

“Welcome to the family, Angie,” Pa said.

She smiled, though she had a pale look to her. Probably the only sensible one in the group. Upset by a gunfight. Imagine that.

Pa’s eyes slid to Seth, who’d come wandering out of the barn behind them. “You look like you’re kin to Heath, is that right?”

“I’m Seth, Heath’s big brother.” He gave a wild grin that seemed to say a shootout was about the most fun he’d ever had in his life. “I’m the man who burned down your house. Looking at things now, I reckon I didn’t need to do that. Sorry.”

Pa closed his eyes as if he was in pain.

Sadie disengaged from Ma and said, “Heath and I have been

living in the ramrod's cabin. Let's go there now. Pa, how's your leg?"

Mel came up to Cole's side as his family headed for a place to sit down. It looked like Pa could stand to get off his feet for a while.

"I'm going home now." Mel patted Cole on the back. "I suppose it's safe to ride the country alone again."

She turned to go, but he caught her arm and turned her right back. He pulled her all the way in to a kiss.

"No, Cole, you said it was wrong." Mel pushed against him and turned her head aside, even if it was the hardest thing she'd ever done. "You said you might be leaving and I wasn't fit to go with you back east."

He let her get about an inch away. "First of all, you're about the finest woman who ever lived. I'd be proud to take you anywhere. But I think you'd hate the city, so I might've said you wouldn't fit in. You'd be ready to start shooting people before you'd been there a week. That's a whole different thing than thinking I wouldn't be proud to have you at my side."

"That's probably true about the shooting." Mel had to concede the point.

"Second, nothing has ever felt so right as kissing you, so it's not wrong. In fact, I think it's a big old sign from God that you're the perfect woman for me."

Cole kissed her again, and Mel was about ready to shove him away again. In just a minute . . . or two.

"And third and last, Melanie, I'm not going anywhere."

This time when he kissed her, she didn't even pretend to push him away.

32

"Will you look at that?" Ronnie stood at the window watching her troublesome oldest son kiss the living daylights out of Mel Blake. Ronnie heartily approved.

Chance came up beside her. He was limping badly, and Ronnie was going to hog-tie the man to a chair just as soon as she quit watching her son decide his whole life right in front of her. Kissing Mel like that meant choosing a wife and also choosing the Cimarron Ranch as his home.

Leastways that was how Ronnie read the situation, and since it was exactly how she wanted things, she'd just go ahead and believe whatever suited her.

"Well, what do you know? Never figured Cole was quite smart enough to pick such a perfect wife." Chance turned from the window, kissed Ronnie on the cheek, and whispered, "She's almost as fine a woman as you."

Ronnie understood why he was whispering. Because Angie was nearby and she was a surprising choice for Justin. Yet Ronnie could see her sweetness and the love they shared and knew Justin had chosen well, too.

Cole and Mel quit their kissing and, arm in arm, started

walking toward the ramrod's cabin. Heath trailed after them, on his way to meet up with Sadie. Seth must've stayed in the barn with Rosita and John.

Ronnie wondered how they were all going to fit in this cabin. "Our children have done well for themselves," she said.

Chance turned to face the room. "Yep, and I get all the credit for that."

She slapped him lightly on the back of the head. He grinned down at her. "It was my demanding they all come home that helped them find mates and saved the ranch."

Ronnie stared out the window at the wreckage of her lifelong home and didn't comment.

Cole held Mel close like nothing Ronnie had ever seen from her son before.

"Mel just agreed to marry me," Cole announced.

The little room erupted in cheers and applauses.

Justin shook Cole's hand.

Sadie hugged Mel. A small crowd surrounded them with congratulations. They were all happy, but Ronnie noticed that no one seemed overly surprised. She needed to sit Rosita down soon and get a full accounting of all that'd gone on around here while Ronnie was away.

It was a story she couldn't wait to hear, and she knew good and well it was one Rosita couldn't wait to tell.

As the celebration quieted, Cole's whole face shone with happiness. Mel blushed and leaned closer to him, resting her hand on his chest as if to touch his heart.

"Ma and Pa, we're going to have a wedding ceremony that you can actually attend," Cole said with a smile.

Ronnie nudged Chance into sitting in one of the few chairs in the cabin. When he'd finally gotten off his leg, he said, "I have an idea that I hope you'll like."

All three of their children turned to listen. Chance caught Ronnie's hand and squeezed. "I think instead of rebuilding the ranch house and forcing you to live where you don't choose, we should build four houses."

Ronnie gasped and squeezed Chance's hand tighter. It was a good idea.

Cole glanced sideways at Mel, who looked enough in love to live in a cave with him.

"We can spread them out a bit so you each have a home you can call your own. But we'll still be close, able to see each other often and all share in the legacy of the Cimarron Ranch." Chance paused and drew in a deep breath. "No, that's not right. You can each live where you choose. I want us all together, but I also know you're grown men and women. You can live where you want. I hope that'll be close because I love you all and would miss you if you're gone, but it's your choice. No more of your pa being a tyrant."

Heath nodded and said, "We can share the legacy but maybe not while living right on top of each other."

That brought a burst of laughter.

"In the meantime, I do have a house in town," Cole said. "It's a long ride, though, and I've found I actually prefer it out here." He looked at Mel. "We can stay there while we build closer to your parents, near the property line our ranches share. Because you're a much better rancher than I am, and you're going to have the running of your own land."

"I'd like that," Mel said.

Cole walked over to where Chance sat resting his leg. Ronnie had seen this between them all their lives, the closeness they had since the day they'd pulled a covered wagon into her yard and stayed to win her heart.

"You're gonna have to change that will, then, Pa," Cole said.

"It's a legal document. And if I take Mel to town or to the mine and stay, or to her own folks' house, and something happened to you before the will's changed, we could lose the ranch."

"I'll do it before anyone leaves today," Chance promised. He shifted in his chair, and Ronnie knew he needed to put his leg up. There was only one other chair in the room, and she was sitting in it beside him. She stood and, despite his protest, helped prop up his leg.

"I know that will I wrote was wrong," Chance said quietly.

Everyone fell silent until they could have heard a lark singing on top of Mount Kebbel.

Justin pulled Angie close. "We understood your reasons, Pa."

Cole nodded. "And we were mighty upset at first."

"But, Pa, it turned out to be a blessing," Sadie said. "We needed to move back here. And living here helped me to get to know Heath better. That will you wrote led me to the man I love."

Ronnie saw Sadie rest her hand on her middle, right over the child growing there. Sadie had told her the news within a minute of their first hug. Ronnie couldn't wait to tell Chance that he was going to be a grandfather.

"Sadie coming home is what prompted Sister Margaret to send for Angie. So it led me to the woman I love."

Angie added, "And saved me from a terrible life."

"All of this trouble would have been worse if we'd been spread out." Cole glanced out at the now-smoldering ranch house. Little was left of it now but ashes and a jumble of charred adobe bricks. The walls still stood mostly, but the building had been reduced to ruins. "Instead, because of you, we were together to face the trouble as one, which made all the difference. You didn't punish us with that last will and testament—you saved us. Thank you, Pa."

Epilogue

"I now pronounce you man and wife. You may kiss the bride."

Cole turned and kissed Mel with a gentleness that made her heart ache. "I love you, Mrs. Boden. Thank you for the honor of marrying me." Cole rested his hand on her cheek. "You're especially beautiful today—even for a woman who's beautiful every day of her life."

Mel looked down at her golden-brown dress. Ma had wanted a new dress for her in this color to match her hair and eyes and skin. It was the dress more than anything that had held up their wedding for the last two weeks. The fabric was found in Skull Gulch, but it needed to be sewn up, and Ma wanted to add special embroidery and lace.

"I love you, too. You've made me the happiest woman on earth." She thought Cole's dark suit and shining white shirt, necktie, and new black Stetson—which he'd set aside for the ceremony—was a perfect match for her dress. Of course, he dressed like this most days, while she'd really fancied herself up.

They shared a smile before turning to face their family and friends.

Ma was crying, as was Ronnie. There might be a tear in Pa's eye, too. Uncle Walt winked at her.

The tears were pure sentiment, since she and Cole lived close enough to everyone, never to be missed for very long. In fact, Mel planned to be home working with Pa when Cole was working at the mine. With help from the Blake Ranch hands, they'd managed to build a small cabin already with plans to add on later. But they'd needed to get roofs over everybody's heads before they did more to their place.

Ma and Pa had built a more reasonably sized home. Justin and Angie lived on the ranch with them, and so far Sadie and Heath showed no sign of moving out of the ramrod's cabin. With Justin and Heath around, and John Hightree healing fast, they probably didn't need a ramrod anyway.

Cole and Mel linked arms. Sitting at the piano, Sister Margaret played "Come Thou Fount of Every Blessing" as the couple strode proudly down the center aisle. As they passed the front pew in the tiny church sanctuary, Mel heard Ronnie whisper to Chance, "Can you believe it? We got to witness one of our children getting married."

"Yep," Chance responded. "A mighty fine day."

Mel had Sadie and Angie stand up with her during the ceremony. Justin and Heath had stood as attendants for Cole, though heaven knew the whole town of Skull Gulch was here witnessing it.

Mel smiled at John Hightree, still moving slow but alive and healing. He sat beside Rosita, and there seemed to be something between them since John's brush with death and Rosita's tender care of him.

As they swept down the aisle, Mel saw Ramone in one of the pews, well-dressed and looking happy. He'd been tracked down and told he'd inherited a healthy sum of money from his father. Once he was sure Señora de Val was locked up, he'd traveled to Mexico City to claim his inheritance. He'd grown a tidy beard and wore an eye patch. Though he'd always have that brutal scar, he seemed content now, no longer bothered by all that'd happened.

There was an inheritance for his late sister Maria, too. Ramone had given it in full to Sister Margaret, for the orphanage had provided a good home to Maria while she lived and worked there. Ramone had come back with the information that all the talk of revolution was part of Lauressa's scheme to throw suspicion onto others.

Mel, on the strong arm of her husband, emerged into the March sunlight and the warmth of early spring that always blessed New Mexico Territory.

A whole beef was roasting out at the Blake Ranch. There'd been little reason to invite the guests to the Bodens', what with the main house a heap of ashes. And their new cabins were still raw and lacking in most everything a good-sized party needed. Buckboards and carriages and saddled horses lined the boardwalks of Skull Gulch.

The prisoners had been sent to Santa Fe, and with their confederates either dead or locked up, it didn't look like these folks had any influential friends who'd find a way to set them free.

Hattie June had gone into a fit when they'd tried to put her in front of a judge. Now the judge had claw marks on his face, the lawyer had teeth marks on his jaw, and Hattie had the rest of her life to spend in prison, with half the folks near the courtroom that day having lost their hearing from all her screaming. The judge had been heard to say on several occasions that life in prison wasn't harsh enough for her, and he probably owed the other prisoners an apology.

Cole helped Mel up onto the seat of his fine carriage. "Aren't you glad now you didn't wear trousers to your wedding?" he asked as he swung up beside her.

She smiled as she put a hand on his chest. She loved the feel of his beating heart under her hand. He'd come very close to death too many times. "I am indeed," she replied.

"Are you going to stop busting broncs once there's a baby on the way?"

Mel blushed. "Such talk. Hush now."

Sadie had told her their news, and Mel overheard Ronnie and Rosita whispering something about Angie. It seemed as if the next generation was well on their way.

Cole leaned close to his bride. Before he settled his lips on hers, he whispered, "We'll have our own children to add to the Cimarron Legacy just as soon as we can."

"We will. And we'll teach our children to love the land and remember all that it cost, and to remember that faith is the most important thing in the world."

"And that love is the true legacy of any happy family." Cole kissed her again, then slapped the reins on the horse's back.

They were headed to a reception now that would last out the day, but then would come their time to celebrate marriage privately—to begin their own Cimarron Legacy.

About the Author

Mary Connealy writes romantic comedies about cowboys. She's the author of THE KINCAID BRIDES, TROUBLE IN TEXAS, and WILD AT HEART series, as well as several other acclaimed series. Mary has been nominated for a Christy Award, was a finalist for a RITA Award, and is a two-time winner of the Carol Award. She lives on a ranch in eastern Nebraska with her very own romantic cowboy hero. They have four grown daughters—Joslyn, married to Matt; Wendy; Shelly, married to Aaron; and Katy, married to Max—and four precious grandchildren. Learn more about Mary and her books at:

maryconnealy.com
facebook.com/maryconnealy
seekerville.blogspot.com
petticoatsandpistols.com

Sign Up for Mary's Newsletter!

Keep up to date with Mary's news on book releases and events by signing up for her email list at maryconnealy.com.

More from Mary Connealy

Disguised as a man, Kylie Wilde is homesteading for profit so she will be able to live comfortably when she moves back East. But both love and danger threaten to disrupt her plans.

Tried and True, Wild at Heart #1

Also Available!
Now and Forever, Wild at Heart #2
Fire and Ice, Wild at Heart #3

BethanyHouse

Stay up to date on your favorite books and authors with our free e-newsletters. Sign up today at bethanyhouse.com.

Find us on Facebook. facebook.com/bethanyhousepublishers

Free exclusive resources for your book group! bethanyhouse.com/anopenbook

You May Also Like . . .

While fleeing the villain who killed her father, Grace Mallory is waylaid by Amos Bledsoe, who hopes to continue their telegraph courtship in person. With Grace's life on the line, can he become the hero she requires?

Heart on the Line by Karen Witemeyer
karenwitemeyer.com

When ballroom wallflower and gossip columnist Permilia Griswold overhears a threat against Mr. Asher Rutherford, she tries to warn him. Away from society's spotlight, they discover there's more going on behind the scenes than they anticipated.

Behind the Scenes by Jen Turano
Apart From the Crowd, jenturano.com

When paid companion Gertrude Cadwalader is caught trying to return items pilfered by her employer, her friend Harrison's mother jumps to the wrong conclusion. But Harrison quickly comes to Gertrude's defense—and initiates an outlandish plan to turn their friendship into a romance.

Out of the Ordinary by Jen Turano
Apart From the Crowd, jenturano.com

Returning home for her father's funeral, Jessica faces the Amish life—and love—she left behind. As she struggles with regrets, she learns about a Revolutionary War–era ancestor who confronted similar choices. Will she find peace along with the resolution she hopes for?

A Plain Leaving by Leslie Gould
The Sisters of Lancaster County #1, lesliegould.com

BethanyHouse